PRAISE FOR

If You Can't Stand the Heat

— ✕ — ✕ — ✕ —

"First-timer Allen delivers a breezy and likeable menu."

—*Kirkus Reviews*

"Ideal for fans of culinary mysteries."

—*Booklist*

"A delightful mystery, full of regional charm and kitchen spice. Robin Allen has served up a delicious debut."

—David Liss, *New York Times* bestselling author of *The Devil's Company* and *The Whiskey Rebels*

"Robin Allen delivers big time, with colorful characters and an intriguing plot that keeps you turning the pages. Can't wait to see what Poppy Markham cooks up next."

—Ben Rehder, author of the Edgar Award finalist *Buck Fever* and other Blanco County mysteries

"Poppy Markham hits the mark! This fast-paced tale of an aspiring eatery, an insufferable Michelin chef, and the crew of Texas hipsters, hotheads, and raw talent that keep the kitchen going is great fun, rich with character and conflict."

—Nadia Gordon, author of the Mystery Writers of America Mary Higgins Clark Award-nominated *Lethal Vintage* and other Napa Valley mysteries

©LEIGH-ANN SHRUM

About the Author

Robin Allen lives and writes in the great state of Texas.

ROBIN ALLEN

Stick a FORK IN IT

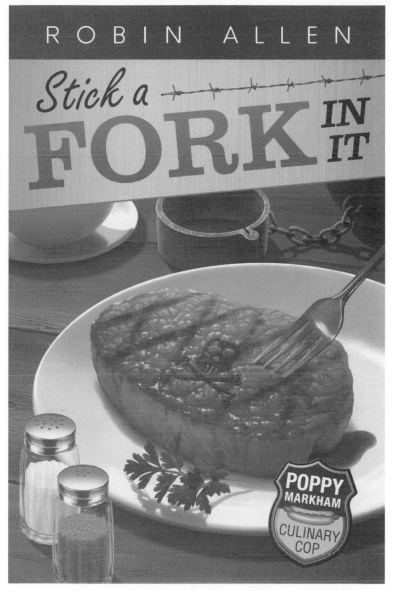

POPPY
MARKHAM
CULINARY
COP

MIDNIGHT INK
WOODBURY, MINNESOTA

MIDNIGHT
INK

First Edition
First Printing, 2012

Cover background: iStockphoto.com/loops7 and
barbed wire: iStockphoto.com/oblachko
Cover design by Kevin R. Brown
Cover illustration by Desmond Montague

Midnight Ink, an imprint of Llewellyn Worldwide Ltd.

Library of Congress Cataloging-in-Publication Data
Allen, Robin, 1964–
  Stick a fork in it / Robin Allen.—1st ed.
    p. cm. — (Poppy Markham: culinary cop; 2)
  ISBN 978-0-7387-2795-0
1. Women in the food industry—Fiction. 2. Murder—Investigation—Fiction.
3. Austin (Tex.)—Fiction. I. Title.
  PS3601.L4354S75 2012
  813'.6—dc23

                                                          2012005496

Midnight Ink
Llewellyn Worldwide Ltd.
2143 Wooddale Drive
Woodbury, MN 55125-2989

www.midnightinkbooks.com

Printed in the United States of America

for the Darling of Heaven

Acknowledgments

My heart is full of love and gratitude for my friends and helpers, Tina Neesvig Pfeiffer, Letty Valdes Medina, Paul Allen, Nicole Allen, Jackie Kelly, Hannah Matthes, Lorie Shaw, and Melody Valadez; for the Austin WriterGrrls, especially my talented brainstorming partners Wendy Wheeler, Jennifer Evans, and Kimber Cockrill; for my yogis; and for my editor at Midnight Ink, Terri Bischoff.

Special thanks to Detective Brian Miller with the Austin Police Department for not issuing an arrest warrant for me after answering so many detailed questions about murder; former Austin/Travis County senior health inspector Susan Speyer, RS, owner of Safe Food 4 U in Austin, Texas, for making Poppy look like a real health inspector; Jackie Kelly, MD, for medical advice; and Bosco Farr for tattoo advice. They all provided expert information when I asked for it, but I didn't always ask and I didn't always listen, so any errors or inconsistencies are my own.

"There is no requirement that someone
be physically fit to be executed."

—A spokesman for the
Illinois Attorney General

ONE

A couple of weeks ago, an employee at my father's restaurant tried to kill me by setting my bedroom on fire. He wanted to keep me from discovering that he had murdered a famous French chef and set up my territorial stepsister, Ursula York, to take the fall. When that didn't work, he tried to lock me in the restaurant's walk-in refrigerator and freeze me to death. That didn't work either. And now he's awaiting trial and I'm back at work, doing what I love: health inspections—in this case, a food permit inspection for a new restaurant going up on the southeast side of Austin.

It was a muggy morning fit for orchids and alligators when I pulled up to the front gate at 7:58 AM, grabbed my inspector's backpack full of necessaries, and hopped out of my Jeep. Inside the locked gate, I saw several dusty construction workers shouldering wooden planks and pushing banged-up wheelbarrows. I caught the attention of one of them and waved him over.

He approached me as if walking through a field of land mines toward a lynch mob. When he got within shouting distance, I held up my badge and shouted, "Is this fifty-five fifty East Slaughter Lane?"

He shook his head. "No let you in," he said in heavily accented English.

"I need to speak with someone in charge."

He took a step back.

I tried Spanish. "*Por favor, tengo que hablar con el jefe.*"

Then he started running.

When the rest of the workers assessed the situation—me, my badge, their fleeing coworker—they took off, too. All of them.

A short, hefty man ran out of the building in time to see the last of the guys fly through the back gate. He barked something at the two construction workers who followed him from inside, and they went after the escapees. Then he came up to me and threw his belly against the fence, his sweat-stained blue T-shirt announcing Miles Archer Construction Company in fat yellow lettering.

"What in the name of Davy Crockett are y'all doing?" he demanded. His white hard hat read "Boss/*Jefe*" in black marker.

"Poppy Markham," I said. "Austin/Travis County health inspector. I showed my badge and your guys ran." Banged-up cars and trucks roared past us. "Now why do you think they did that?"

He glanced back at the building and his manner lost some of its bluster. "Don't know why they'd be 'fraid of a health inspector."

"I didn't tell them who I was, just that I wanted to speak with *el jefe.*" I waited as another car sped away. "You know you can get into a fair amount of trouble for hiring undocumented workers."

He displayed both palms. "I have papers for ever' single one of them, lady. If they lied, I don't know nothing about it."

"Lucky for you I'm the food police, not Homeland Security. I need to inspect this place before you can get your Certificate of Occupancy."

He reached into his pocket and pulled out a set of keys along with a new tone. "Oh, right, the boys said you were coming today." He unlocked the gate and swung it open to let me pass. "Miles Archer, construction manager."

I shook his hand. "I know it's a holiday, but is there a restaurant manager or owner on the premises?"

He smiled. "Only all of 'em." I followed him to the double door opening at the front of the building, but he stopped a few feet away and unclipped a walkie-talkie from his waistband. "Archer to eighty-eight," he said into the mic, "health inspector's here."

"Roger that," came the reply. "Send him back."

Miles pushed the button on the side of the device and brought it up to his mouth, then let it go. "We'll let you be a surprise." He pointed to the right. "Kitchen's around back."

I didn't want to walk around the building. It was only the last day of May, Memorial Day, and already the temperatures had climbed into the mid-eighties. I haven't had time to get the air conditioner in my Jeep fixed, so I had already been sweating like a mail-order bride stepping off the plane. One of the treats, sometimes the only treat, of doing an inspection is that first blast of air so cold it crystallizes the sweat on your skin.

"But these doors are open," I said.

"I can't let you in the dining room without a hard hat, ma'am." He pointed again to the right. "They're waiting on you."

Ma'am. Ugh.

———— x   x   x ————

"There's nothing wrong with that sink," Todd Sharpe said. "It's brand new."

"I can see that," I said. "But it only has two compartments, and code requires that you have three."

"Nobody told us that."

Of all the duties of a public health inspector, a food permit inspection is one of the cushiest. Unlike surprise inspections that take up the majority of our time, performed in kitchens as pleasant as an active volcano, we perform these permit inspections in the relative comfort and quiet of an empty restaurant. No heat or sour grease traps, no rodent droppings or expired milk, no complaints or arguments.

I loathe them.

And this is why: rookie restaurant owners. They hurry through everything, rarely paying attention to the rules and regulations—the "boring stuff," they like to call it—and then whine or argue when their lack of attention leaves teeth marks on their flanks.

I had, however, looked forward to this particular permit inspection when I found out that the Sharpe brothers owned the restaurant. I wanted to see how the past twenty years had treated them. I was two years behind Todd and his identical twin, Troy, in high school. I never could tell them apart except on football game day, when Troy wore his number 8 quarterback jersey and Todd, his receiver, wore number 88, so it was more economical and practical to have a crush on both of them.

Todd had not reacted to my name or my face, which didn't surprise me. He and his brother had preferred haughty cheerleaders to serious loners. Physically Todd had turned out fine—still tan and overprocessed, still carrying himself like a star athlete strutting through the corridors. He wore his light brown hair military short, and the lines around his dark blue eyes made him look as intelligent as he was. But something about his manner didn't seem right.

Most people are nervous during an inspection, even if they aren't trying to hide something. Todd wasn't nervous so much as anxious. Every time I passed by the door that opened into the dining room, he went on defense, putting himself between me and it like he was afraid I would break through—which didn't make sense because I had to go into the dining room eventually to inspect the wait station, bathrooms, and bar.

That Todd and I were already discussing the sinks was my fault because I had broken one of my own rules. Instead of handing him my report and going over each item at the end of the inspection, I was pointing out issues to him as I found them. Not because I forgot how to do a food permit inspection, but because Todd stayed glued to my side, gnawing his thumbnail, asking me, "Did it pass?" every time I turned a knob or shot my infrared thermometer into a reach-in refrigerator.

He wasn't going to like what I had to say next. "You also need a separate mop sink."

"Why's that?" he asked, breaking eye contact with me when he reached down to scratch his knee.

"Because you can't thaw chicken or cool pasta in the same sink you empty the mop bucket into." I recognized the look on his face: *how much is this going to cost, and how long will it take?* He also looked ready to kill somebody. Before I lost him, I said, "You can make this one the mop sink and have your guy install a three-compartment sink. Just make sure he installs the proper backflow valve."

I squatted down to open one of the lowboy coolers on the cooking line. "What kind of food are you going to serve?" I asked, trying to take his mind off of whatever it had started to chew on.

"Comfort food," he said.

I shut the door and stood. "That covers a lot of ground."

He stepped closer to me. "Did it pass?"

"It's cooling to the proper temperature."

When Todd started to follow me into the walk-in, I suddenly felt hot and sweaty. A hot flash? No. I'm only thirty-eight. My hand throbbed, and I realized it was a flashback. Before I had turned the tables on my would-be murderer and locked *him* in the walk-in, I had sliced the palm of my hand grappling with a bread knife. Eleven stitches.

Everyone had cautioned me not to go back to work so soon afterward, but I hadn't suffered any after-effects—certainly not emotional ones. I dealt with the incident the same way I deal with everything: I cowgirled up and moved on. It wouldn't do for a health inspector to squall like a starlet in a slasher movie every time she encountered a walk-in. So why did I feel distressed now, when I had been the one to triumph?

Maybe it was something else. The flu or a latent schoolgirl reaction to finally speaking to Todd "the Catch" Sharpe or simply the general feeling of unease that had been nagging at me since I pulled up to the building.

Most restaurants make an effort to be inviting, with glass front doors, painted exteriors, and cheerful landscaping, but everything about this place shouted "Go away!" Its two stories of gray cinder block were surrounded by a moat of blacktop parking lot protected by a high chainlink fence topped with barbed wire.

Regardless of the reason for my sudden flush, I didn't want to work through it in front of Todd. I stopped and turned around. "How about we go see the facilities?"

He ran a manicured hand over his salon-streaked hair. "Facilities?"

"You put in bathrooms, didn't you?"

"Upstairs and down. But we're trying to keep the concept under wraps until the grand opening."

A lot of restaurant owners are protective of their concept before they open, believing that it's so unique and genius that no one on earth has done it before. But really, everything has already been done. Twice. There is nothing new under the sun, and there is certainly no idea that some restaurant owner somewhere hasn't already considered and tried or considered and rejected.

"I don't need to see your menu," I said, "but I do need to see where the entrées will eventually end up."

His smile eased the concerned creases on his forehead. "Yeah, okay, but I need you to sign a confidentiality agreement."

He went into an office near the kitchen door and returned with two hard hats and a single sheet of paper. I read standard language that made me promise not to divulge anything to anyone about what I saw, heard, or believed about the restaurant. I didn't think a lawyer wrote it, but it got the point across.

"You mentioned an upstairs," I said, handing him the signed paper. "Is there a second kitchen I need to see?"

The kitchen we stood in was quite large. Take away the ovens, stoves, and prep tables, and the Dallas Cowboys could have run drills in there. My father's restaurant, Markham's Cocktails & Grille, uses six cooks during the week and nine on the weekends. This place would need at least twice that to keep it going on a busy night.

7

"Just this one," Todd said.

"What are you calling it?" I asked as we crossed through the kitchen.

"That's still under discussion," Todd said.

I figured that was something else they wanted to keep under wraps. And I was pretty sure from the bleak exterior it wouldn't have bistro or café in the name. "It would be nice to have the name for my report," I said.

"We'll tell you when we decide," he said. "Put this on."

He handed me a pristine white hard hat with "Troy/*Jefe*" handwritten across the front in black marker, then put a scuffed "Todd Sharpe" one on his own head. My hat fit loose and dropped down over my eyes. Todd pushed open a floor-to-ceiling swinging silver door and indicated that I should pass through ahead of him.

If you had asked me what I didn't expect to see, what I saw would be the answer.

A huge dining room—no, not a room, an expanse—of concrete floors and gray walls. Made of cinder blocks, it looked like the exterior. No artwork, beer neon, televisions, or knickknacks on the walls. No tables, chairs, booths, or benches. Not even carpet. They would need to serve comfort food to make up for the soullessness of the ambiance.

And then I noticed something even more odd. Each of the letters A, B, C, and D were painted fifteen or twenty feet high in black on each of the four walls. It looked like Stephen King and Tim Burton had collaborated on a daycare design.

A flash of light drew my eyes up to a sidewalk squaring the perimeter of the second floor and accessible by metal staircases on each side of the room. A catwalk? In a restaurant?

In spite of losing about ten guys in the outdoor exodus of illegals, Miles Archer Construction Company still had several workers inside sawing, nailing, assembling, welding, and trying to outdo each other in the noise department. It sounded like a war zone.

"Todd!" a man yelled from above. I looked up to see Todd's twin, Troy, on the catwalk. He sat on the black railing, his legs dangling over the edge, with what looked like a noose around his neck. "I can't take it anymore!"

I saw another flash of light, then Troy pushing himself off the railing.

I surged toward him screaming, "Nooooo!"

TWO

I HEARD LAUGHTER. TWIN laughter coming from in back and in front of me. Then surround-sound laughter as the construction workers joined in. Troy had landed on a large, black, billowy pillow, like the kind stuntmen use.

Troy held his belly and guffawed. "That…was…awesome." He wiped tears of hilarity from his eyes. "The way you ran and screamed." He made his voice high. "Nooooo!"

Something really must be wrong with me. Practical jokes are a rite of passage in restaurants, and with all the ones I've seen and perpetrated over the years, I should have at least suspected a setup. I didn't like being humiliated so publicly, but I especially didn't like being off my game.

Todd caught up to us, and when he saw the look on my face, he did the right thing and stopped laughing. "Poppy Markham, meet my brother Troy, the practical joker. Troy, meet the health inspector."

Troy scooched himself off the stunt pillow and removed the noose from around his neck. Except for bloodshot eyes, he still looked exactly like Todd. He held up the other end of the rope. "It's not attached to anything. I was just having some fun." He gave me the same look he had given his girlfriends in high school, a look that said, *Don't be mad. I'm just a dumb, adorable jock.* It always worked on them, and, surprisingly, it worked on me.

"That was pretty good," I admitted.

"Did we get the permit?" Troy asked.

"We need three sinks," Todd said.

See? They never pay attention. "You need a three-*compartment* sink and a separate mop sink," I said. "Two sinks. One if you reuse—"

"You know," Troy said, grinning, "I remember a cute blond from high school named Poppy Markham. Would that be you?"

Troy "the Train" Sharpe had noticed *me* in high school? And he thought I was cute? I felt flush again.

"I was two years behind y'all." My voice sounded strangely delicate. "My cousin, Daisy Green, was in your class. She's Daisy Forrest now."

Troy nodded. "Right, right. Daisy." He leaned toward me, and I pulled back from the odors of stale beer, cigarette smoke, and the same sweet cologne Todd wore. He lowered his voice. "So, Poppy, can't you just…"

I looked up at him, and the hard hat fell over my eyes. I pushed it back. "Can't I just what?"

"You know."

My regular voice returned. "No, I do not know."

But of course I knew.

It didn't concern Troy that the dining public might swallow hair with their hamburger or crunch on a little grime from the bathroom floor with their mozzarella sticks. He wanted me to ignore what he thought was a minor detail compared to finishing construction and earning profits.

11

And then it came. And he wasn't even subtle about it.

"I can make it worth your while," he said.

"Unless you can get me a date with Keanu Reeves, there's nothing you can do to make it worth my while."

Troy smiled as if a date with the star of *The Matrix* would be the easiest thing in the world to arrange. Before I was faced with a choice between a dream I had never outgrown since *Bill & Ted's Excellent Adventure* and keeping my oath of office, I said, "And even a date with Keanu wouldn't do it."

I could feel Troy's body temperature rise into triple digits. He balled his fists and threw his head back like a sleepy three-year-old who had been told it was bedtime. "Archer!" he bellowed. "Archer! Archer! Archer!"

"Right here, Troy," Miles said, coming in from outside, through the double doors he had refused to let me enter earlier. He was followed by a lanky, dark-haired man with soft features, dressed like the twins in a red polo shirt and shorts. I didn't need to see the name on his hard hat to know that he was another guy I had gone to high school with: Danny MacAdams.

Danny had been in the same grade with the Sharpe twins, but he hadn't been friends with them. The twins had mentally and physically tortured Danny for the two years I was there with them. Everyone called him Danny Dull. And now they were opening a restaurant together? An ocean's worth of water must have passed under that bridge in the past twenty years.

Troy crossed over the line of scrimmage, cursing a blue streak of insults I had never heard and ones I would never repeat. The inside construction workers had stopped moving as soon as Troy started yelling for Miles, but they honored their *jefe* by going back to work and pretending he wasn't getting verbally flayed in front of them.

Todd and Danny tried to calm Troy down, which turned Troy against them, too. Soon everyone became infected by Troy's hostility, yelling over each other, pointing fingers, getting nowhere.

"Hey!" I yelled, clapping my hands like a kindergarten teacher. They stopped bickering and swiveled gargoyled faces toward me. "It doesn't matter whose fault this is," I said. "You can send someone over to CapTex Restaurant Supply and get a three-compartment sink. If it's installed by the time I'm finished with the rest of the inspection, you can have your permit. Assuming everything else passes."

Miles, who'd had the most fingers pointed at him, said, "Done."

Troy looked at him. "*Done*," he mimicked. "You said 'done' *yesterday*." He swatted away the hand Todd put on his shoulder. "'Everything but the second floor,' you said. 'You can open tomorrow as far as I'm concerned,' you said. I've got a photographer here right now, food vendors coming tomorrow, and—"

"I'll handle it," Danny cut in.

"You do that," Troy said. He pulled a red box from his wrinkled shorts and jerked his hand up to eject a cigarette. He pointed a final hard finger at Miles. "June eleventh, Archer. June freakin' eleventh."

"I'll go get them sinks right now," Miles said, then took off.

Troy put a flame to his cigarette. Danny blew it out. "Jeez, Troy!" he cried, gesturing to the welders. "They're using propane in here."

Danny hadn't been fast enough, and Troy answered by unloading both nostrils of smoke into Danny's face. I sneezed like I always do at my first whiff of cigarette smoke. Troy said "Bless you," but I could tell he didn't mean it. Then he walked past us toward the kitchen.

Todd gave Danny a look that could have been either an apology or a challenge, and he was about to say something when Miles came back.

"What now?" Todd said.

Miles put his hands in his pockets and looked at the floor. "I need money."

"Cripes, Archer!" Todd said. "Charge it to our account like you always do."

Miles looked up. "It's like this, Todd. Last time I was in there, Jesse said we were cash-and-carry."

That's a harsh burden for a fledgling business. It meant that they had somehow ruined both their credit and their good will with the vendor. Ruining credit is easy to do: don't pay your bills. But ruining good will with Jesse Muñoz? The man who encourages restaurants to trade in their old ovens and stovetops so he can refurbish and donate them to at-risk youth programs? That's hard to do.

"Since when?" Danny asked.

"Must've been last week, when I went to get a microwave. Paid for it with my own cash money."

"Why am I hearing about this now?" Todd demanded.

"I figured y'all knew," Miles said.

Todd took a deep breath, then shook out both hands as if he had washed them but didn't have a towel to dry them. I remembered him doing that on the football field while he waited for a play to start. I always thought he was flashing his assets to the other team.

"Come on," Todd said to Miles, heading through the kitchen doors.

"Sorry about that," Danny said to me after they left.

"Forget about it," I said. "If you're opening on June freakin' eleventh, you've got plenty of time."

He grunted. "Twelve days. We still don't have our liquor license, and we just now decided on a chef." He looked toward the kitchen door that both Sharpes had passed through. "We need about four weeks to get the restaurant finished out and the rest of the staff hired, but Troy won't budge on the date."

"What's so special about June eleventh?" I asked.

I watched Danny debate with himself whether to tell me. Good grief! So what if that date was the twins' birthday or the anniversary of the first time they ran Danny's tighty whities up the flagpole.

"I signed a confidentiality agreement, Danny."

He crossed his arms over his chest. "Paranoid freak."

"Pardon?"

"Troy coming up with that stupid agreement. I told him we need to tell everyone about this place—give interviews, get some buzz going—but he wants to keep it a secret as long as possible."

"Why?"

"He thinks there are roving bands of restaurateurs waiting to pounce on his idea."

"What does that have to do with June eleventh?"

Danny's eyes darted around the dining room. "He'll kill me if it leaks out."

"I understand." I pulled a rubber glove out of my backpack and snapped it onto my right hand with a calculated flourish. Danny flinched. "I'll be in the kitchen finishing that part of my inspection," I said.

"I guess I could tell you."

15

I pushed the hard hat back and looked at him. "Only if you want to."

"I'd like to know what you think, actually. Todd and Troy are crazy, and this whole idea seemed cockamamie when they first told me about it. They have this way of making you buy whatever they're selling…I don't know what's normal anymore."

A rev-up like that was sure to crash at the end. I waited for him to tell me that they were fusing Italian fare with Hawaiian cuisine to come up with Pineapple Pasta Primavera and Coconut Manicotti, which would make a certain kind of sense if they had only recently decided on a chef. That's what happens when amateurs set a menu without the help of a professional.

I beckoned with my gloved fingers. "Unburden yourself, Danny."

He took a deep breath, then said, "June eleventh is the day Timothy McVeigh was executed."

"The Oklahoma City bomber?"

Danny started pacing. "I told those guys the date was too much, but they blew me off like they always do. And now Troy wants to serve nothing but mint chocolate-chip ice cream on opening night…"

I tried to make something of what he said, but I couldn't even locate tab A to insert into slot B. "Are we still talking about the restaurant?"

Danny stopped in front of me. "Didn't they tell you about our concept?"

"Todd told me you're serving comfort food."

"In a way."

"What way?"

"We're serving the last meals of death row inmates."

16

I looked around at the cinder block walls, the catwalk, the high fence visible through the open doorway. "And this is a prison," I said.

Danny started pacing again. "It was just going to be the waiters dressed up as prisoners and guards, you know. Toy guns that shoot ketchup and mustard. But then Troy got that stuntman pillow so we could do hourly hanging executions. Once he got going, he decided to bring in gurneys and syringes, put in a firing squad shooting gallery for the kids. Add a gift shop, except he wants to call it a gift *chamber* and fill it with dry ice. Like a Hard Rock Café for death. Every day he comes up with some demented new idea." He pointed to the far side of the room. "See those crates over there? It's an electric chair. It's been sitting for a month because none of Archer's guys will touch it." He wrapped a hand around his forehead. "We're bleeding money and behind schedule, but Troy…"

Venting had reddened his face and warmed him up. He took off his hard hat and fanned himself with it. "What do you think?" he asked.

I could only tell him the truth. "I think it's sick and twisted, and—"

Danny pushed me. "Look out!"

A hammer landed where we had been standing, taking a bite out of the concrete floor. I looked up at the catwalk but saw no one.

"Happens all the time," Danny said. "That's why we wear these." He knocked on his hard hat, then put it back on his head.

Death row inmates, prison cells, fake suicides, and now a hammer almost carving out a pound of my flesh. No wonder I had felt creeped out earlier. I adjusted my hard hat. "How about I see the bathrooms now."

Danny pointed across the dining room. "Cell block D, next to the elevators. They're not working, so you'll have to take the stairwell in the wait station to the ones on the second floor."

I started across the room, then thought better of being out in the open and stayed under the shelter of the catwalk. I passed by a worker standing a few inches from the wall. He was using an awl to scratch graffiti into the cinder blocks, referring to a piece of paper on a clipboard. I read "Im innocent" and "I dint do it." He had gouged tick marks to count off the days.

So I was wrong. This was something new under the sun.

I started with the downstairs women's room, which looked more interesting than the rest of the place, if you find white porcelain toilets and matching sinks interesting. I always turn on the hot water at each sink and then flush the toilets to check that they work, and to draw cold water out of the pipes to send the hot water out faster. Except there was no water. Not in the men's room, either.

Strange, because the kitchen and the bathrooms usually share a plumbed wall, and the water had worked in the kitchen. Hadn't it? Before performing any inspection I wash my hands and put on gloves, but my bandaged hand is a burden to wash, so I may have skipped it. I couldn't remember. Todd shadowing my every move had me flustered and forgetful. And after the flashback situation in front of the walk-in, I was almost willing to believe I hadn't checked the water. If the water on the first floor wasn't working, the second floor wouldn't be working either, so I saved myself a trip upstairs and went to tell the boys the bad news.

THREE

WHEN I CAME OUT of the bathroom, I saw Troy standing in the center of the dining room, talking to two of the construction workers. As I approached them, he took a swig of something in a green bottle. Ten o'clock in the morning, and he was drinking beer.

"Excuse me, Troy," I said.

"There's Poppy!" he exclaimed, as if he had been looking for me. He turned to the two guys who had followed Miles outside when I first arrived. "Do you know Poppy?"

They looked at him.

They may not even know English.

"Poppy, this is Rudy and Mingo. Rudy and Mingo, this is Poppy."

We smiled hello, then I said, "I inspected the bathrooms, and there's no water."

"Rudy and Mingo are going to be our drivers," Troy said.

"Okay," I said.

"Rudy's the fastest, aren't you, Rudy? *Mucho zoom-zoom.*"

Rudy nodded.

"You can have Mingo," Troy said to me.

"What if I don't want Mingo?" If he wasn't going to make sense, then I didn't have to either.

Troy waved his hand around the restaurant. "Then pick one of the other guys."

"I want Rudy," I said.

Troy drained his beer. "Negative. Rudy is my driver."

"If I can't have Rudy, then I'm going to finish my inspection."

"Okay," Troy said. "You can have Rudy." He pulled a walkie-talkie from his waistband. "Eight to eighty-eight. Come in, eighty-eight."

"Eighty-eight here," came Todd's response.

"Me and Mingo against Poppy and Rudy," Troy said.

"What are you talking about?" I asked.

Danny shot through the kitchen door. "No way, Troy!" He forced long strides across the room. "They have too much work to do."

"What are you talking about?" I asked again.

Todd had been right behind Danny through the doors. "Danny's right, bro, so just one lap."

"These guys are getting paid double because of the holiday," Danny said.

I'd had success with shouting and hand-clapping earlier, so I did it again. They looked at me. "What are y'all talking about?"

Troy handed his empty bottle to Danny. "Go get me another one," he said, then turned to me. "Over here."

With all the talk of drivers and laps, I thought Troy would take me out to his car, but everyone headed toward cell block C in the back of the dining room. I suspected another practical joke, but curiosity wouldn't let me stay behind. He wouldn't get me this time, though.

Troy rolled two long silver tables away from the wall, then patted one. "Hop on."

"A gurney race?" I asked.

Troy pointed to the floor, where two lanes had been lined out with bright blue painter's tape, dirty and missing in some places. The track went in an oval all the way around the room.

"Outside lane gets a two-length head start," Troy said. He pulled a quarter from his pocket and flipped it into the air. "Call it."

What I should have said was "You're crazy and I need to get back to work." But I felt the pressure of dozens of eyes on me and said, "Tails."

The quarter landed at Todd's feet. "You won," he said to me. "Inside or outside?"

I looked at Rudy and pointed to the floor. "*Afuera*," he said. Outside? That was interesting. Wait, what was I doing?

Danny returned from the bar and handed an open beer to Troy. "One lap," he said, "then everyone gets back on task."

Troy brought the beer to his lips and leaned his head back, guzzling half of it. "Two laps," he said. He wiped chin dribbles on his sleeve, then held up peace fingers to Rudy and Mingo. "*Dos lapos.*"

Danny crossed his arms over his chest, possibly to restrain himself from punching Troy in the throat, but he didn't say anything. Even I knew that the number of laps in the race would increase with every protest Danny made.

Rudy whistled to get the other guys' attention, then gave an order in Spanish. They began clearing the lanes of building materials, moving tools, paint cans, nails, and boxes into the center of the room. Lights flashed again on the second floor. The workers stood in the center looking uneasy, probably anxious for the race to be over so they could get back to work before Miles returned.

Troy chugged the rest of his beer, then waved the bottle at Danny. Danny snatched it from him, then went back through the kitchen door, apparently done acting as Troy's bartender/babysitter.

Troy hopped aboard one of the gurneys, then flopped onto his stomach. He hung his head off the front and his arms over the sides to hold onto the table legs. "It's better when you can't see where you're going," he said.

"Doesn't it make you dizzy?" I asked.

He looked up and grinned. "Oh yeah."

As everyone waited for me to get on the second gurney, I came to my senses. I couldn't be in a race with a customer. What if someone got hurt? What if this got back to my boss? What if I beat Troy? "Better not," I said, holding up my bandaged hand. "Eleven stitches."

Troy dropped his head. "You referee, then. I'll race Todd."

Todd handed me his hard hat, then laid prone on the other gurney, putting his chin on the table so he could see.

Rudy and Mingo arranged the gurneys on the lanes, and after Troy made a last-minute driver switch so Zoom-Zoom Rudy was pushing him in the inside lane, he said, "Time for the kickoff."

I had never officiated at a gurney race, and I wasn't sure if the correct start should be "Ready, set, go," or "Three, two, one, go." I decided to do it like in auto racing. I picked up a red grease towel, then walked a few paces up from the gurneys. I made eye contact with Rudy and Mingo, then raised the towel and brought it down quickly.

Had I been a real referee with authority and the proper hardware, I would have blown my whistle every few seconds on technicalities. Team Troy/Rudy took off a split second before the flag dropped. Team Todd/Mingo had the head start because they were in the outside lane, but Troy and Rudy caught up to them quickly.

As Troy passed Todd, he reached out his hand and shoved Todd's gurney, sending it swerving to the right. Rudy shouldered Mingo, throwing him off balance. Mingo recovered and got Todd back in the lane, but not back in the race. On the straightaways Troy stretched his arms out to the side like a deranged magpie, whooping and giggling.

When Troy and Rudy crossed the finish line after the second lap, I waved the flag to bless them as winners. Todd and Mingo stopped where they were, about half a lap behind.

Troy rolled off his gurney, bent over, and threw up.

x   x   x

I went to inspect the bar. After they got cleaned up, Troy and Todd sat on barstools across from me and walkie-talked Danny to join them. "Monday morning muster," Troy said.

I checked the beer coolers, which were stocked with expensive German beers that practically shivered in their frigid containers. The bar had a three-compartment sink for soapy wash, first rinse, and second rinse, and the water worked. It wouldn't surprise me if Troy had Miles build the bar before he built the kitchen.

"Get me a beer while you're back there," Troy said.

Danny groaned. "Jeez, Troy."

"Oh, sorry," Troy said. "And one for yourself. My treat."

"I'm a county employee on official business," I said, "and it's ten thirty in the morning."

"Gotcha," Troy said, tapping the side of his nose with a forefinger. "Vodka, then. Pour it into one of those syringes and squirt it in your mouth. It's going to be our signatory cocktail, the Lethal Injection."

"Signature cocktail," Danny said, sounding like he had corrected Troy about two thousand times. "And not if we don't get our liquor license."

"It's a myth that vodka doesn't smell," I said, handing a beer to Troy.

He put the bottle against the edge of the bar and slammed his hand down on it, lopping off the cap and letting it stay where it landed on the floor. He took a long pull, then wiped his mouth on his shoulder. "Tell us, Poppy," Troy said, "what would a health inspector order for her last meal?"

"I don't know. I guess maybe some rice and beans, and jalapeño cornbread."

"Snoozeville," Troy said.

"I'm a vegan, and this is the first time I've thought about it," I said defensively. "What would yours be?"

Troy held up the bottle of beer. "You're looking at it."

"They don't serve beer on death row," Danny said.

"Gary Gilmore got bourbon," Troy said. He finished his beer and signaled me for another—his fourth that morning that I knew of.

"That was contraband," Danny said.

"Let's not get into that again," Todd said. "It's all hypothetical. If Troy wants a beer, he can have a beer."

"Or a signatory cocktail," Danny muttered.

"Getting back on track," Todd said, "let's ask Poppy what she thinks."

They nodded, in agreement for the first time since I had been there, which immediately made me wary. Whatever I gave my opinion about would surely divide them.

"We need a name for this place," Todd said.

I stared at him. "You really haven't decided? You're opening in less than two weeks."

Danny threw a scowl at Troy. "Unless someone comes to his senses."

"Belay that, Danny," Troy said sharply. He slammed the top off his fresh beer. "You keep telling employees and vendors—*and Archer*—we're opening on June eleventh."

Now that I'd had a look around the place and could see the unfinished state of their operation and their incongruent owners' triangle, I thought their timeline seemed optimistic. They hadn't asked for my opinion about their schedule, but I didn't wait for them to. "That might be difficult, considering Mr. Archer lost half his guys earlier."

"He what?" Troy spluttered. "Why?"

"They misinterpreted my badge."

"You have a badge?" he said. "Cool. Does it have a hot dog on it?"

Now, my reaction would have been to call Miles and ask him the same question I had earlier: why were his guys afraid of a badge? And then find out how he planned to finish the restaurant in less than two weeks with half a crew. But Troy seemed to have the attention span of a Labradoodle puppy.

"No, it does not have a hot dog on it." I showed him the silver-plated oval attached to a black leather holder.

He took it from me, held it at arm's length, and then made a finger gun with his other hand. "Food police! Freeze!"

Todd plucked the badge from Troy's hand and slid it across the bar to me. "Which name do you like better?" He pointed to Troy, who smiled and said, "End Zone"; then to Danny, who said, "Ol' Sparky's"; then to himself and said, "Ciao Chow," and spelled it for me.

I felt like I had been asked to make a choice between them personally. Should I pick Troy the Train, Todd the Catch, or Danny Dull? "All of those are clever," I said, "but I think it's pretty obvious what you should call it."

Troy and Todd smiled, assuming I would pick their restaurant name. Danny looked away as if he had already lost.

"Capital Punishment," I said.

The smiles faded as they processed that I had not chosen their name, then they looked at each other when they realized I hadn't chosen any of the names. Then Troy saluted me with his empty beer bottle. I hadn't seen him take the first sip.

"Excellent!" Troy said.

Todd looked at Danny. "I like it."

"Finally!" Danny said. "I've got to order menus, uniforms, stationery…"

"Stuff for the gift chamber," Todd said.

"I need to check on that guillotine," Troy said.

They stood and went into the kitchen, slapping each other on the back.

"You're welcome," I said to the swinging door.

x   x   x

I finished my inspection of the bar and wait station, then went looking for them in the kitchen. I found Todd and Danny in the corner office, each speaking into a cell phone. I stood in the doorway and removed my hard hat.

Todd pulled his phone away from his ear and asked me, "Is it Capital with an A or an O?"

Jocks. "A as in Austin," I said, "the capital of Texas."

"A," he repeated into the phone.

They ended their calls at the same time, then came out of the office.

"How did we do?" Todd asked.

I tossed my hard hat through the doorway, landing it next to theirs on the floor. "You have no water in the bathrooms."

Todd looked at Danny. "Your buddy Archer strikes again. You get to tell Troy."

Danny rolled his eyes. "Where is he?"

"He went out to the snack truck."

The back door swung open and we all turned, expecting Troy, but one of the construction workers ran inside. "*Andale!*" he cried. "*El guëro se murió!*"

I ran toward the door, then looked back at Todd and Danny, who hadn't moved. How could they stand still at news like that? Unless they didn't understand Spanish. "He said the honky is dead."

FOUR

TROY LAY ON THE blacktop near the back fence, facing away from us. Todd reached him first and dropped to his knees, then put his hands on Troy's shoulder and hip. I tried to imagine what Todd was going through, about to look into, well, his own lifeless face.

"Don't move him," Danny cautioned.

I thought that was good advice, but Todd ignored it. He turned Troy over, but before he could feel for a pulse, Troy scrunched his face into a grimace.

"Troy!"

"Right here, bro. No need to yell."

"What happened?" Todd asked as he helped his brother sit up.

A similar scene had played out on the football field every time Troy dropped out of the pocket and got sacked. Except this time there were no teammates and coaches running onto the field, no cheerleaders nervously quiet on the sidelines, no crowd in the stands chanting "Train, Train, Train," until he popped up, invigorated by the sound of his nickname repeated like a mantra by hundreds of strangers. I never believed he was as hurt as he appeared to be.

Troy raised a shaky hand to the back of his head. "Someone knocked me out."

Danny snorted. "Who was it this time? Jack Daniels or Jim Beam?"

"Shut up, dork," Troy and Todd said. Then Todd glanced up without looking at us, which was unfortunate, because instead of apprehension or worry on Danny's face, he would have seen what I saw: satisfaction.

"Danny, get some water," Todd commanded.

"I'll go," I offered, glad for an excuse to get out of the sun.

"And a cold beer," Troy called after me.

I wound my way to the sink through a network of expensive stoves, prep tables, and ovens. I turned on the water, solving one mystery—it worked—but I immediately turned it off because it presented a new problem. They hadn't purchased any kitchen supplies. No bowls or glasses, pots or pans, not even a ladle. I didn't remember seeing drinking glasses at the bar, but maybe I would find something that could hold water. I knew I would find cold beer.

I pushed through the kitchen door and ran straight into someone soft and exasperated.

"Can I help you with something?" asked a woman with short blond hair that looked blonder against a tan as dark as her brown eyes.

Ginger Krueger. She hadn't gained a pound since high school. In her expensive tennis whites, she still looked like a head cheerleader. And was still as intimidating.

"I'm, uh, looking for beer," I said.

She raised an eyebrow.

"For Troy."

She put her hands on her hips. "Troy Sharpe has had enough beer to last him to his grave." Then her face changed, and I recognized the look. It was one of uncertainty and mistrust that had recently slid into my own eyes whenever I encountered a woman I thought could be the one with whom my now ex-boyfriend, Jamie, had cheated on me.

Ginger had to be either Troy's or Todd's wife, instinctively protecting her husband or her brother-in-law. She had dated both of them in high school, and neither twin wore a wedding band, so I couldn't be sure who she belonged to.

"Who are you?" she asked.

Of course she didn't remember me. She had been too busy applying lip gloss and breaking hearts to notice a sophomore nobody. I put my hand in my pocket and wrapped my fingers around the answer. "Austin/Travis County health inspector," I said, holding up my badge.

"On a beer run for Troy?"

"I'm also looking for a glass for water." I explained that Troy had passed out behind the restaurant. "Todd asked for water, then Troy asked for a beer. I couldn't find—"

"Todd's here?" she said, pushing open the kitchen door.

I followed Ginger through the kitchen, her short tennis skirt popping against the backs of her legs with every step. They still looked strong enough to propel her to the top of a human pyramid. I picked up an empty beer bottle from a prep table, then filled it with cold water at the sink.

The back door opened and the twins came through it, Todd saying, "But he's the only one of us who knows what he's doing. We're in the crosshairs if he doesn't come back this time."

"He'll be back," Troy said. "And if he can't take a little hazing, he'll be relieved of his command. He's not the only manager in Austin." He put a hand to the back of his head, then checked it for blood.

"I know," Todd said, "but just take it easy, man. Okay?"

Ginger waited for them to notice her, as did I, but unlike me, she wasn't dying of curiosity to know which one had put that iceberg on her left hand.

"Ginger," they said at the same time. Todd sounded surprised; Troy sounded guilty. That didn't tell me anything.

"Boys," she said. I was standing behind her, so I couldn't see her face, and her tone didn't tell me anything.

"Ginger, Ginger," Troy said, like a little boy. "I came up with a name for my restaurant. Guess what it is."

"Capital Punishment," I said. If he wanted to claim my credit, then I would claim his thunder.

"It's about time," Ginger said, then glanced back at me. "That one was wandering around looking for beer. She told me you passed out."

"I got *knocked* out," Troy said.

Ginger must have looked at Todd for confirmation, because he twitched one shoulder into an almost imperceptible shrug. Twins are supposed to be able to sense the truth about each other, and it appeared that Troy's didn't believe him.

"By whom?" asked Ginger, sounding doubtful.

"If I knew that," Troy said, "I'd be on the phone with the police."

"Probably some kids," Todd said.

"Did they take anything?" Ginger asked.

"Take?" Troy echoed. He patted both back pockets of his shorts, then looked relieved.

"Surely they didn't hang around in the heat for who knows how long, waiting for you to stroll out back so they could knock you out and run off into the brush." Ginger sounded like a lawyer who won a lot of cases, and I thought I had my answer. She had to be Troy's wife.

"Since you know everything," Troy said, "why don't you tell us what happened."

"The same thing that's been happening since you got kicked out of the marines. You started drinking when the sun came up, and instead of admitting that you passed out just now, you're making up some story about being attacked by kids with no discernible motive other than kicks."

"Todd said they were kids. And I didn't get kicked out of the marines." Troy jumped a cigarette out of its pack. "Is that my beer?"

I had been following the grenade launches so intently, it took me a moment to realize that he had changed the subject and was now talking to me.

"How about an AA meeting instead?" Ginger said.

Troy looked at her with several antonyms of love in his eyes, stuck the cigarette between his lips, then left through the back door.

"Watch out for those meddling kids!" Ginger called after him.

It was only when Todd relaxed his shoulders that I realized he had been as silent as I had during their face-off.

Ginger looked at Todd. "Sorry," she said.

"That brother of mine has been on everyone's nerves lately."

Including mine, and I had been there for only a couple of hours. I handed Todd the beer bottle, then removed a business card from the side pocket of my backpack and gave it to him. "Call me when the sinks are in and the bathrooms have water."

"It'll be done after lunch," he said.

I had agreed to a lunch date with my ex-boyfriend, so the timing worked perfectly. "I'll be back around two o'clock," I said.

I had the leisure of unrushed inspections and weekday lunch dates because my boss, Olive, had me on light duty. A couple of days after my skirmish with a murderer, I had gone back to my regular duties as a Special Projects Inspector, an SPI, filling in for absent colleagues and doing follow-up inspections.

The first time I didn't allow a restaurant to reopen after being shut down by another inspector, the owner called Olive to whine that my hand wasn't safe to be around food. It was their pest control system—several cats controlling the roach and rat infestation—that wasn't safe to be around food, but Olive said she didn't want to field any more complaints about me. I suspect it was more like she didn't want to interrupt the continual insertion of luridly colored snack foods into her mouth or take a break from the intellectual challenge of computer solitaire.

Her first solution had been to put me on disability leave, but having nothing to do all day every day for days on end sounded like a vacation. No, thank you. I convinced her to let me do food permit inspections, which is why I was at the Sharpe place on Memorial Day.

I left Todd and Ginger to their Troy troubles and walked through the restaurant to the main entrance, hotfooting it when I remembered that my borrowed hard hat was in the office, which left my noggin exposed to raining tools.

Outside, Miles Archer stood near a wheelbarrow conferring with Rudy and Mingo. They must be the job foremen. No wonder Danny had protested using them as gurney drivers.

I waved to them as I headed for the front gate, and Miles fast-walked to catch up with me. "I got to let you out, ma'am," he said, then unlocked the gate.

I passed through, then decided I should tell him about the water in case the Sharpes didn't get around to it. I turned back to him. "You have no water in the bathrooms, either."

His eyes grew as big as charger plates. "No!" he bellowed.

Behind me I heard voices shouting, "Go! Go! Go!" and I realized Miles was reacting to something besides that news. Then everything happened at once.

FIVE

A BLUR OF BODIES rushed the fence. Miles grabbed my hand and jerked me inside the gate. He yanked so hard, I had to hold onto him to stay on my feet. He pushed the gate closed with his free hand, but I had pulled him off-balance. We both fell. Miles cursed. Guys whooped and wahooed as they galloped past us toward the building. Illegal construction workers returning to rescue their *amigos*?

Miles hollered, "Lock the doors!"

Rudy and Mingo ran into the restaurant and slid a metal door shut from the inside a millisecond before the mob reached it.

"What's happening?" I yelled.

Miles grasped the fence with both hands and pulled himself to his feet. "Tree…huggers," he said, huffing from his effort.

He ran toward them but wasn't fast enough. Some handcuffed themselves to the door handle while others clicked handcuffs around their free wrists, linking themselves into a voluntary chain gang.

Miles bent over to catch his breath, then pulled his walkie-talkie from his waistband. "Miles…in the yard. We have…a breach."

"Location?" came the reply.

"Front…parking…lot."

"Copy that."

The group began chanting, "Keep Austin green! That's what we mean! Keep Austin green! No in between!"

I heard distant sirens.

"Hear that, boys?" Miles asked them. "Cops are on the way."

"Green not greed! Construction is destruction! Green not greed! Construction is destruction!"

A couple of minutes later, two police cars pulled up next to my Jeep. The officers stepped out of their vehicles and took confident steps through the open gate.

Troy came out another door near the corner. Probably the gift chamber. "Todd's securing the back door," he said to Miles. "Get John to come out here and take some pictures of these guys."

"Will do," Miles said, then unlocked the gift chamber door and went inside.

While Troy spoke with the police, I surveyed the handcuffed crowd. Eight twenty-something guys wearing jeans or shorts, flip-flops, logo T-shirts, and pierced facial features. Their look fit nature-loving protester dudes, but it also fit band dudes, skateboarder dudes, cashier dudes at any store, waiter dudes at any restaurant, and computer software developer dudes. All but the last group would have the leisure or desire to gather and gripe on a holiday Monday.

And I knew one of them. After working almost every day in my father's restaurant—in every job from busgirl to waitress to manager to chef since I was old enough to hold a ramekin—I had worked with thousands of people. Still, I'm surprised when I see someone I know from there outside the walls of Markham's.

"Philip Anthony," I said, standing close to him to block the sun. His co-huggers snarled at me.

He looked up through a shaggy fringe of dirty blond hair, then snapped the fingers of his free hand. "Don't tell me." *Snap, snap, point.* "Poppy Markham."

"What's going on?" I asked.

"Are you working for these greedy jerks?"

"Greedy jerks! Greedy jerks! Greedy jerks!"

I squatted down in front of him, wincing at the reminder from my tight quads that I had missed too many yoga classes recently. "I'm a health inspector now. Doing a permit inspection so they can open."

He narrowed his dark eyes. "Yeah, well, we're here to make sure that doesn't happen."

"I heard y'all chanting that construction is destruction."

The dudes started on that chant again.

"It is!" Philip tapped the blacktop with his finger. "This used to be green grass. Now look at it. Ruined."

"Aren't y'all a little late with this protest? They're almost finished. The grass has been gone for months."

I became aware of the dudes getting restless. They started booing and yelling, "Get away! Get lost!"

"We're sending a message to future greedy jerks that their businesses will fail," Philip said, "so don't even bother breaking ground."

I figured that Philip and his friends didn't have jobs, and they had kept up their protest many months after groundbreaking so they would have something to do. "Markham's lost a few waiters recently," I said. "Go talk to Mitch about a job."

I heard someone behind me say "Smile," and Philip flung his free arm in front of his face. Thinking he was going to hit me, I reared back and lost my balance, falling sideways at the same time a light flashed.

My brain had been baking inside the kiln of my skull for about ten minutes, but I wasn't hallucinating what I saw when I squinted up. And even if I was hallucinating, I would like to think that my scorched mind would have conjured Val Kilmer or John Cusack or, considering the restaurant's theme, John Wayne Gacy or Ted Bundy. Anyone but my next-door neighbor, temporary roommate, and forever nemesis, John Without.

Stunned, I asked the first thing that came to me. "Why are you using a flash outside?"

"It stops the action." He said it as if I were the densest cow in the solar system, which is how he says everything to me. Not only is he without hair, which earned him that nickname, he is without charm, height, and manners. He snapped a picture of a police officer using bolt cutters on handcuffs attached to the front door.

The dudes began making barnyard sounds—snorting, oinking, and mooing. Mooing? The whole thing felt scripted, like they had read about the protest movements of the sixties and were doing what they thought they should. I guess not everyone could be Abbie Hoffman and the Chicago Eight.

"What are you doing here?" I asked.

John Without pointed his camera at a policeman hauling Philip to his feet. "A job," he said.

I reached out my hand to John so he could help me up, but he ignored it. "You have a job," I said, struggling to stand. "Running an art gallery with your boyfriend."

He turned to me and very deliberately pulled the camera away from his face. Then he exhaled slowly and fixed me with a surly blue stare. "Troy Sharpe hired me to document the erection of this facility."

I waited for him to hear the pomposity of his words, but he just blinked at me. "You mean take pictures of the construction?" I asked.

He smirked. "That's what I said."

Troy walked up to us as the police officers marched the protesters out the front gate. "Did you get all of them?"

"Yes, sir!" John said. I had been to his art gallery, Four Corners, many times and recognized those words in that tone he reserved for people who were about to spend an obscene amount of money on a piece of art.

"Good man," Troy said, patting him on the shoulder. "Print up some mug shots for me. I don't want any of those goldbrickers sneaking into a job later."

"Shall I have them framed?" John said with a chuckle so obsequious I waited for him to add "milord." "I need to take a few more pictures inside, then I'll pack up my things and be on my merry way."

John and Troy went through the gift chamber door, and I left through the open gate. It wasn't the roughest permit inspection I had ever done, but it was certainly the strangest and most violent. I had twice used my injured hand to break a fall, and spots of blood dotted the white bandage.

My lunch date with Jamie wasn't for another hour, so I fired up the Jeep and prepared for my next appointment. But then I stopped. For the first time since I became a health inspector, I didn't have a next appointment. So I took off for the most comforting place I know.

SIX

My father's house would be comforting only under one condition: if my stepmother, Nina, was off spending money to pamper herself with unnecessary clothes, an undeserved massage, or a gossip session with her cronies over an overpriced diet plate at her country club.

Ever since my father, Mitch, ignored my sensible advice (and later, my strongly expressed opinions) and married Nina only fourteen months after my mother died, he has clung to the sweet but deluded hope that any day now, Nina and I will finally get to know each other and become friends. And we'll include Nina's daughter, Ursula, in our quadrangle of happiness.

Mitch forgets that I did as he asked and got to know them, and that's where we ran into trouble. It took about 1.8 seconds for me to determine that they were shallow and spoiled, and not people I wanted to include in my circle of friends.

Granted, my circle is more of a semicircle that includes my ex-boyfriend, Jamie; my cousin, Daisy, and her family; and John Without's boyfriend, John With, but I couldn't imagine myself in any situation that would require the kind of advice Nina and Ursula were qualified to give.

I would never want to know what color to wear with peacock blue or if a French pedicure is too last year or whether it's unclassy to use all of your ex-husbands' last names on your bank checks. And they wouldn't seek advice from me about what dishes to make with textured vegetable protein or how to live within your means. Neither would I want to do either of them a favor—except for proving that Ursula didn't kill the famous French chef Évariste Bontecou, but I did that for Mitch, not Ursula.

I called my father, who told me that Nina had gone to meet her friend CiCi at the Palatine for shopping and sushi. Traffic up north to Hyde Park could hardly be called traffic because of the holiday, and about twenty minutes later I walked through the front door of my father's house. Nina would have the locks changed if she knew that I let myself in with my own key instead of ringing the doorbell and waiting to be admitted like a proper visitor.

I found Mitch outside, sunning himself by the show pool. I call it that because my father can't swim and Nina doesn't like to get her face wet, so no one has ever been in it as far as I know. Nina's two Hairless Chinese Cresteds, Dolce and Gabbana, were balanced on each of Mitch's thighs, intent on a plate of cheese and crackers that sat on the table just out of gobbling reach. Mitch had a cell phone to his ear and a sweating highball to his lips. His eyebrows said *hello* to me and mine said *hey* back.

"I'm glad this worked out," Mitch said, wrapping up his call. "See you tomorrow."

"You're glad what worked out?" I asked as I took the drink from his hand and sniffed it. Water. One thing Nina and I and my father's heart doctor agree on is that he should moderate his drinking. Not that he would normally be drinking hard liquor before noon, but when the warden turns her back, you couldn't blame her only prisoner for pouring a taste of freedom.

My father took his glass from me. "I think I found a new GM."

"Someone local, I hope."

"Recently returned to town," Mitch said.

He broke a cracker in half and threw the pieces in different directions. Both dogs hurled themselves to the ground and toward the same piece. They have separate food bowls, but they tussle with each other over the food in one, then do the same thing with the other.

"It would be very easy to train them to eat their own food," I said.

"Honey," Mitch said, stroking his white goatee, "there are two kinds of people in this world. Those who like to do things the right way and those who like to have fun."

"Are you saying I don't like to have fun?"

"Not at all," he said, his smile letting me know he thought the exact opposite. That wasn't news to me.

"I suppose if you had to choose a last meal, you wouldn't ask for rice and beans."

"Maybe as a side dish next to a porterhouse steak smothered in blue cheese dressing."

"Is the GM anyone I know?" I had worked in our family restaurant or the industry all my life, so the chance of me not knowing the new hire was slim.

"Possibly."

"Oh, Daddy! You know I don't like games. Do I know him or not?"

"Could be a her."

"Do I know this person?"

"Let's wait and see if things actually do work out," he said, then began humming a tune that sounded like "That's Amore."

I have a different kind of relationship with my father than most girls have with theirs. I'm his daughter, but I'm also his employee—or I used to be until I changed careers. Mitch knows why I chose this particular one, and he doesn't mind that I'm one of the most detested people in a restaurant owner's life. What he can't forgive is the fact that I left Markham's in the first place. But after two and a half years, he's coming around.

In his role as my father, Mitch enjoys devising life lessons for me. He thinks I'm too serious and rigid, and that I would be much more fun if I could learn to roll with the punches. So even though I'm two years shy of forty and have lived on my own for almost twenty years, and even though his lessons often have unintended results, he hasn't stopped trying to shape my worldview.

When he thought I should be more patient, he had me start an herb garden for the restaurant. When he thought I should learn to get along with people I don't like, he made Ursula the executive chef of Markham's kitchen and demoted me to sous chef, her second in command. He had other reasons for demoting me, like the fact that I'd had my heart broken and couldn't manage the kitchen, and that I had stopped eating animals, but getting along was the "life lesson" reason.

I killed everything but the rosemary, and I quit the restaurant altogether after enduring Ursula's one-upmanship, tantrums, and general crabbiness for seven months, but his lessons worked. I had learned both patience and how to get along with others. Whoever Mitch hired to manage Markham's, I would roll with it.

"How is Trevor handling his demotion back to sous?" I asked.

Trevor Shaw is Ursula's twenty-five-year-old sous chef and some-times paramour who had taken over the kitchen during Ursula's brief stint as an inmate. He kept Markham's running during one of the worst times in its history.

"He'll be fine," Mitch said, breaking and tossing another cracker.

"I hope Ursula is treating him like the hero he is. I haven't had a chance to tell you how he came through. I saw him in action. He's got the chops to run his own kitchen."

"And he's a pretty good cook, according to Jamie Sherwood's review."

"Trevor deserves a raise."

"Already done. And I'm naming a drink after him."

Mitch is always naming drinks after people. It's a way to get cus-tomers and their friends and family into the restaurant. And it's an easy way for a bartender or food server to build rapport when some-one asks, "Why do they call it a Harvey Wallbanger?" No one ever asks about a Cosmopolitan or a Manhattan.

If Mitch likes you, he'll give the drink your name—say, the Lance Armstrong, or, if the honoree is shy about such things, Yellow Jersey. If you complain that his prices are outrageous for such paltry por-tions, you get the Hair on Ann Richards's Chest.

Mitch had never named a drink after me. *Or Ursula,* I thought smugly. "What's in it?" I asked.

"I'll leave that up to you," Mitch said, standing up. "Come by the restaurant tomorrow and work your usual magic."

I started to protest that I would be busy with inspections morning, noon, and night, but was again caught by habit rather than fact. I had nothing to do the next day. "How does Trevor's Treat sound?" I said.

"I like it." He squeezed my shoulder on his way into the house. "Can you stay for meatloaf, honey?"

He always forgets that I don't eat meat. "I'm meeting Jamie for lunch."

He stopped in the doorway, Dolce and Gabbana each getting a snoutful of hairy shin. "Are you two back together?"

During recovery from a recent surgery to put a stent in my father's heart, he had started singing. The doctors told us that surgical patients sometimes show an interest or even an aptitude for things they had never done before, like singing or pantomime or air guitar. So I could believe that Mitch's sudden interest in my relationship with my ex-boyfriend was a similar result of the surgery, or I could scan the sky for winged pigs.

"We're on a slow mend," I said.

He entered the house, singing, "'When the moon hits your eye like a big pizza pie…'"

SEVEN

I HAD RECENTLY INSPECTED a restaurant near my father's house that served raw vegan food and knew that the kitchen was sanitary. I called Jamie from Mitch's driveway to suggest we meet there. "Have you reviewed Awstin Rawsome?" I asked.

"If you read my website," Jamie said with a certain amount of testiness, "you would know that I haven't reviewed it and have no intention of doing so."

Jamie Sherwood is a former newspaper journalist and current freelance food writer. His website, Amooze-Boosh—the Texas spelling of the French *amuse-bouche*, which translates to "mouth amuser"—gets thousands of hits each day from people all over the world hungry for his opinionated take on the Austin food scene: grand openings and undignified closings, chefs who call all the shots or who had to call a bail bondsman, behind-the-kitchen-door reports, food trends, manager movements, scandals, and plain old restaurant reviews.

"That's on your website?" I asked.

"My opinion about raw food is on there. But since your house burned and you're living with your neighbors, I'll tell you what I think. It's absurd."

"You sound a bit constipated, Jamie. Some fiber might do you good."

"Vegan is bad enough, but raw vegan? How is that even food? Why would anyone do that?"

"Isn't your website's tagline 'everything food, amusing or not'? Aren't food writers supposed to have an open mind?"

"I do about real food. Raw food isn't real food."

I knew where this was going. Jamie likes to engage me in verbal swordplay as a way to sharpen his thinking for his reviews and articles, which I normally enjoy. But he was making his thrusts and parries while sitting in an air-conditioned office, and I was making mine in a doorless Jeep in south Texas in the late spring.

"How about Mother's Café?" I suggested.

Thirty minutes later, I had delicious artichoke enchiladas on a plate in front of me and a very handsome man on the other side of the booth.

"Did you dress up just for our lunch date?" Jamie asked.

I still wore my personal inspection uniform of black jeans and black T-shirt. "Olive sent me over to that new place on Slaughter for a food permit inspection."

"You're kidding!"

"I never kid about permits," I said.

"No, about the new place. What is it? I've been trying for weeks to find out about it. No one's talking."

"I can't tell you."

"Hmm. I don't see any cats running around with your tongue, so do you have amnesia?"

"I don't remember."

"Funny," he said. "Gimme."

"They made me sign a confidentiality agreement."

Jamie sat back in the booth and let out a soft whistle. That was ripe information in and of itself. He could spend two or three articles speculating about what it meant. *Blast!* I needed to be more careful.

He looked out the window and watched four soldiers wearing fatigues from nearby Camp Mabry approaching the front door, but that was just a cover for what he was really doing. He uses silence as an interview tactic for reticent interviewees. They don't know he's waiting for them to fill the uncomfortable silence, but I did. Still, I said, "I'm no stool pigeon, Jamie. You'll have to find another informant."

"There isn't another. I've run through my contacts twice and can't find one person who works there or even knows someone who works there." He looked down at his plate and said casually, "It's like they're going to hire the entire staff on opening night."

He raised his eyes to see if my reaction told him whether he had guessed correctly. A couple of years ago, a restaurant had perpetrated that disaster. "Close, but no," I said.

"Just tell me what their menu is like so I can prepare my palate."

I couldn't tell him anything about Capital Punishment, but I needed him in a receptive mood because I wanted to talk about our relationship. I told him what Todd had told me before I signed the agreement. "They're serving comfort food."

"Like pork chops and fried apple pies?"

"Is that how your mom comforted you?"

"Every time Fluffy ran away," he said. "Mashed potatoes and chicken noodle soup?"

"If it were a hospital, which it's not."

"It looks like one from the outside. What about the inside?"

Yes, there were gurneys and syringes inside, but they weren't there to save people. I didn't want to lie, so I said, "Yes, there's an inside."

"Just give me a hint," he said.

"Sorry, but I have to obey the gag order."

He lifted a bite of food on his fork. "This spinach lasagna is comforting. Love the pecans."

"Good enough to be your last meal?" I asked.

He thought for a moment. "That would have to be a filet mignon, sautéed spinach, and sour cream cheesecake. Rare on the filet."

"No cherry-stuffed duck breast or fried eel fritters?"

"Simple is better," he said, taking another bite. "I'm going to double their business with my review."

"What review?" the waitress asked as she refilled our tea glasses. She'd had the same dreamy smile on her face since Jamie sat down at her table.

Jamie looked at me with uh-oh in his eyes.

"He didn't say review," I said. "He said he got a gnu."

Our waitress frowned. "A new what?"

"Could I please get a cup of potato soup?" I asked.

"Beckham would envy your footwork," Jamie said when she walked off. "Sometimes I forget we're not hanging out at your kitchen table."

He was letting me think I had gotten him off the topic of the new restaurant, but I knew he would eventually come at it from another angle. Jamie never gives up. And he knew I knew, so he would have to be extra crafty. We sipped our iced teas and smiled at each other.

I had second thoughts about initiating a conversation about our relationship unprovoked. Nothing had been said, and there were no awkward silences to spur such a discussion. In fact, things had become quite comfortable between us, which is what worried me.

The answer I gave my father earlier about being on a slow mend with Jamie was the truth, but it didn't tell the whole truth. When you mend something, you must first decide if it's worth keeping, then you decide whether it can be fixed. If you want to do a good job, you look for other breaches so you can fix everything at the same time. You figure out the best way to put it back together, which sometimes isn't its original form. You decide whether you can fix it yourself, then gather the best tools for the job. And then you take your time mending it because if it breaks again, you might have to throw it out and get a new one.

Jamie and I had spent a couple of years together. I knew that our relationship was worth keeping, and I knew it could be fixed, but I needed time to look for other breaches. What had unraveled in Jamie that allowed him to make such a disastrous decision one night? What was fractured in me that wouldn't let me forgive him after all these months?

Jamie dipped his spoon into the soup our waitress had brought. "How many hamsters you got turning wheels in there, Poppycakes?"

He knows me too well for me to even attempt to slide around that. "We need to talk about our relationship," I said.

He swallowed. "Do you mean the relationship we're in right now where you don't trust me because I was unfaithful to you, and you're still deciding if you ever will, so we need to take things slow, and you'll come back when you're good and ready?"

"That about sums 'er up."

"Just saving us some time," he said. "I know where we stand."

"When are you going to get a haircut?" I asked. "You're looking a little Ted Kaczynski these days."

"You don't like my Unabomber look?"

"Is he on death row?"

"Doing life. Why?"

"Just curious."

✗ ✗ ✗

It was 2:15 PM when I pulled up to Capital Punishment, and the first thing I noticed was how dead it looked—like it had been abandoned. Did Troy tick off everyone and they walked out? Or did Miles lose the rest of his guys to rumors of *la migra*? Surely the protesters hadn't succeeded in shutting them down. Maybe everyone decided to take the holiday off after all.

The only sign of life was a red convertible BMW with the vanity plate GSHARP. Ginger.

The sound of metal clanking brought my attention to the front gate, which had been left unlocked. Anyone could just walk through, and I was anyone, so that's what I did. I tried the sliding metal entrance door. Locked. Same thing at the gift chamber, so I hoofed it around the building to the kitchen door, which had been propped open with a cinder block.

"Ginger?" I called as I crossed the threshold. "I'm here to finish the inspection." The door must have been open for a while because the kitchen felt like a hug from a sweaty aunt. "Hello?"

The room was darker than a black steer's tookus on a moonless prairie night, but no lights came on when I flipped the switches. By the time I reached the cooking line, I ran out of daylight from the open door.

If you're not the curious sort of person—the sort of person who must know how things end, who finds it difficult to sleep at night if everything isn't sorted according to size and color and placed in its proper compartment—then you would have gone home and come back another time. But if you're the sort of person who has to know why a restaurant that needed to complete thirty days' worth of work in eleven days had been deep-sixed in the middle of a workday, you would have pulled a flashlight out of your inspector's backpack and gone Indiana Jones in search of an answer.

I decided to come at it like I would a surprise health inspection, if the surprise were on me and I had to start doing them in the dark. I painted broad sweeps of light around the kitchen, taking in the big picture, then I spotlighted countertops. Except for four empty beer bottles sitting together in a puddle of their own sweat, they were bare. I made a quick check of the sinks. A new one had not been installed, so they wouldn't be passing their food permit inspection. But with no electricity or construction workers, that would not be their worst news of the day.

I pointed my flashlight at the floor and saw that I had a straight shot across the kitchen. "Food police! Freeze!" I said as I burst through the kitchen door. No one but me laughed at my silliness. I swept the light over the dark space and saw that the crates that contained Ol' Sparky had been moved to the center of the room.

I lifted the flashlight and ran the beam along the catwalk. It looked much as it had earlier, except now there was a body hanging by the neck from a rope.

EIGHT

"Girl on the premises," I called out of habit as I let myself into the Johns's kitchen.

My voice sounded like what you would expect it to after spending the past couple of hours answering official questions. I had already been through a police interrogation when Évariste Bontecou was killed at Markham's, so I tried to be helpful by offering more details from the start so they didn't have to ask for them. That worked against me, however, because they became suspicious of my precise memory and asked even more questions to trip me up. It also didn't look good that they found two people on the property when they arrived and I was the one still earthbound and breathing. After giving them my father and Jamie as alibis, they let me go.

The clock on the stove showed 5:17 PM. The Johns had decided to keep Four Corners open until 8:00 PM for the holiday, so they would be gone for a few more hours. *Goody goody gumdrops.* I needed a long soak in some warm water, and I didn't want my peace or my thoughts disturbed.

I went to the bathroom and started filling the tub, then sprinkled in some expensive-smelling bath crystals that, to my delight, turned into bubbles. As I waited for my bubble bath to mature, I browsed the titles of books resting on the back of the toilet: *The Catcher in the Rye*, *To Kill a Mockingbird*, *Anna Karenina*. That last one was probably put there by John Without just for show. There were also a couple of Western novels, a book on dog obedience, and one that made me smile: *A Confederacy of Dunces*. It so perfectly described Troy, Todd, Danny, and Miles.

I settled into my bath and reflected on the day's unsettling episode. The detectives hadn't told me they thought it was a suicide, but I heard the word. And that's what it looked like—Troy Sharpe hanged himself in an empty restaurant. They didn't have to tap into a keg of brain power to come up with that.

But it takes time for cops to investigate a person's life, and they can know only what they're told by friends, family, and official files. They would find out that Troy had been a star high school quarterback fawned over by everyone from the lunch ladies to the school nurse, the prom king who married his queen, a US Marine—reasons to live. If they sifted through another layer of sediment, they would uncover a drinking problem, a discharge from military service, an unhappy marriage—enough tarnish on his shiny life to make their suicide theory not unlikely.

The thing about a theory, though, is that it mixes facts and speculation to come up with the most likely possible outcome. You might say that the more facts you embrace, the better the theory. And you would be wrong. A liberal dose of guesswork can be just as effective because it, too, requires facts. Facts mixed with intuition.

I had not spent much time with Troy, but it was enough to know that he was a hero. Not like Boo Radley, who came out of the shadows to save the day and then quietly returned to them. Troy had heard crowds chanting his name every Friday night. He drove a flashy German coupe with the vanity plate 8SHARP. He liked practical jokes, which require victims and witnesses for maximum impact. He was opening a death-themed restaurant on the anniversary of a notorious mass murder's execution.

No, Troy was more like Holden Caulfield, who is the hero of his own life, and that type of hero always needs an audience. It was possible that the rotten stuff in his life had putrefied enough to prompt a suicide, but there was no way Troy the Train would have taken his own life all alone in an empty restaurant. That was my theory, anyway.

Before I could entertain alternate theories about how Troy got dead, the bathroom door swished open and there stood John Without, looking like an Oscar in shiny gold bike shorts and matching shirt, a folded newspaper in his hand.

I threw my arms across my chest. John Without screamed and brought his free hand to his mouth.

"Why aren't you at work?" I demanded.

"I'm setting stuff up for tomorrow night before I go to the gym. Why aren't *you* at work?"

I had parked at my house under the carport, so he probably hadn't seen my Jeep. "Didn't you hear about the accident?" I asked.

"Oh, please," he said. "When are you going to stop using that hurt hand excuse for everything?"

"When are you going to stop dressing like Barbie's hairdresser?" He could find out about Troy on his own.

Cool air had worked its way over to the tub and settled onto my skin, giving me goose bumps. It made me aware of the absurdity of having this conversation with my neighborhood archenemy while under a thinning blanket of bubbles. John deserved what I did next.

I sunk lower in the water, then put my hands on the sides of the tub and made to push myself up. "Can I get dressed, please?"

A crimson flush vaulted up his neck, past the sparse ring of drab brown hair and over his fallow scalp. He extended the palm of his free hand in front of him, then slapped the newspaper over his eyes. Sports section. "Stay!"

I ignored him bossing me like a dog. "Sorry, John, but I can't stay in the bath *and* put clothes on."

John turned his back to me. "I'm leaving."

"Don't bust a bicep," I said as he slammed the bathroom door. Then he slammed the front door.

I had just finished drying and dressing myself when Jamie called. "Are you okay?" he asked.

"So far." I knew he wanted to ask me a bunch of questions about Troy's death, and I wanted to bounce my theory around with him, so I asked if he would bring a movie over to the Johns's house. "Something dark and moody," I requested.

—✗——✗——✗—

"You went to the same high school as Troy, right?" Jamie asked.

"He was two years older," I said. "I didn't really know him, though."

We sat facing each other on either side of the center cushion of the Johns's green microsuede couch, drinking fresh orange juice that Jamie had brought for me. I never get tired of seeing him in faded jeans and a black T-shirt.

He had already done some inquiring and knew a lot about what had happened. His police scanner had alerted him to the death, then his sources at the Austin Scuttlebutt Factory embellished the story. He seemed disappointed that I couldn't confirm the rumor of a pentagram on the floor under the corpse. "But it was dark, and I didn't get that close," I said.

"What happened to the electricity?" he asked.

I sipped my juice. "It worked earlier. I can't imagine what happened to it in the three hours I was gone."

"Are you sure you're okay?"

"Yes," I said, but I wasn't, and I didn't know why I was putting up a brave front. I didn't need to be rawhide around Jamie. But I did need to be cautious. This was one of those occasions that could easily rush the mending of a broken relationship. A vulnerable sniffle from me, a consoling hug from him, and then the Johns would be walking in on hanky-panky. "It just sucks to see a dead body again."

"Police are saying it looks like a suicide."

"Looks like. It could also have been an accident." I told him about Troy's floor show but not the gurney race because the fake hanging would be hard enough to explain without breaking confidentiality if Jamie decided to probe. "The rope had been tied to a pole on the catwalk."

"Why was he playing around with a noose?" he asked.

"Apparently Troy liked practical jokes."

"And he was playing one on himself?"

"Troy was the loudest and the least stable of all of them. And he drank. He was probably goofing around."

"Did you tell that to the police?"

"I figured I'd let someone who knew him better tell them. But what does it matter? Accident or suicide, he's still dead."

"It matters to the beneficiary of his life insurance policy. They usually don't pay off for suicide."

I reached for the bottle of juice, but Jamie got to it first and refilled my glass. It felt good to be taken care of, and I smiled my thanks.

"So there's a catwalk, huh?" he said, quite happy to have another ration of black market information. "Are they doing burlesque?"

"Please don't post about the catwalk!" I said. "You're going to get me into a heap of trouble if that comes out."

"How would anyone know it was you who told me? Did they make the EMTs and police officers sign nondisclosures before they entered the building?"

"You're not dating those city officials."

"I'm not dating you, either."

"Jamie."

"Okay, I won't use it. But give me another hint."

"Can we please confine ourselves to Troy's early release from this world?"

"Troy. The guy who built a catwalk in his restaurant and is not doing burlesque. Would you tell me if it were burlesque?"

"Jamie!"

"Okay, okay. Was he the kind of guy who would take his own life?"

"From what I saw, no. But it takes a long time to understand the nuances of someone's behavior. When Jeffrey Dahmer bragged on the playground 'I eat little boys like you for breakfast,' who thought he meant it literally?"

"Penelope Jane!"

It's not easy to shock Jamie, and I was so pleased to hear him call me by the fake full name my father made up to admonish me, I leaned over and kissed him on the cheek. He smelled good. "Gallows humor," I said. "Is he on death row?"

"Dahmer? He got something like a thousand years. But he's dead already. Another prisoner beat him with a broom handle."

"What do you think was his last meal?"

"Manwiches. You hungry?"

"Not anymore," I said. "Really, though, I can't see Troy killing himself after all the time and money he put into the restaurant."

"You're ruling it an accident?"

"That doesn't seem right either, but I can't say why."

"That leaves homicide."

"Or Dick Powell and Claire Trevor," I said. We play a trivia game where one of us names two actors and the other has to come up with the movie they starred in together.

Jamie smiled when he finally figured it out. "*Murder, My Sweet*." Then his soft copper-brown eyes hardened, and his beautiful face went from triumph to concern. "Poppy."

"I wonder if this is related to the power being out."

"It was one thing to help your stepsister, but you don't even know this guy."

"You're right."

"But you're going to look into it anyway, aren't you?"

"You know I don't like uncrossed Ts," I said. "I'll make a few discreet inquiries. All of my suspects are tied to the restaurant."

"You already have suspects?"

"Three or four. What I don't have is a motive. I might need your help, okay?"

Jamie shook his head, which could have been his answer but was more likely his opinion about my desire to involve myself in something that was none of my business.

He had brought *The Green Mile*, and we both moved closer to the center cushion to watch it. The Johns came home during the ending credits, John With apologizing for interrupting us, John Without banging things around in the kitchen to disturb us further.

I walked Jamie out to his car, then went to bed, but I had a hard time falling asleep. Thinking about Troy's death contributed to my insomnia, but I also heard a faint whining sound that could have been either John Without talking about his favorite topic—himself—or another puppy the frat boys down the street had adopted.

I also realized that I was falling in love with Jamie. Again.

NINE

THE NEXT MORNING, THE Johns left early for their art gallery, as they had done every morning since I moved into their guest bedroom. I've lived next door to them for almost three years, but if you asked me if that was their normal routine, I couldn't tell you.

I have two relationships with the sunrise. I'm either starting my day before it happens or I'm sleeping through it after working into the early morning on a "sneak and snare" project—my name for the kind of project that snares restaurant employees doing sneaky things, like throwing dead rats into the dumpster when they think that all of the county health inspectors are snug in their beds. But ever since Olive put me on light duty, I had been keeping banker's hours. I didn't like it.

After the first few days of living with the Johns, they had finally stopped treating me like a houseguest, but every morning before they left, they placed a coffee cup, a spoon, and a bottle of maple syrup on the counter, and prepared the coffee maker to brew two cups. All I had to do was press a button. I say "they," but I know it was John With—the tall one *with* dark, wavy hair and a crooked smile—the nice one. The one I have a harmless crush on, which is why his boyfriend doesn't like me.

Olive had called twice while I was in the shower, and she called again as soon as I started peeling a banana. I don't like speaking to my boss on the phone. She usually gets right to the point, which I appreciate, except she rarely has a point to make. She says stuff like, "He called about your report and wants to know what you mean about the ice scoop. Fix it, Markham." Then she hangs up before I can remind her that a lot of my reports mention an ice scoop and does she want me to fix the report or fix the ice scoop situation at the restaurant or fix things with "him." She never answers when I call back, so I do what I think is right, which usually prompts another call from her, and we start all over. This is one of the reasons she thinks she has to micromanage me.

I hadn't written any reports in the past few days, so I let my phone ring while I paged through the reasons she could possibly be calling. Just to say hi was out of the question, as was checking on me to see how my hand was healing. She could want me to fill in for an inspector on vacation, but that would require full duty. Full duty! I couldn't answer the phone fast enough. "Purgatory Pool Hall. You whack 'em, we rack 'em." I keep hoping that one day she'll play along.

She didn't play along, and she didn't want to put me back on full duty. She wanted a report on my permit inspection of the Sharpe place. "In person, Markham."

"My hand hurts when I drive," I said.

"Fast-track me, then."

"I think what you mean is 'bottom-line me.'" I explained to her about the sinks and the water.

"They just called and want to know where you are."

"Isn't it a crime scene?"

"Police cleared it an hour ago. I told them I'd personally make sure you showed up." And then, to my horror, "Come pick me up."

As I silently denounced having my baffling boss on a ride-along, the sunny side of this fried situation found me: Olive would now see that I knew my stuff and appreciate that I handled myself as a professional. Troy wouldn't be there to bribe me or challenge me to a gurney race, but Todd might argue with me about the sinks or a blade saw might fall from the catwalk and slice off my ear. Once I healed and returned to work, Olive would start to trust me, and I wouldn't have to account for every hour of every day. Maybe she would take my side once in a while against those crybaby cooks who think it's okay to keep a Mason jar full of gasoline in the reach-in because gasoline, they assure me, loses its combustible properties in cold temperatures.

— x   x   x —

The sound of the highway roaring through the Jeep's missing doors made conversation impossible, but Olive appeared to be content with her large bag of crispy orange doodle things, and I was content to marvel at the eating machine that is her mouth. It occurred to me that this meal of empty carbohydrates and artificial everything might be her breakfast.

As we sat at the light at I-35 and Slaughter, I asked, "Is that what you'd eat for your last meal?"

She adjusted the air-conditioning vent toward her face. "What do you mean, last meal?"

"The AC doesn't work," I said, which should have been obvious. "If you were going to die, what would you have as your last meal? Anything you want."

"Right now, I'd kill for a Popsicle," she said, fanning her face. "Then lamb chops with mint jelly and a champagne cocktail." So she wasn't a complete food ignoramus. "And a whole mess of tater tots."

The light turned green, and I made a left onto Slaughter. Rice, beans, and tater tots sounded good.

Around 9:00 AM I pulled up to the front of the restaurant as Olive leaned her head back and emptied the bag's crumbs into her mouth. Most of it landed on her Hanging Tree Golf Club shirt, and she brushed the orange confetti onto the floor of my Jeep. She always wears golf shirts, and everyone in the office calls her Golferina behind her back, even though the only club we've ever seen her hold is a sandwich.

"That…the…restaurant?" she asked between licks of her fingers.

"Yes ma'am."

The front parking lot was empty of cars and people, but I could see activity behind the back fence. I caught glimpses of white and silver, which could only be a mobile snack truck that had set up behind the restaurant to sell breakfast to the workers. I wondered if they had seen what happened to Troy back there the day before. It would really help my investigation to know if he had passed out or if someone had knocked him out, as he claimed.

Olive balled up her empty bag and dropped it among the crumbs, then hopped out of the passenger seat and hitched up her black polyester pants. I noticed an Ace bandage around her left ankle, but she didn't favor either leg as she marched up to the gate, put her hands around her mouth, and yelled, "Yoo-hoo! Health department."

Olive turned back to me and called, "Shake a shank, Markham." But I stayed right where I was, safe from the werewolf bounding toward the front gate. A German shepherd up close, homing in on Olive as if she owed him money.

"Holy doglegs!" Olive cried as she sprinted back to the Jeep and heaved herself into the seat. I had never seen her move with such enthusiasm.

"What's so funny, Markham?"

"He's behind a fence."

"I see that now."

"Not on a long chain or roaming free around the property like some restaurants I've been to." And where had he been the day before? He would have deterred the protesters.

"What's your point?"

"He can't get to you."

"Don't know why you're busting a gut over it." She picked up the snack bag from the floor, uncrumpled it, and mined the bottom for crumbs with her finger. "I'll wait here." She struck gold and stuck her finger in her mouth.

I was sure that Olive thought that waiting for me in my Jeep would be an incentive for me to get in and get out, but it had the opposite effect. I wanted to take my time and keep her braising in the hot sun so she would think twice about wanting to come with me on another inspection. I unzipped my backpack and took out my badge.

"What's the restaurant like?" she asked.

I tried to put her off by pretending she had asked about Markham's recent upgrade from a humble Bar & Grill to a fancy Cocktails & Grille. "Nina did a nice job redecorating, actually. White tablecloths and candles, leather chairs. I don't think we need the extra 'e' after Grille, but she didn't ask me."

"I don't care about your daddy's restaurant, Markham. *This* place."

"Oh. It's a big gray square with lots of shiny new equipment in the kitchen."

"What kind of food? Uhtalian, French, fusion, what?"

"I can't tell you."

Out of crumbs and patience, she jolted to life and turned toward me. "What are you trying to pull, Markham? You trying to make a fool of me? Think 'cause I'm not out in the field all the time I won't understand what you're saying? I've eaten in plenty of restaurants."

"It's not that, Olive. They made me sign a confidentiality agreement. I can't talk about the restaurant. You don't need to know anything except what I reported about the sinks and the water." Right away I realized I shouldn't have started that sentence the way I did.

"Don't need to know!" she yowled. "I need to know everything."

"Sorry, but I have to honor my word. There's really nothing to tell. The dining room wasn't finished, and I—"

"I'm your *boss*."

"I'm sure if you signed your own agreement, they'd let you look around."

"Don't think I won't." She swung her legs to the right and hopped out of the Jeep, then immediately hopped back in when the dog growled at her. "Take me back to the office, Markham."

"I thought they were in a hurry for their permit."

"They can wait."

I did not argue with her, and I did not sigh as I pulled away from the gate.

By the time I dropped her off, it was noon, which meant that traffic would be slower than beach erosion from Airport to Oltorf. Since this permit inspection was the only thing I had on my schedule, I decided to kill some time at Markham's, work on Trevor's drink, check out the new general manager, then head back to the house of horrors in the afternoon. If Todd or Danny called looking for me again, Olive could explain why I hadn't shown up.

x x x

My phone rang with a call from Mitch as I pulled into the front parking lot of Markham's, but I didn't answer because I would see him in thirty seconds. Nothing was so imperative that it couldn't wait that long. I unlocked the front door of the restaurant, then stepped into the cool, dim dining room, despising Évariste Bontecou's killer for robbing me of the peace I felt when I walked into the place I love.

Ever since I left Markham's to become a health inspector, I've stayed out of the restaurant's business, but if I had a single reservation about the new GM—even if I didn't like his name—my father would hear about it.

Mitch walked out of the office and saw me across the dining room. "Hi, hon!" he called. "Come say hello to Coop."

I hoped I hadn't heard him right. Maybe he said boop or poop or goop. But I knew he hadn't. The only reason Mitch wouldn't tell me who he had been talking to on the phone the day before was because the new general manager of my family's restaurant was Drew Cooper.

My legs wanted to run for the front door, but that was impossible because they could no longer support my weight. I felt a change in cabin pressure, but no oxygen masks dropped from the ceiling. I grabbed for the seatback in front of me.

Mayday!

TEN

If I bolted, I could take some time to get my mind around this, but it would look like I still cared, which I did not. If I stayed, I would have to do something I had given up on ever being a possibility: talk to the brute.

"Poppy honey?" Mitch called.

I couldn't decide what to do. "*Momentito*," I said. "Going to the ladies."

Indecision made my legs work, and they carried me to the bathroom. I started breathing again, then checked myself in the mirror. I looked, well, comfortable. When did that happen? Not just my clothes, but me. I hadn't colored my hair in a few weeks, and dark blond roots mixed with gray framed my face. And even though I felt furious, it showed up as pain in my green eyes.

Why did he have to come back now? Why come back at all? And how could Mitch even consider letting him through the door? I had racked up three years' worth of reservations about Drew Cooper, and my father was going to listen to every single one of them.

I was calculating my chances of making it to the bar unnoticed for a quick jigger of calm when the door opened and Ursula squealed, "Poppy!" She rushed toward me with her arms out, all crinkly eyes and exposed teeth. "Oh, Poppy!" she said, wrapping her arms around me.

When my father started spending time with Nina and I heard Ursula's name for the first time, I pictured Ursula Andress, the Bond girl actress. Except for the hair and skin tone, I wasn't far off. Ursula York is tall and elegant, with long, red curly hair framing a pale face, and fierce blue eyes that don't usually glitter.

She is also the product of a privileged childhood and prodigious talent in the kitchen, which makes her the very definition of a prima donna chef. She does not squeal. She does not smile. She does not embrace anything—critiques of her food, menu ideas, new employees, friends. Yet there I was, being rocked side to side in an Alpha Delta Pi sorority hug. The residents of Pearl Harbor could not have been more surprised than I was at that moment.

Perhaps it was National Practical Joke Week and she was playing one on me. Or my father was, and he had sent Ursula into the bathroom to tell me that Drew wasn't really waiting outside. I relaxed, but only a little. The memory of Troy's delight at my spirited reaction to his rope trick made me stand still and do nothing lest I make a fool of myself again.

Ursula pulled back but held onto my shoulders, her blue eyes searching mine. "How are you?"

She sounded sincere. Maybe she wanted me to do her a favor. Although if we were tallying who owed who what, my side would be lifted high with favors done and Ursula's dragging the ground with favors owed.

"Good," I said.

"And the Johns's? Are you happy over there?"

"Mostly."

"Great!"

She released me to look at herself in the mirror. Ursula did not look comfortable. She looked radiant, her face lit up from within, and she moved with a lightness and ease that I imagined angels did as they bounced from cloud to cloud on their way to meet up for a cappuccino.

"Did you get a Michelin star?" I asked.

The tinkle of her laughter seemed to flutter the air in the bathroom. She turned and pulled me to her again. This time I hugged her back.

"Oh, Poppy!"

"Wait," I said, drawing back. "Did Mitch send you in here to put me in a good mood?"

She looked like I had crushed her wings. "No. Why would he?"

He wouldn't. He knows how I feel about Ursula. She would triple my agitation, so maybe Mitch had sent her to tump me off balance so I would be discomposed and docile when I saw Drew and wouldn't give him what-for afterward.

"What's with all the hugs and the Poppys?" I asked. "Why are you talking in exclamation points?"

She threw her hands into the air. "I'm free!" Then she lassoed me again. "Thanks to you."

"Oh, that," I said into her shoulder. "You would have gotten out eventually."

She hugged me tighter, then gave me a kiss on the cheek. Not a faux air kiss like she gives Nina, but a loud smack. "I'm out *now*! And I have an offer to write a cookbook!"

She released me, and I stepped out of grasping range. "An offer from who?"

"Évariste's publisher. I'm going to be famous!"

"Isn't that kind of…never mind." Why should that surprise me?

She wetted a paper towel and wiped her face. "Have you seen the new GM?"

There were so many ways to answer that question. "Yes," I said, "I've seen him."

"He's going to be perfect," she said, then floated out the door.

Unless I took holy orders and became a nun, I would have to talk to Drew eventually, so it may as well be now. I pulled out my pony-tail and finger-combed my hair. I wasn't wearing any makeup and didn't have any with me, so I pinched my cheeks and bit my lips to draw color. Then I washed my hands with lavender soap and dried them on my shirt and pants, hoping the fragrance would overpower my eau de highway exhaust.

I took one final look in the mirror, then went to say hello to the former love of my life.

x x x

"You won't believe our food costs from the grand opening," Mitch said. I found him sitting in the manager's office, shuffling through a pile of papers. Alone. He resumed crooning, "'Like the fella once said, ain't that a kick in the head.'"

"Where's Drew?" I said.

"I sent him to the bank."

I dropped into a chair across from my father and gave him a look that would have made anyone else stand and salute me.

"I know what you're going to say," he said.

"That not even Benedict Arnold would have done this to his own daughter?"

"We need him, honey."

After an argument a couple of weeks ago that preceded my father's collapse, I had promised myself I wouldn't be so quick to anger with him, but I couldn't keep my promise. Not after Drew Cooper.

"*I* don't need him," I said. "What kind of drugs did they give you in the hospital? Don't you remember what he did to us? How he disappeared? No notice, no explanation?"

Mitch leaned back in his chair. "I'm under doctor's orders to take it easy for a while. I need a manager I can—"

I shot out of my chair. "You can't swing a bullwhip in Austin without lashing a thousand restaurant managers. Why Drew Cooper?"

"He knows Markham's, and he's good. He can start with almost no training."

"You and Nina had to cut your honeymoon short when he left!"

"Are *you* going to come back and manage the restaurant?"

"This isn't employee stuff, Daddy. This is daughter stuff."

He looked down at the desk and sighed. He can be so bad at the daughter stuff.

I wiped a sneaky tear that had started down my cheek. "You should have told me."

"Nina said the same thing. I tried to call you." He came around the desk and gave me a hug. "I was wrong, and I'm sorry."

Yes, my father was wrong, but the boss was right. Drew has a gift for managing restaurants and could be trusted to run the front of the house. He could hire and schedule the wait staff, hostesses, and bartenders, deal with customers, pay bills, lock up after midnight. With Ursula back in the kitchen, Mitch could rest easier and focus on getting stronger. This was father stuff, too.

Mitch leaned against the desk. "Can I count on you to help him if he needs it?"

"I'd sooner be friends with Nina," I said, crossing my arms and putting some extra poutiness into my words.

Mitch patted my shoulder, then returned to his chair. We were okay.

"Did Drew tell you why he deserted us?" I asked.

"Yes, but I think you should hear it from him."

"It won't matter. The damage has been done. To me, at least."

"I believe you'll feel differently once you hear his story."

"I doubt it." I took a step toward the door, then turned back. "Daddy?"

"What is it, honey?"

"Don't hold me to being friends with Nina."

— x   x   x —

You wouldn't know it from seeing my own house, but cleaning soothes me. Doing any mindless activity, really, which was what this ambush called for. When I worked in the kitchen and needed to occupy my hands, I would prep vegetables. Never mind we didn't need them. They would eventually find their way into a soup or a lunch special. In fact, some of my more creative dishes sprang from having three pounds of diced tomatoes or a garden's worth of chopped tarragon in the walk-in.

I found a clean grill towel in the wait station and started with the coffee maker. I turned off the burner, which is exactly what it does—burn coffee—and violated health code by pouring the stinky brown liquid into the hand sink. Then I filled the coffee pot with soda water, salt, and lemons, and set it on the counter.

"Well, well, well," said a man's voice behind me.

My stomach had plunged at the first "well," thinking Drew had returned from the bank, but then I recognized the drawl.

"Hey, Trevor," I said uneasily, turning to face him.

Trevor had been one of my suspects in Évariste's murder, and I hadn't seen him since the last time I questioned him. He'd had several days to work up a nice harangue heavily weighted with "How could you" and "I told you so."

Trevor leaned against the reach-in and crossed his arms, his left forearm wrapped in gauze and clear plastic. He smiled slowly, and I dropped my eyes to the floor, glad that I wouldn't have to take my medicine in front of an audience.

"You just poured out my lunch," he said.

"Sorry," I said, which is what I was going to say at the end of his reprimand.

"It's time to switch to the good stuff anyway." He reached under the counter for a glass, then filled it with the official drink of people under thirty—Dr. Pepper.

"I suppose that would be part of your last meal request," I said.

"With about a hundred of Ursula's salmon cakes."

"That's my recipe, you know," I said. "And dessert?"

He lifted his glass. "More of this."

"That stuff will wreck your taste buds," I said. "What happened to your arm?"

"New ink." He held eye contact with me as he took an extra big gulp of his drink.

Like most people who are really into tattoos—a group that specifically excludes girls who put a quarter-sized rose on their shoulder or guys who think that a barcode on the back of their neck is clever—Trevor has illustrated his body with words and images of personal significance: a paw print to honor his favorite puppy, a man riding a tricycle along a path of six stars in memory of his father's death when Trevor was six years old.

"What's the subject?" I asked.

"It's a commemoration of recent events in my life."

"Can I see?"

He unwrapped the plastic and pulled the gauze back to reveal the words *non coupable* in the shape of a knife healing on the tender inside of his forearm. "It's French for 'not guilty,'" he said.

"Is that a poppy flower on the tip?"

He smiled.

"You never actually said you didn't do it," I said.

"You never actually asked me if I did."

"It was my first murder investigation. I went with the evidence I had." I looked up at him. "I'm really sorry, Trevor."

"Two apologies in one day. Lucky me." He topped off his soda, then said, "And for the record, I didn't kill Troy Sharpe."

Ursula came through the swinging doors holding a spatula and looking like a red-headed Tinkerbell. "Oh, hi, Poppy," she said, then to Trevor, "I didn't realize you were busy. Can you please come talk to me about the specials when you're finished here?"

"Sure thing, babe," he said.

Ursula backed through the doors and Trevor looked at me, grinning like Alexander the Great after he cut the Gordian knot.

"So it's not just me because I got her out of jail."

77

"Check this out." He leaned over the counter so he could see through the pass into the kitchen. "Hey, babe," he called, "I thought your marinade could use some extra garlic, so I added about ten cloves."

"Thank you!"

"You two must be on again," I said.

"Like that ever gave me privileges with her food."

"True." Simply expressing an opinion other than "perfect" about one of Ursula's recipes would be a death sentence even for Trevor, regardless of relationship status.

"Plus, she's not thrilled about me and Belize," he said, reproaching me with a raised eyebrow.

I had been the one to tell Ursula about his secret affair with the waitress, but only because of my investigation. "That makes a hat trick of apologies I owe you."

"She's almost over it," he said, rewrapping his arm. "I'm pretty irresistible when I want to be."

"I know she's excited about the cookbook, but that doesn't explain why she's channeling Mary Poppins. The pressure should make her sourer, not sweeter."

He glanced through the pass into the kitchen, then lowered his voice. "Care to wager on when she'll turn?" He pulled a piece of paper from the front pocket of his chef's coat and showed me a list of names, each followed by a date. "Your ten will take the Diva Pot to two hundred. My money's on June sixth."

As Ursula's sometimes boyfriend, Trevor has inside information and knew that June 6 is her birthday. No doubt he was counting on the big three-five to trigger a meltdown. I'd already cruised past that mile marker and knew something Trevor, at twenty-five, couldn't know. The day after is when you wake up and realize that you're halfway to the town of Elderly.

"Put me down for the seventh and an IOU."

x   x   x

Talking to Trevor had injected some sunshine into my disposition, and I no longer felt compelled to clean the wait station. It had also reminded me why I had come to Markham's in the first place.

I went to the bar to work on Trevor's drink. Mitch wouldn't care what I came up with, but I wanted the drink to be a singular tribute. I already didn't like the name I had proposed. Trevor's Treat was a drink for someone who parted his brown hair on the side and drove a hybrid, not a blue-eyed, sinewy flirt who wore his long blond hair in a ponytail and rode a motorcycle.

A drink for me would be easy: something deep red, like a Manhattan, heavy on the grenadine, with a dark roasted espresso bean or splash of dark cacao in the center to complete the look. Poppy's Red Alert or Opi-yum. Ursula's drink would be equal parts dry vermouth and pickle juice over lots of ice with a slice of lime. The old Ursula anyway. The new Ursula would be sweet and frothy, some sort of pink spiced rum daiquiri topped with a cloud of whipped cream. Ursula's Undone or Angel's Parfait. Both versions were extreme and equally unpalatable.

Trevor, however, wouldn't be so easy. I picked up a shaker and started mixing, thinking of names—Trevor's Truce, True Blue, Blond Adonis. After an hour, I didn't have a drink or a name, but I had nipped enough of each contestant that I felt a little tipsy. After cleaning up behind the bar, I made myself an Americano and sat on a barstool, sipping my watered-down espresso in the cool hush of the restaurant.

I didn't want to think about Drew Cooper, but how could I not? The bar at Markham's may have been upgraded, all granite and squeaky leather, but the space would always harbor the memory. Here, on March 18, in the wee hours after St. Patrick's Day, after the restaurant had closed, Drew had added Owner's Daughter's Boyfriend to his curriculum vitae. Just the two of us, me behind the bar mixing margaritas, explaining how to make the perfect one, Drew sitting on one of the seasoned wooden stools, watching me with something on his mind.

That there was a story behind Drew's subsequent disappearance, a story that Mitch had already accepted, meant that I might have to consider an attitude other than righteous anger. Of course, my father is quick to forgive people he's not related to. He also has a Y chromosome, which would make him more inclined to accept a story about Drew running off with another woman. But even Mitch couldn't be so thick as to believe that such a story would smooth things over with me.

And, aha! That's why Mitch had asked whether Jamie and I were back together.

Jamie.

Drew had been four months gone by the time Jamie and I had started dating, yet he had hung over our budding relationship like a shroud. Drew is the reason Jamie had to work so hard to gain my trust in the first place, and I realized now that Drew was the reason I couldn't easily forgive Jamie for his indiscretion.

I heard movement in back of me and looked up at the mirror behind the bar and into the familiar hazel eyes of Drew Cooper.

ELEVEN

"Hello, Sugar Pop," Drew said.

I cursed myself for not being ready for this, for not thinking through every possible scenario between us and preparing a reaction so I could direct the conversation. Or at least not look foolish. I did time in the Girl Scouts, but I had forgotten the most important lesson: don't get caught with your pants down.

"My name is Poppy," I said. I placed my hand over my carotid artery to cover the pulse that cosmonauts at the Space Station would be able to see if they looked down.

"What happened to your hand?" he asked.

Nothing about Drew had changed. Three years hadn't aged him, hadn't fattened him up, hadn't loosened any skin or chiseled any wrinkles. Not even a gray hair among the black waves. But there was a tired sadness in his eyes that I had never seen before.

"Long story," I said.

The flaming anger I had directed at my father would have come in handy right about then because all along the target had been Drew. But the coals of my mind had cooled and wouldn't serve me anything but clichés: How are you? It's been a long time. Nice to see you. I slipped off the stool and behind the bar, hoping movement would spark something more scorching. It didn't.

"So, you're back," I said.

"Looks like it."

"It's been a long time."

"Yes, it has," he said, matching my neutrality and distance.

From the first week Drew started at Markham's, I suspected he was interested in me, but we worked together for months as friends. I figured he was too much of a professional to go after the owner's daughter, but he told me that night he hadn't wanted to rush me. He said he was waiting for me to come to him, that I was worth the wait. That he would have waited forever.

"Are you getting the hang of things?" I asked.

Drew looked around the bar. "Markham's may be dressed in a fancy evening gown and pearls now, but the bones are the same. I'm already ready to send Mitch home."

Watching the easy way Drew held himself, the way his shoulders moved beneath his white dress shirt, I thought about what I felt the first time I saw him: nothing.

It's the same way most women react to him. He's just there. Not unattractive, but nothing to make you look twice. But after a time, after you get to know him, feel his quiet steadiness and strength, you wonder how you overlooked him. You remember how you weren't always on your best behavior around him. You start to regret all those times you had a beer with him after a long day in the kitchen and didn't brush your hair or wash your face. You begin to ask him questions about himself, like how he spends his time when he's not working and if he has a dog. Then, after a long, busy holiday night when you tell him that the secret to your margaritas is that they're made with love, he knows it's time to express his feelings for you.

And then one day, after he has erased all doubt from your mind that he's the one you want to spend the rest of your life with, he vanishes.

It was my turn to say something; however, any topic not restaurant-related could be dangerous. But I was still tipsy, and when I'm tipsy, I like a little danger. "Where have you been for the past three years?"

"It's been thirty-five months," he said. Always so exact. "It's a long story, too."

"How long could it take to explain that you ran off with another woman?"

His eyebrows scaled his forehead. "Is that what you think?"

"I had also allowed that you were in the witness protection program, but that's seriously cliché and doesn't seem likely now, seeing as you're standing here."

He eased himself onto a bar stool and looked at me.

"Well?" I said.

He took a deep breath. "The night before I left, I got a call from a hospital in Denver. My mother was really sick. I couldn't get a flight, so I drove all night."

"You couldn't have called me?"

"After all the calls back and forth with the airlines and the hospital, my cell phone died. I planned to call you when I got there."

"That's your excuse?" I said, suddenly very angry. "A dead cell phone? I called you every day for two months." The memory of making those calls and hearing the same cheerful voicemail greeting agitated every chamber of my heart. "You fell in love with your mom's nurse, is that it?"

He looked away like he always did when he was choosing his words carefully. "You still think you know everything."

"Just tell me so we can move on."

Drew's face hardened. "Like you moved on with Jamie Sherwood, what, four months later?"

"Don't tell me you expected me to wait around in my wedding gown until you tired of your fling!"

"Poppy, it wasn't a fling."

"So there's a Mrs. Drew Cooper. How nice. Are there baby Coopers, too?"

Drew stood quickly and almost lost his balance. "Let's talk about this another time."

He walked off, a slight limp and the lack of a wedding band the only indications that things had not been entirely perfect for him during his time away.

My mind began to sizzle and spit as it cooked up choice cuts of *should*. I should have left the bar as soon as I saw him. I should have told him that Mitch's forgive-and-forget gene skipped a generation. I should have said yes to Mitch—I would quit my job and manage Markham's.

No, not that. I love my job.

Even though I had no clue what to do about Drew, I knew that his very presence was sure to complicate my already-complicated relationship with Jamie. Even though Ursula turning over this confusing new leaf meant that I had to rethink how to handle her. Even though I hadn't slept in my own bed for weeks and was instead living in the guest room of two gay men. Even though I had to prove myself to Olive daily. Even after all of those things that I had not asked for and could not control, I could still follow rules, write reports, and keep Austin restaurants safe for the many thousands of diners eating meals away from home.

And if those people were going to eat the same meals as death row inmates, Capital Punishment would need a food permit.

—x—x—x—

On the drive south, I kept myself from dwelling on the heat by compartmentalizing the day's events according to color and size. I started with Ursula and her potential-famous-cookbook-author-induced sugar-and-cream routine with me and then with Trevor, which made me think about Trevor's drink, then Drew invading my thoughts at the bar and then my space—my life!—about his return to Markham's, and how I was glad I wasn't there anymore because I had another job, leading to Troy's body dangling from a rope like a Salem witch, which brought me full noose back to the Wicked Witch of the Southwest.

The old Ursula would be too self-involved to give Drew a second thought, but with her new generous spirit, she might take notice of him as a man rather than as simply another person to bend to her will. Those two working together so closely every day and every night…well, it was none of my business what they cooked up.

I arrived at Capital Punishment grateful to stop thinking about the motives of love and to start looking for a motive for murder.

—x—x—x—

Everyone responds to difficult situations in their own way, so I don't understand how someone can say that their friend or family member or neighbor or coworker didn't act normal in the aftermath of a tragedy. Because what defines normal? Movies or television shows that manipulate every bit of emotion out of our jaded hearts? Or news anchors who can narrate a story of child abduction with a somber face and then break into a smile when they announce, "Coming up after the break, a barbershop quartet…with an ice skating giraffe!"

Todd Sharpe met me at the back door, as he had done the day before. I wouldn't say he wasn't acting normal, but he didn't act as if he had lost his brother and best friend. Which was good, because if he had been gnashing his teeth and carrying around Troy's old football jersey like a blankie, I would have felt like a jerk as I tried to discover where he landed on the suicide versus accident hypothesis. Or if he had a reason to kill his twin brother.

"Thanks for coming," Todd said as we walked into the kitchen. "Sorry about yesterday."

"I'm sorry, too," I said.

"I can't believe he's going to miss the grand opening."

That was weird. "Is it still going to be on the eleventh?"

He frowned. "Why wouldn't it be?"

"I thought…let me take a look at the sinks."

"You know where they are," he said. "I'll be in the office."

A three-compartment sink and a mop sink had been installed, so I turned on the hot water faucet. Nothing. Cold faucet. Ditto. Before I concluded that they had trouble paying their utility bills, which would explain the blackout the day before, I looked under the sink and saw the problem.

Todd wasn't in the office, so I went to the silver door and looked out into the dining room. Filled with busy construction workers making a lot of noise, it took me a moment to locate him. He stood in the open doorway on the other side of the dining room speaking to someone I couldn't see.

With a 100 percent chance of raining tools, I wasn't about to leave the kitchen without a hard hat, so I went back to the office. There was only one hat on the floor.

It's just a hat, I told myself.

A dead guy's hat, myself told me.

I had no choice but to put on Troy's hat and go out to meet Todd. As I got closer, I saw that he was conferring with Miles Archer. Both of them stopped speaking and stared at me as I walked up.

"It was the only hat in the office," I said. "If you have a—"

"It's fine," Todd said. "What about the permit?"

"Almost," I said.

"Now what?"

"The sinks are in," Miles said, "just like I told you."

"Yes, the sinks are in," I said, "but the plumbing isn't hooked up."

"My guys were just about to get to that," Miles said.

Todd's eyes had voltage in them when he looked at Miles. "Get it done. Now." I had started to think of Todd as the nice one, but today he sounded a lot like Troy. "While she's here." He looked at me. "Can you wait?"

"For a little while," I answered, as if I were doing them a favor. But they were doing me one. I now had more time to investigate Troy's death.

TWELVE

MILES HURRIED OFF, LEAVING me with Todd. I followed his gaze up to the catwalk. Ribbons of yellow police tape surrounded the area where Troy had gone over.

Todd sighed.

I didn't know what to say, but I had to say something. "Are the police still looking for evidence?"

He shook his head. "There wasn't much to find."

"Then I think you can take down the tape."

When Évariste Bontecou had been killed, the police had put tape around parts of the crime scene at Markham's and taken pictures of little plastic numbered triangles next to evidence. They were finished within twenty-four hours and said it was up to us whether we left the tape up.

"It's kind of fitting in this place, don't you think?" Todd looked past me at nothing. "We've never done anything like this before."

Who was "we"? What had they done? I waited, but he didn't confess to anything, so I said, "There's a first time for everything."

"We've done some impulsive things, sure. But this…" He waved his hand around the dining room. "If only I hadn't let him talk me into it."

"Couldn't you have stopped it?" I asked. I had no idea what we were talking about.

Todd grunted. "When he decided to do something, it got done. You joined up and manned up or you got left behind. He wanted us to be marines, and suddenly I was at boot camp. He wanted us to open a restaurant, and I was cosigning a loan. Doesn't matter we have no idea what we're doing."

"Are those things you wanted to do?"

"Troy never asked what I wanted," Todd said. "He always got his way."

I didn't point out that they weren't Siamese twins and he could have lived his own life. "Did you get kicked out of the marines, too?"

He grinned. "That Ginger. No, Troy got a medical discharge and made me take early retirement."

"I didn't know Troy well, but I can't see him taking his own life."

Todd tensed. "Never."

"But the police—"

"It was an accident."

I was about to ask about Troy's medical discharge when Miles came up to us, damp and puffing from the effort of walking faster than leisurely. Miles looked down at the floor and put his hands in his jeans pockets.

"This isn't the army, Archer," Todd said. "You don't have to wait for permission to speak."

"My plumber took off." Miles looked out the double doors toward the back gate, indicating that his plumber had been part of the illegal immigrant panic.

"Then you do it," Todd said.

"Only if he's licensed," I said. Checking trade licenses is part of the building inspection, but as I was present and privy to this conversation, and as I didn't want them to pass my permit inspection quite yet, I mentioned it.

"Of course he's licensed," Todd said.

"I'm licensed as a general," Miles said. "I hire the plumbers and electricians."

Todd shook out his hands. "Figure something out," he said, then walked away.

Which left Miles and me looking up at the yellow tape.

"It can't be easy working around that," I said.

"Nothing about this job is easy."

"Besides spontaneous gurney races holding up construction?"

He snorted. "One delay after another. And right when I think I have a handle on it, Troy up and changes ever'thing."

"Like what?"

"Like he decides he wants a second floor right after we break ground so it'd look more like a real prison. Had to draw up new blueprints, order more materials. And all the while he wants to know how come I haven't started building yet."

We both stopped talking as we worked through the irony of Troy requesting the construction of the very thing that would eventually cause his death. That's what I was thinking about, anyway. Miles could have been thinking about Roger Staubach's game-winning Hail Mary pass in 1975.

"What happened with the electricity?" I asked.

Miles looked at me as if I had asked him the square root of pi, but first he had to figure out what pi was.

"It was off yesterday," I said.

"How'd you know that?"

It was possible that Miles didn't know I had been the one to discover Troy, and I wasn't sure if telling him would help or hurt my investigation. So far, there was no reason he couldn't be on the suspect list, and I needed to be careful. He would find out eventually, though. "I was here. I found Troy."

"Sorry, ma'am," he said. "No one was supposed to be here yesterday afternoon."

"When did you lose power?"

"Right after the cops hauled off them protesters." Miles pointed to the corner. "Thanks to Ol' Sparky over yonder."

I chided myself for not noticing an assembled *electric chair* in the restaurant, but when I looked where Miles pointed, I saw a mound of black plastic that appeared to be Troy's deflated stuntman pillow. It could also have been a tarp, which isn't so unusual at a construction site and therefore not worth special notice. And then I remembered Jamie saying that everything is worth noticing.

When my thoughts had finished with that, the impact of what he said hit me. "That thing works!"

"Tripped ever' breaker when Troy and them plugged it in."

I stared at the black blob. Troy hanging from the catwalk was nothing compared to what I could have shined my flashlight on if the chair had worked properly and Troy had been curious.

"Couldn't you flip the breakers back on?" I asked.

"Took out the transformer," Miles said. "The power company said it'd be a while 'cause of the holiday, so ever'body left. Acourse they got them lights turned on pronto when the police called."

"Why was Troy here?"

Miles looked up. "Besides to do what he done, I couldn't say."

We stood quietly for a moment, then I said, "Where was the dog yesterday?"

"Ma'am?"

"I saw a German shepherd here earlier today, but not yesterday."

"It belongs to one of my suppliers."

Todd's voice boomed through his walkie-talkie, startling both of us. "Archer! Sinks!"

"'Scuse me, ma'am," Miles said.

I 'scused him, then took out my cell phone and walked around the job site until I found a signal—which was, of course, in the middle of the unshaded parking lot—then called Jamie.

"Do twins commit…twinicide?" I asked.

"For brothers, it's fratricide, and it's not common."

"But possible."

"Anything is possible," he said. "You think it's the brother? Have you come up with a motive?"

"I haven't come up with anything except a case of the creeps from wearing Troy's hard hat…" I just stopped myself from saying "and seeing a working electric chair." Which I hadn't actually seen, but still.

"Hard hat?" he asked, as if I had leaked a clue.

"It's a construction site."

"Construction site, huh?"

I could have jostled with Jamie a little longer, but the sun had turned my hard hat into a hothouse and I wanted to get back inside. "The restaurant is under construction, and I have to wear a hard hat while I'm in the dining room."

"So…there's a dining room."

"Oops. Don't know how I let that slip. Please don't quote me as your source."

"What else can you give me?"

"Nothing. I wish you'd abandon these appeals."

"Never," he said. "Can you meet for lunch?"

"I'm waiting for them to hook up some plumbing, and I want to look around while no one is paying attention to me."

"Please be careful," he said, dialing up his tone to the serious setting. "If you're right and Troy was murdered…why don't you go to the police with your theory?"

"They can conduct their own investigation. I'll notify them when I solve the crime."

"Martin Short and Annette O'Toole?"

"*Cross My Heart*," I promised.

—✕—✕—✕—

Access to both metal staircases in the dining room was denied by a chain and a sign that warned Authorized Personnel Only. I figured it was part of the prison décor, and I did have a certain amount of authorization, but since I was sneaking around, I used the stairwell in the wait station that had no such restriction. If anyone asked, I would say I had come up to inspect the bathrooms. Not that I expected anyone to ask.

With the office door closed, I assumed that Todd had shut himself inside while he figured out how to play the fourth down without a quarterback. Miles had left through the front doors even though the sinks were in the kitchen. And I hadn't seen Danny. Was he the only one too rattled by Troy's death to carry on? Or was he afraid to show his guilty face because he had killed him?

The stairs let out at the opposite end of the crime scene, but I couldn't see anything else. A dim light came up from the first floor, which gave the second floor the illusion of being one of Dante's circles of hell. The seventh circle of violence, perhaps, or the ninth circle of treachery.

I pulled my flashlight out of my backpack and got my bearings. Bathrooms to my left, elevators ahead on the right, and ringing the catwalk were several individual prison cells, complete with metal bars. I always imagined that real inmates on death row spent their free time behind solid beige doors with little slits for food trays to slide through. But that wouldn't be easy to service in a restaurant situation, and it really wouldn't work for claustrophobic diners.

I walked straight ahead and shined my light into a couple of cells. Each had been furnished with a large round table, a semicircular six-person booth made from shiny black vinyl, and a single bare bulb hanging from the ceiling. Black tar paper covered the small windows I had seen from the outside, which explained the absence of light. All of the cell doors stood open, except for the one closest to the elevator, closest to where Troy went over. That cell held stacks of cinder blocks, bags of cement, masonry tools, and a couple of large brown boxes with dirty shipping labels.

The crime scene had been taped off-limits in a pie shape from the railing to an orange pylon in the center of the walkway, which took up a lot of floor space. How long did Todd plan to leave that up? As macabre as the very idea of the restaurant was, forcing guests to dine near a memorial shrine to his dead brother increased the grisliness by a factor of about twenty-seven.

As I approached the railing and caught my first glimpse of the floor below, my skin felt suddenly drenched in sweat, but my body shivered. At first I thought the effort of climbing the stairs two at a time had induced a myocardial infarction, which didn't seem very far from possible given my father's recent heart troubles, but also didn't seem very close to likely given my clean vegan diet and general good health.

I took another step toward the railing and finally comprehended why I felt like I was dying. I'm so rarely in a situation that puts me significantly higher than ground level that I had forgotten about my fear of heights. I can ride an elevator to the top floor of the tallest skyscraper and fly in an airplane, but I cannot look down. If you want me to confess to anything, threaten to put me on a ski lift.

I turned around and pondered whether I really needed to solve the mystery of the death of a narcissistic jerk who treated his own twin like a member of his entourage and spoke to his wife as if she were his ex-wife. I had no particular love for Troy Sharpe, and I couldn't bring him back, but I do have a love for justice, for keeping the universe balanced, and I knew I couldn't live with the burden of "what if." I had to know for sure what happened. If I wanted to see what Troy had seen from up here before he died, I needed to be where he had been, which meant that I would have to step closer.

I told myself I wasn't afraid of heights, which, circle-of-hellwise, placed me in the eighth, fraud. Plus it didn't work. I couldn't talk my mind out of something my body insisted on, so I stuck my flashlight in my mouth and took a couple of slow, deep breaths like we do in yoga class. I dropped to my rump, scooted to the edge, and grabbed the vertical bars of the railing with both hands.

The hard hat felt like a second head, compounding my dizziness and panic, so I leaned back and shook it off. It felt like a weight had been removed, which made things worse. I needed that weight to keep me grounded. I squeezed my eyes shut and released my hands so I could pivot around and turn my back to the abyss. I kept my eyes closed and felt around on the floor for the hat. My fingers didn't touch anything but grit.

I marshaled myself by visualizing what I would see if I opened my eyes. Cells in front and to my left, elevators in front and to my right, and farther down, the stairs that would take me back to where gravity was less terrifying.

I opened my eyes to slits to make sure I hadn't gotten turned around and was accidentally facing the void, then opened them all the way to see one thing I hadn't seen with my mind's eye and did not want to see with my real eyes.

THIRTEEN

A PAIR OF FRECKLED knees, pale, dry, and hairy.

Danny MacAdams squatted down in front of me. "Are you okay?" The overhead lights were on.

I took my flashlight out of my mouth. "Where's my hard hat?"

It had landed on its dome and rolled into the crime scene. Danny reached for it and saw Troy's name on it. "What are you doing with this?"

"It was the only one in the office," I said.

"This was in the office?"

"Yes, why?"

Danny placed the hat on my head. "We couldn't find it this morning."

He stood and held out his hand to help me up. My mind flashed on Évariste's killer making that same gesture before I had to scramble for my life, but I batted it away. This was a new investigation, and I needed to interview my suspect.

There we were, alone on the catwalk, standing in front of the very place Troy had died. What more perfect setting could there be to ask Danny pointed questions about his relationship with Troy? Except I couldn't think of anything but plunging over the railing.

"What are you doing up here?" Danny asked.

"I came up to inspect the bathrooms and thought I'd take in the view."

Danny rested his elbows on the railing and looked down at the activity. I took a step back for him, willing him to come with me, but he stayed put. "It's pretty cool, huh?" He seemed more relaxed than he had been before, and not at all like he was mourning the death of his business partner.

I took another step back, which took the drop out of my view, and my mind went back to work on thoughts other than staying alive. Where had Danny gone after Troy went down behind the restaurant? Todd and Troy had been arguing about him when they walked through the back door, and I had assumed Danny left in a huff over something Troy did or said. Did his huff boil into a fury and he came back later and killed Troy?

Danny looked over his shoulder at me. "Do you need to sit down?"

I nodded.

He went to an open cell and sat at a booth, motioning for me to join him. "You afraid of heights?" he asked as I slid in across from him.

"A little." In the cell, with Danny leaning back against the booth, we could have been having this conversation anywhere. "I'm really sorry about Troy," I said. "Todd indicated that you're still shooting for the eleventh?"

"We won't make it," Danny said, "but right now it's better to let Todd think we will."

"I'm surprised to see you with these guys. Did you become friends after high school?"

He looked at me with a question on his face, and I recalled that he hadn't been around the first time I refreshed Troy's memory about our alma mater. "I was two years behind y'all."

"I don't remember you," he said, "but I don't remember much about high school."

"Not even how bad the Sharpes treated you?"

"They weren't so bad."

I took off my hat and placed it on the table between us. "Are you taking some memory-erasing meds?"

He laughed. "Life's easier if you forget how unfair it is."

"How did you hook up with them?"

Danny told me he had moved to Dallas after high school and started working in restaurants, and eventually became a manager. He worked at a few high-volume restaurants around the city and was managing a Planet Hollywood when Troy and Todd walked in one night.

"I don't think I've changed that much since high school," he said, "but they didn't recognize me. It was getting on to closing time, and I let them buy me a beer at the bar. You know the type—the ones who think they're helping you get away with drinking on the job because you're with a customer."

"They also think they've bought your undivided attention," I said.

"Exactly. So they do a couple shots of tequila, which starts them reliving all these high school memories, and I finally tell them I'm Danny MacAdams, and they have no idea who I am. It takes a while for me to jog their memories, but they finally make the connection when I remind them about that time they replaced my clothes with Ginger's cheerleading uniform while I was showering after gym. 'Danny Dull,' they say. Troy starts talking about other tortures, embellishing as he goes along, but Todd apologizes."

"That must have made you feel good," I said.

"I really didn't care anymore. Besides, Troy was always the instigator. We have another drink, and they tell me they just got out of the marines and have this great idea for a restaurant, something nobody has ever done before, and ask if I want to run it for them. By that time, I could see they hadn't changed in twenty years, and they won't tell me what they're planning. I figure I don't need to get involved with amateurs, so I tell them I'm happy where I am and wish them good luck."

"Obviously not the end of the story," I said.

Danny laughed. "They didn't win so many football championships because they like to give up. The next day they come back and ask what it would take for me to say yes. Todd is doing all the talking this time. I figure they're grandstanding like they always did, so I name a monster amount of money and tell them I want to move back here at their expense and I want a new car."

"And here you are," I said.

"They didn't even blink."

Since Danny and I were buddies now, I figured it would be okay to say, "I hope you don't mind me saying, but for all that trouble to hire you, they don't listen to your advice."

"They do about some stuff, but Troy had grand plans and didn't like them sidelined, no matter how crazy they were."

"Like buying an electric chair?" I said. "How did he get a real one?"

"He had a replica made. Spent a bundle on it, too. I tried to tell him that we'd never be able to get insurance, but he did whatever he wanted. I didn't know it was juiced until Monday." Danny absently tapped Troy's hard hat. "Next thing I know, we're getting deliveries for eight-foot gallows replicas to hold the lights over the tables."

"Sounds like every day was a challenge."

"More like a grudge match," he said. "I finally figured out it was better if I didn't say anything, but that wasn't always easy." He jerked his thumb toward the cell behind him. "That one's got boxes of medieval death implements in it. I had to hide them from Troy because he wanted to plan a raid on some of the construction workers while they were napping after lunch."

What else had Danny done to derail Troy? "I can't believe he killed himself."

Danny looked out the cell toward the orange pylon and yellow tape. "If you knew him better, you would believe it."

I slumped against the booth, disappointed that everything was what it seemed and there was nothing to investigate. "Was he upset about something?" I asked, then waited for Danny to tell me a country-western song's worth of reasons why Troy would have wanted to end it all.

He looked back at me. "What? No. He was always drunk and always messing around. I'm sure he did it to himself, but whether it was an accident or intentional, we'll never know."

I sat up straight. Troy's truck didn't break down, his dog wasn't dead, and his wife hadn't left him. My investigation was still on. "Why do you think he was messing around up here while the power was out?"

"For his own amusement," Danny said. "Which is pretty much why he did anything." Seeing the disgusted look on his face, I wondered whether he had remembered the trauma of his high school days or recalled something more recent.

The walkie-talkie hanging from his pocket crackled. "Miles to Danny, over."

Danny answered, "What's up, Miles?"

"Is that lady inspector still here?"

"I'm with her now."

"I got the water working."

"We're on our way down," Danny said into the mic, then to me, "Feeling better?"

I put on my hard hat. "It's only bad if I look down."

Danny stayed between me and the railing as we walked to the stairs. Whether he assumed I had already inspected the bathrooms or it had escaped his attention, nothing was said by either of us. I now had a free pass back to the crime scene whenever I needed it.

x   x   x

In the few minutes it took for us to get down the stairs and into the kitchen Miles had disappeared, but Todd was waiting for Danny. He wore a smile that made me wonder if he had received news that St. Peter had commuted his twin's death sentence and Troy had been brought back to life.

"Suzi Grimm will see us if we can get to her office by three o'clock," Todd said.

"I'll drive," Danny said.

"I checked every sink, and the water works," Todd said to me on their way out the door. "Find Archer when you're done."

"Sure," I said.

What I really wanted to find out was why those two wanted an emergency huddle with a criminal defense attorney the day after their business partner died. Were Todd and Danny in some trouble together? Like maybe they had killed Troy and needed to do some what-iffing with Suzi Grimm?

I started with the three-compartment sink and turned on the cold tap. Water came out, as promised by both Miles and Todd. I turned on the hot tap and pulled out my thermometer while I waited for it to heat up to 110 degrees. A few minutes later I went in search of Archer.

I hadn't seen Miles in the dining room when Danny and I had walked through earlier, so I checked the back alley first. An unmarked snack truck rested in the shade of the building. Miles stood under the truck's silver awning holding something wrapped in paper. Veggie wraps are not usually the go-to fuel for hot, hungry construction workers, so I knew that his belly would be getting a significant number of fat grams in the next few minutes.

"Miles," I called, starting toward him.

He handed his lunch back to the snack truck operator, then met me halfway. "We got them kitchen sinks hooked up, ma'am."

"The plumbing is hooked up, but there's no hot water."

"There's not?"

I searched Miles's face for signs of mental disability. How could someone with so little concern for detail read a blueprint, much less oversee the complex construction of an entire restaurant to spec? Miles had blamed Troy for construction delays, and yes, having to add a second floor at the eleventh hour, suspending construction every time Troy indulged his inner six-year-old, and dealing with a power outage for an entire afternoon so close to deadline were out of Miles's control, but the man was sloppy and lazy. It would have taken less than sixty seconds to check his work on the sinks. Why did I have to be the one to tell him?

Because I am a health inspector. "It's not working in the kitchen," I said. "I didn't check the bar, wait station, or bathrooms."

"Sorry, ma'am. Does Todd and them know?"

"Todd and Danny left, so you're the first."

"They left?"

"They had an emergency appointment. How long before the water is fixed?" I pointed to the snack truck. "Do I have time to do a surprise inspection while I wait?" And ask the vendors if they saw what happened to Troy the morning before he died.

Miles looked back at the truck, then took a step toward me. "Sorry, ma'am, but you can't do that now."

"Now is the perfect time. They're so well-hidden back here, they'd never expect a health inspector to drop by."

He took my arm. "Troy doesn't want anyone but me and my guys here when they're not at the site."

I took my arm back. "Troy is dead."

"I mean Todd." He looked down, and I noticed a shiny patch of skin on the very top of his head. "Look, I'm in the doghouse for the building taking so long, and I don't want them to holler at me about you, too."

"I'm hardly a stranger, Miles." Wait, what was I doing? If he fixed the water and they passed the inspection, I would need to be sworn in as a police officer to keep investigating Troy's death. Miles had handed me a good reason to come back. "But I don't want you to get in trouble."

"Much obliged, ma'am."

"I can come back in the morning."

"We're staining the floors tomorrow, so it'll have to be the day after."

"Thursday," I confirmed. I started for the back door, then wondered what he could tell me about Troy. Miles had worked closely with him for a few months, or at least in close proximity. He could wait a few minutes to eat lunch. I turned around. "Miles?"

"Ma'am?"

"Was Troy around the job site much?"

"Yep."

"Every day?"

"Yep."

"Did you get to know him very well?"

"Nope."

That's what I got for asking yep or nope questions. "How did he seem to you?"

"What do you mean?"

"Was he sad or depressed?"

"I really couldn't say, ma'am. We weren't friends exactly."

I learned from Jamie that when conducting an interview, you should start with questions you already know the answers to so the subject feels comfortable talking. I had seen Troy dress down Miles the first day I was there, so I knew Miles would have plenty to say about that. "Did you have problems with him?"

"Nothing I can't handle, but I'm all over the site, especially now that we're finishing out. I can't help but see stuff."

"Like what?"

He looked toward the back door as if he expected Troy to come through it. "It don't seem right for me to speak ill of the dead."

That's what he said, but I could tell he was going to anyway. I didn't have to wait long.

"Troy got into it with ever'body, seems like. Todd and Danny, that snooty blond wife of his, even those guys letting him try their food. Troy'd eat ever'thing and ask for seconds, then tell them thanks for the free lunch but he already had a supplier. They'd be packing up their things, madder'n hornets. Troy'd be laughing at them like it was the funniest thing."

I knew how they felt. "Did any of them threaten Troy?"

"Not that I heard, but like I said, I'm all over the site."

"What did he argue about with Todd and Danny?"

Miles looked toward the back door again. "The usual stuff."

"Business or personal?"

"They'd start out talking about the restaurant, like what color chairs did they want. Seemed like Danny and Todd never agreed with Troy. Troy'd say red and they'd say black. Then Troy'd say they were always double-teaming him, then Todd'd say he was being paranoid, then Danny'd try to get them to stop bickering and pick a color, and they'd tell Danny to shut his pie hole." Miles shook his head. "Ever' doggone day it was something."

"And Ginger?"

"Who?"

"His snooty blond wife."

Miles pulled a red bandana from his back pocket and wiped the sweat from his face and neck. "That one's meaner'n a skilletful of rattlesnakes. One day they're sweet as pie, loving on each other, the next, she's yelling and saying he's a no-good scoundrel."

"Was there anyone Troy *did* get along with?"

He laughed without mirth. "With the right number of beers in him, he could get along just fine. Ever'body was his buddy then."

"What about the protesters?"

"The prosti—"

"Tree huggers."

"Oh, them. He didn't like them either."

Miles looked like he had more in him, so I stayed still, quietly perspiring. But I had gotten all I was going to get because Rudy whistled to him from the back door.

"I need to get back to the job, ma'am."

It had not been a productive interview. Miles didn't tell me anything I couldn't have deduced had I taken time to think about it. I had already seen Troy's comedy/tragedy act, his love affair with alcoholic beverages that he carried on without shame in front of everyone, and his bumpy relationships with Todd, Danny, and Ginger.

I had a lot of work ahead of me if I wanted to pursue my scrawny theory about Troy's death not being what it seemed. Unless I ignored it. That would be easier. But if I had ignored my suspicions that a gourmet sandwich shop had been secretly substituting cheap pork for prime veal in their Better Calf sandwich, who knows how many more kosher Jews would be filling up their bathtubs for a *mikveh*. It's not against health code to cheat the public, but it's wrong. Within hours of Jamie posting his "You've Been Porked" exposé on his website, several rabbis had called for a *cherem* of the deli, and justice had been served.

No, I couldn't turn my back on Troy's murder. Better to keep grinding away at clues until a solution started to percolate. I could let Troy get away with accidentally killing himself, but I wouldn't let one of his inner circle get away with murder.

x — x — x

I went into the office to return Troy's hard hat, which had always been available for me to use only because he never wore it. That would make sense if he wanted to end his life and hoped to have his skull crushed by a falling cinder block or a hammer, but that was no guarantee he would die. It could blind him or leave him paralyzed, wearing adult diapers and drooling. If it were me, I would think through the consequences of being that reckless.

But this was Troy. He seemed to enjoy being careless—negligent, even. And everyone around him put up with it. Why? Todd was an equal partner and had as much say in how things were run as Troy did. I didn't know if Danny had a money stake in this venture, but he had given up a good job in Dallas. He was the only one with the kind of restaurant experience this place needed, yet Troy had shut him down every time he spoke up.

I put the hard hat on the desk but didn't want them to think I had left without finishing the inspection. Not that I didn't trust Miles, but the hot water not working was another blunder in a long list. It would be easy for him to save face by fixing the water and then claim it was working the whole time.

I was out of business cards, so I attached a yellow sticky note to the hat: *Checked sinks. No hot water. CU Th at 8.* My handwriting with my hurt hand had improved a little, but it still looked like a tipsy ten-year-old had written it.

I seemed to be quite alone in the kitchen, so I decided to do some covert snooping. In case anyone appeared, I pretended to check my backpack while I scanned the desk for anything interesting, like a million-dollar life insurance policy on Troy, dunning notices from suppliers, bank statements with a negative balance, or a suicide note. I saw nothing but restaurant paperwork: order confirmations from meat and produce vendors, a half-finished application for a liquor license, and equipment catalogs.

I "accidentally" slid my backpack over the top layer of papers and shuffled some of them to the side, revealing handwriting on a legal pad. The pad was upside down, but I could make out the words *corpse* and *last rites*.

Jackpot!

FOURTEEN

I COULDN'T BELIEVE SOMEONE would leave something like that laying around for just anyone to see! But I suppose if you're dumb enough to take notes on a murder, you would be dumb enough to leave them out in the open.

Sadness immediately replaced my elation at this discovery because a plan meant that Troy's death was premeditated, and Todd and Danny had ganged up on him one last time.

I poked my head out the door to make sure I was still alone, then pulled on rubber gloves and walked around the desk so I could read the paper right-side up. They were notes about death, but not Troy's. I had momentarily forgotten the restaurant's theme.

It was the beginnings of a menu. It looked like Troy had started it because *End Zone: Food to Die For!* was written at the top, but the paper had the handwriting of three or four people. They listed their "visiting hours" as *24/7 365*, then wrote menu headings, but with death-related words substituted for traditional ones, like *First Offenses* instead of appetizers, *Main Corpses* instead of entrées, and *Last Rites* instead of desserts.

Then it appeared they had scrapped those headings because actual last meals include a little bit of everything and don't lend themselves to separation into categories. The names of executed inmates were listed, followed by their entire last meal request.

Dieters or vegetarians could order the Harry Charles Moore and get two green apples, two red apples, a tray of fresh fruit, and two 2-liter bottles of Coke, or the Karla Faye Tucker and get a salad with ranch dressing, a banana, and a peach.

If you were in the mood for seafood, the Allen Lee Davis got you one lobster tail, a half-pound of fried shrimp, six ounces of fried clams, fried potatoes, half a loaf of garlic bread, and 32 ounces of A&W root beer.

If you wanted breakfast, you could order the Mark Dean Schwab and get fried eggs over easy, bacon, sausage links, hash browns, buttered toast, and a quart of chocolate milk, or the Frank Coppola and get a cheese-and-egg sandwich.

Really hungry and in the mood for Mexican? Ask for the David Castillo and get twenty-four tacos, six enchiladas, six tostadas, two cheeseburgers, two whole onions, five jalapeño peppers, a quart of milk, and a chocolate milkshake.

If you wanted a little bit of everything, you could get the Dennis Wayne Bagwell: a medium-rare steak with A1 Steak Sauce, fried chicken breasts and thighs, barbeque ribs, French fries, onion rings, bacon, scrambled eggs with onions, fried potatoes with onions, sliced tomatoes, salad with ranch dressing, two hamburgers, peach pie, milk, coffee, and iced tea with real sugar, or the Robert Smith: steak, lobster, shrimp cocktail, chicken livers, meatballs, fried eggplant, a salad with blue cheese dressing, a small loaf of bread, a whole Boston cream pie, and three cans of Trevor's favorite, Dr. Pepper.

For the kids, there was the Margie Velma Barfield: Cheez Doodles and a Coke. Olive would enjoy that one. Or the Roger Dale Stafford: six foot-long hot dogs with chili and cheese, a large order of French fries, and two chocolate milkshakes. The Timothy McVeigh was two pints of mint chocolate-chip ice cream.

Death row inmates have years to plan their last meals, which, I imagine, accounts for the culinarily incongruous combinations. They probably keep a running list of foods they're dying to eat and when the time comes, ask for everything on it. I would still like to have rice, beans, and tater tots, and maybe a chocolate soy milkshake. I had heard of some death row inmates refusing to order a last meal. They were either in denial about their future or very hopeful for a last-minute stay of execution.

Under the heading *Name Your Poison*, the guys had started a list of bar drinks. Their "signatory" cocktail, the Lethal Injection, was two shots of any liquor served in a syringe; Ol' Sparky was a vodka martini with Tabasco sauce and jalapeño garnish; Contraband was a shot of Jack Daniels bourbon, neat; Executioner's Song had a question mark after it, as did Guilty As Charged and Solitary Confinement. It reminded me that I still needed to come up with a drink to honor Trevor. Maybe call it Non Coupable?

I stood by the opinion I had given Danny earlier: their concept was sick and twisted. Austin would love it.

I heard a whump as the door leading in from the dining room flew open. "Todd?" Ginger called.

I had two seconds to strip off my gloves and dart around to the front of the desk before Ginger appeared in the doorway looking like she had finished running four laps around Town Lake, a tight black tank top and matching shorts the only indication that she might be in mourning.

"You again," she said. "How long does an inspection take?"

She had just lost her husband, and I thought I should be delicate with her, so instead of saying "It takes as long as it takes," which is the answer an attitude like that always deserves, I said, "Usually not this long. They've had some construction delays."

She rolled her eyes. "Thanks to Miles Archer. Why Troy let those guys talk him into using a home remodeler to build this place, I'll never know. And now they're weeks behind." She looked around the empty kitchen. "What did he muck up this time?"

"There's no hot water."

"Does Todd know?"

"He's not here."

"His car is out front."

"He and Danny left about thirty minutes ago."

Ginger smoothed her ponytail. "Do you happen to know where they went?"

I waited for her to look at me before I answered. I didn't want to miss the tiniest nonverbal reaction. "Todd mentioned an appointment with Suzi Grimm."

Nothing. Not even a twitch of an eyebrow or an involuntary intake of breath. Either she didn't recognize the name or she was a better poker player than Johnny Chan. Or I was wrong about Suzi's area of expertise.

"Did he say when he would be back?" Ginger asked.

I had been so sure Suzi's name would break through her icy scaffold that I didn't have a plan B. So I answered her question. "Nope."

And then I had a whole bunch of questions for one of my prime suspects. "Ginger, did you and Troy—"

A phone rang, and she put hers to her ear before I could determine if it was her phone or mine. "Hello, Ginger Sharpe," she said. She listened to her caller, then waved me out of the office and shut the door behind me.

I stood on the other side and listened with all my auditory nerves, but she kept her voice low. A couple of workers came into the kitchen with paint buckets. They turned on a radio, blowing any chance of me overhearing anything through the office door. I waited for about five minutes, but Ginger never raised her voice or emerged, so I went out to my car, frustrated by yet another blockade.

I knew that my murder theory was based on conjecture rather than facts, but so was the accidental death theory Danny and Todd believed. Both theories relied on Troy's behavior and what the theorist believed about that behavior. I saw Troy as a hot dog who had probably never spent time alone except to go to the bathroom, and even that may have happened in front of an audience on a few occasions. Everyone else saw him as a hot dog who drank too much.

I needed a new plan. But first I needed food.

I called Mitch to see if he wanted to have a very late lunch or a very early dinner. Now that Drew had the restaurant under control, Mitch had his free time back. It would have happened regardless of who Mitch hired as general manager, but it happened a little faster with Drew, which was the only good thing, as far as I could tell, about Drew coming back.

I wanted to apologize to my father for my earlier behavior, and I missed dining out with him. Nina believed she had permanent dibs on what little time he had away from the restaurant and kept him busy with needless shopping trips, boring country club parties, and inane complaints about her masseuse making her lie on 300-thread-count sheets rather than 600-count.

"I'd love to, honey," my father said, "but it'll be awhile. I'm about to tee off at the back nine with Ari and Ira." Mitch's attorneys, the Gross brothers, were the only two seasoned golfers in Texas with enough patience to play with a man who thought they were talking about lettuce the first time they offered to split the greens fees.

"That reminds me," I said. "Is Suzi Grimm still the Grimm part of Grimm, Grimes, and Gross?"

"She is, but let's talk about this at dinner, okay?"

"Okay, but just tell me if she's still doing criminal defense."

"Vis-à-Vis at six o'clock," he said.

Overpriced and high-hat, Vis-à-Vis sounded like something Nina would choose, but I had to take my father where I could get him. "I hope you're buying," I said.

x   x   x

I had a couple of hours until dinner, but I didn't have any work to do, and I had never developed any hobbies because growing up in a restaurant and working breakfast, lunch, and dinner doesn't leave a person with much time for anything other than sleeping and eating and worrying themselves sick about labor costs and customer satisfaction. I needed groceries, clothes, and housewares, but I didn't have a house to put them in. So I called Jamie to see if he wanted to meet for coffee.

"I'm tied to my desk finalizing a proposal for *Deliciousness Magazine*," he said. "But if you'll bring me some *pan dulce* from La Tita Blanca, I'll break away for a few minutes."

115

Thirty minutes later, after a quick trip to the east side, Jamie and I were the only warm bodies in the downtown office he shares with two freelance writers and a graphic designer. He took a bite of the Mexican pastry. "This sure is comforting," he said. "Is it a *panadería*?"

"Yep, you guessed it. Troy Sharpe was about to fulfill his life's dream of opening a gigantic two-story bakery."

"Have you solved the Mysterious Case of the Dangling Dude?"

"Not yet," I said. "I'm starting to think that maybe there isn't a mystery."

He widened his eyes in mock shock. "You don't say."

"*Starting* to think. I'm not ready to give up. I know you think I'm trying to stay busy, and maybe I am, but you know how you know something even though you don't know?"

"Like how I knew something was wrong when I heard about all those dishwashers at chain restaurants quitting their jobs."

"Exactly. This whole thing doesn't feel right to me. I mean, if your twin brother or business partner or husband had died suddenly and tragically, would you be back at work or keeping up with your exercise program the next day?"

"People handle grief in different ways."

"I guess," I said, frustrated that he didn't give me an answer. "If you thought I killed myself yesterday, would you be sitting here today working on this proposal?"

"I don't know. Maybe."

"Really? You wouldn't be wondering why my life was so bad that I didn't want to live it anymore? You wouldn't be asking yourself if there were signs you missed, if there was something you could have done?"

"They think it's an accident."

"I'm making a point, Jamie. If I had died yesterday, wouldn't you be devastated?"

"Yes, I would be devastated to lose you." I heard genuine sorrow in his voice. He wasn't talking about my fictional death. He almost did lose me. We almost lost each other.

"Have you heard anything about a suicide note?" I asked.

"No, but that doesn't mean there wasn't one. If Troy's family asked the police to keep details about the case private, they wouldn't mention it. Or if he wrote something incriminating in the note, the police might keep it quiet."

"Incriminating how?"

"If Troy confessed to being involved in a crime or accused someone else."

"Oh, that's good, like maybe Todd or Danny…" I stopped. "No, if there's a suicide note, that would mean Troy killed himself."

"Unless the note was faked."

"Oh, good idea! So we need to know if there was a note." My eyes landed on the police scanner Jamie kept at his desk, which gave me an idea. "Will you do me a favor?"

He broke off a piece of pastry and handed it to me. "If I can."

"I'm not sure it's possible," I said, which turned it into a challenge and guaranteed he would help me.

"Anything is possible."

"I want to look at the crime scene photos."

He didn't say anything, and I knew he was either deciding whether he should encourage my investigation by getting the photos or trying to figure out if it really was possible. I needed him to at least try.

"Think about it, Jamie. Pictures of the *inside* of the restaurant."

He sighed, then said, "I'll see what I can do. Anything else? Tickets to the Super Bowl? A signed first edition of *Gone with the Wind*? The Hope diamond?"

"You couldn't get the Hope diamond."

"For you, I would try." He tapped my nose with the tip of his finger. "After I finish this proposal."

FIFTEEN

I WENT TO MY office to do drudge work—check email, restock my inspector's backpack, report to Olive in person.

My coworker, Gavin Kawasaki, had emailed me a link to a news report. He collects restaurant stories that have an odd twist and likes to give them a new ending. I read about a chef in Iowa who not only kissed, licked, and stuffed a couple of live toads into his mouth in his restaurant kitchen, but committed the act to video and then posted the file on the Internet so all the toad lovers out there could live frogcariously through him. Local health inspectors found his behavior unsavory and squeezed a $335 fine out of him.

Gavin had written, *When asked about their time inside the chef's oral cavity, the toads croaked about poor dental work and halitosis.*

My cell phone rang with a call from Olive. "Den of Delights," I answered as I walked to her closed office door. "What's your pleasure?"

"Fast-track me on the Sharpe place, Markham."

I knocked on her door and heard it echo in the phone.

"Hold on," she said.

"They don't have any hot water," I said when she opened the door.

She brought the phone to her ear to answer me, then understood the situation a nanosecond before she looked completely foolish. She returned to her chair but didn't invite me to sit. She never does. Maybe because she thinks I'm going to ask to share some of her liver-flavored pork rinds.

"They're staining the floors, so I can't go back until Thursday," I said.

"You're really milking this permit inspection, Markham."

"It's not my fault they don't know what they're doing. Besides, I *want* to work, remember? Put me back on full duty."

"Not with that hand of yours," she said. "I can't read half your reports. Pizza Pig made a deal with L and L, so you can do a mobile tomorrow. Noon."

That would be a mobile vendor permit inspection. This type of inspection is similar to a food permit inspection, but instead of walking around full-size in the vast spaces of a restaurant, I contort myself into a circus acrobat so I can make sure the truck meets specifications. As an independent operator, the owners of Pizza Pig had had a tough time finding an approved location to park their truck when not in use, and they couldn't get a permit until they did.

No, you can't just park it on the street in front of your house. You need access to a commissary kitchen where you can safely dispose of your dirty or "gray" water, and that has a potable water source to supply you with fresh drinking and cooking water. You can also use the space to clean your unit, store raw ingredients, and prepare food. A mobile snack company, Lunch and Larder, had apparently rented them space. And rather than send me to inspect this unairconditioned truck in the cooler morning hours, Olive had thought-fully scheduled the inspection for noon.

An inspection for a "cold truck" is easier because it's for a restricted permit that allows vendors to serve only cold food that is prepared in the commissary, like sandwiches, pasta salads, and fruit cups. An unrestricted permit is for vendors who want to have a grill or oven in their truck so they can prepare hot food to order. Since most people prefer gooey, cheesy pizza right out of the oven, Pizza Pig probably wanted the latter. But I didn't want to assume.

"It's a hot truck, I presume."

"Yeah." Olive licked fragrant residue from her right index finger, then started typing with it. "I'm emailing you the paperwork."

I went back to my desk and printed the documents, then deleted several emails from Olive that had subject lines ending in exclamation points. I added rubber gloves, thermometer condoms, and the last of my business cards to my backpack, then sent an email to Olive requesting "More Biz Cards!!!" Then I headed downtown to the Warehouse District for dinner with my father.

x   x   x

I didn't see Mitch when I walked in, but I did have my second jolt of the week after discovering Troy strung up on the catwalk. Well, third, if I counted Drew Cooper. Fourth, if I counted Ursula's 180 turn from ogress to angel. Okay, fifth, if I counted a small, angry gay man interrupting my bubble bath. I'd had an earthquake's worth of jolts, actually, so I should have taken another one in stride. But I found that difficult to do because this jolt had been calculated and orchestrated by my father. Again.

Nina sat on a bench inside the door, talking on her cell phone and examining her dragon-breath red toenails. Her face looked salon plumped, her lavender linen cocktail dress tamed into unwrinkled obedience. "Have you noticed all the gray in her hair lately?" she said into the phone. "I hear she's on the outs with her hairdresser."

I backed away like a coward from a gunfight and stood in the courtyard deciding among three options. I could retreat and fume, which would make Nina happy. I could stay and fight, which would ruin Nina's dinner, but also mine and Mitch's. Or I could stay and make nice. If Mitch could see that I had gotten his life lesson about holding my nose around people who stink, maybe he would stop trying to force the two of us into smelling range.

I walked inside and tapped my stepmother on the shoulder.

She looked up with one of her fake smiles, then dropped it when she saw me. "Poppy?" she said in a voice as metallic as her short platinum hair. "Are you here to examine the restaurant?" She hadn't asked the person on the phone to hold.

"No, I'm not here to *inspect* the restaurant." I raised my bandaged hand. "I'm on light duty until my hand heals. I got hurt because I was trying to get your daughter out of jail, remember?"

I had given Nina an opening to finally thank me for doing that, but she raised an eyebrow at me and "uh-huhed" into the phone.

"Is Mitch here?" I asked.

"On his way," she said to me and into the phone. "He hasn't been golfing long enough to properly estimate the length of time nine holes should take to play."

A waitress brought her a glass of white wine, but Nina didn't ask if I would like something to drink or indicate that we were together. "Are you meeting someone?" she asked.

I figured she had spoken to the person on the phone, but after a moment of silence, I looked down at her looking up at me. "Isn't it obvious that I'm meeting Mitch?"

"There are my girls," Mitch boomed from behind us. He hugged me, then extended his hand to Nina, who ended her call and took his hand to stand. He kissed Nina's cheek, avoiding eye contact with me.

Mitch goes way back with the owners of Vis-à-Vis, Herb Wolff and Dana White, and he and Nina are regulars for dinner, so the hostess immediately led us to a coveted table by a window. I ordered a glass of Shiraz, and Mitch ordered a martini. Nina didn't veto his selection, so I assumed it was okay if he drank and didn't remind him about doctor's orders.

Mitch sat back in his chair and smiled. "How was your day, Duchess?"

Nina launched into a spellbinding chronicle of her search for a Persian rug to go with the valances in the guest bedroom, her lunch at the club with CiCi Chesterton, and her shoe-ting spree that started at Neiman's and ended at Nordstrom's. "I can't find any sandals to go with my new yellow dress," she said.

"I saw some yellow sandals at the thrift store the other day," I said.

Nina frowned. "The what?"

"Thrift store. It's where they sell used clothing."

"Is that where you shop?" she asked, wrinkling her nose.

"All the time. I find great bargains on all kinds of stuff."

"Bargains," she repeated, making the word sound scandalous. "Are those important to you?"

Mitch blocked my next gambit. "Duchess, love, why don't you take Poppy shopping with you the next time you go?"

The time had come for me to prove that I had learned my lesson. "That would be grand," I said, using Nina's words in the fake-happy voice I had heard her use so often. "When are you going next?"

"Sometime this week," Nina countered in the same voice. I'm sure the only reason she played along was because she thought I would decline.

I showed her my bandaged hand again. "I'm on light duty for a while, so name the day and time."

She consulted the calendar on her phone. "Let's see, I have a mani-pedi Wednesday morning, a tennis clinic Thursday afternoon, garden club on Friday…"

Not to be outdone in the important appointments department, I said, "I have to do a couple of inspections tomorrow."

"Oh, that's too bad," she said, putting down her phone. "Another time."

"But I'll be free after lunch," I said. "Shall I pick you up?" Nina had only so many moves in this chess game. And there is no way she would ride in my Jeep.

She consulted her calendar again. "Oh, pooh. I'm having a seaweed wrap at noon."

I looked at Mitch. "Oh, pooh."

"So let's make it two-ish?" Nina said.

Mitch raised an eyebrow and smiled at me. Checkmate.

Ish is for people who believe that everyone else's schedule revolves around them. I don't do *ish*. "I'll be at your house at two o'clock sharp," I said.

Nina and I looked at the king, but Mitch had played his end game and lowered his head to read the menu, even though he always orders the special when he dines out.

After our waiter delivered our drinks and took our order for the pineapple-marinated portobello mushroom for me and the duchess and the trout special for my father, Mitch put his hand on mine. "I'm sorry about yesterday, Penelope Jane. How are you holding up?"

"What happened yesterday?" Nina asked.

I looked at my father. "Is she serious?"

"I believe I told you while you were unloading the car, love. Poppy found Troy Sharpe dead while inspecting his new restaurant."

"Oh, that," Nina said, no doubt disappointed that we weren't gearing up to further discuss her lack of suitable footwear. "I heard his wife is divorcing him."

I choked on my Shiraz. "Where did you hear that?"

"At the club," Nina said, already bored. "CiCi's daughter is taking tennis lessons from…what's her name…Gina."

"Ginger?" I said, asking rather than correcting because Nina could have been spreading gossip about someone else ending her marriage.

"Yes, Ginger," Nina said. "I'm not surprised she wins so many tournaments with those meaty thighs of hers."

I hated to ask Nina for details, but it was not the time to put pride before a probe. "Do you know if Ginger was just talking about divorce or had she served him with papers?"

"CiCi will know," Nina said.

I cannot abide the interruption of cell phones in general and during meals in particular—for any reason whatsoever—but I didn't say anything to Nina when she picked hers up and dialed. That information about Ginger would be valuable currency when I returned to Capital Punishment and needed to bluff someone out of a secret.

While Nina "Really-ed" and "You don't say-ed" with CiCi, I said, "So, Daddy, tell me about Suzi Grimm. Is she still doing criminal defense?"

"As far as I know," he said. "Why do you ask?"

I couldn't tell him about my suspicions that Troy's death was not an accident, not while the Godmother of Gossip gabbed on the phone with CiCi Chatterbox, if I didn't want Ginger to know about it within ten minutes. And I certainly couldn't tell him that the very fact that Todd and Danny had an appointment with Suzi made me think they might be murderers. I lowered my voice. "I may need her services after my shopping trip tomorrow."

Mitch chuckled. "You'll have a good time." He ate a bite of bread. "But you asked me about Suzi before you made shopping plans with Nina."

At the mention of her name, Nina hung up the phone, then sipped her wine and cast her eyes around the restaurant.

"What did CiCi say?" Mitch asked kindly before I asked un-so.

"She thinks Ginger spoke with an attorney but hadn't served him."

From CiCi's daughter to CiCi to Nina, the rumor had been filtered through three suspect sources, maybe more, but it was all I had. I needed to figure out a way to get it straight from Ginger.

Over salads, Nina recaptured Mitch's attention and the conversation with her opinions about CiCi's Lap-Band surgery (she approved) and the upcoming fall fashion trends (she did not approve of wearing sequins before 5:00 PM), ignoring me and foiling any attempts Mitch made to include me.

It gave me time to stock my inventory of excuses for not going shopping with her: I found another dead body. The Johns are dressing me now. I joined a bowling league and rolled my way into the semis. Any one of them would do, because she wouldn't listen and she wouldn't care. Even if I wanted trendy clothes from a department store, and even if Nina did have a PhD in shopping, I didn't actually want to spend time with her. I just wanted Mitch to believe I did.

The needles on my patience and energy meters had been running in the red zone by the time Nina and Mitch ordered espresso and a dessert of fresh peaches infused with Cointreau, so I said good night and headed home.

× × ×

Once the exterior walls of my house had been repaired, I started doing surprise inspections of the interior to encourage faster progress. It was coming along, but I suspected that my contractor had not connected the air-conditioning unit to discourage me from moving in early so he had the leisure of working in an empty house.

I can rough it in a lot of ways, but sleeping when I'm hot is my least favorite. It's why I try to live right. I would never get a good night's sleep in hell.

So it was back to the Johns, who were both home. Had I not been so tired and annoyed, had my mind not been occupied with the day's events, I would have noticed the sign taped to the back door that read *No admittance until 10:00* PM.

I would have noticed a lot of things and would not have done what I did.

SIXTEEN

THE JOHNS'S RAISED WINE glasses were in mid-clink when I walked through the kitchen door, all of us surprised at seeing what we saw but for very different reasons.

Their kitchen table had been set with a white tablecloth, their M. A. Hadley collectible plates, and a flickering candelabra that looked like it had been FedExed from the Liberace museum in Las Vegas. An extravagantly frosted cake sat between them on the table, inscribed with "Happy Ann," the "iversary" split into two pieces on dessert plates.

That was my surprise.

John With's surprise was the fluffy Maltese puppy squirming in my arm. I had found it whining in a box on the side of the house and scooped it up on my way to the back door. The Johns had owned a Maltese named Judy, who got run over by a moving van a few months ago. I used to take care of her when they traveled. She was always whining, and I was always picking her up to make her stop, so when I heard this one, I did the same thing.

John Without's surprise was that I had ruined his surprise anniversary gift for John With.

I put the puppy on the kitchen floor, closed the door, and crossed the yard to do penance in my hot house. Had I owned a hair shirt, I would have slept in it.

x   x   x

After the fire that had destroyed my bedroom, I had cleared out everything from my house that was smoke- or water-damaged, so I had nothing with which to start my day the next morning except a toothbrush and a load of guilt that would have had a good Catholic wearing out the kneeler in a confessional. No coffee or food, no towels, no shampoo or soap, except for a dirty bar of pumice soap the contractor had left by the kitchen sink. As extra atonement, I rinsed it off and washed my face with it.

I could have eaten breakfast at any of the restaurants within walking distance of my house that served bagels and coffee to everyone, regardless of personal hygiene and thoughtless actions the night before, but I went next door. I knew what was waiting for me there, but I couldn't go a whole day with this hanging over my head. I don't like John Without, but I would never have done something like that on purpose.

I walked out of my house and looked across my yard that had been mowed recently, but not by me, and at their driveway. I didn't see John Without's car, so I went over to test the atmosphere with John With. I reverted myself to houseguest status and knocked on their front door.

John With answered with his crooked smile and a scolding shake of his head. "You don't have to knock." He wore a bright white polo shirt and long blue shorts.

He led me into the kitchen, pulled out a chair at the wooden table that had gone back to looking like it always does, except for the candelabra, and poured a cup of coffee for me.

"Where did you go last night?" he asked. "I was worried about you, but John wouldn't let me call."

"To my house."

"You don't have a bed."

"I don't deserve one," I said. "Where's John?"

"At the gym."

He set a bottle of maple syrup in front of me, but I waved it off. "I'm drinking it black and bitter today."

"Stop it, Poppy Markham," he said, handing me a spoon.

"I am so sorry about last night. It was an accident. I picked it up automatically, like I used to with Judy. And please don't say it's okay, because it's not. I ruined your anniversary."

"You didn't ruin anything." John sat down across from me and poured maple syrup into my cup. "As far as I'm concerned, you bringing in the puppy was part of the surprise, and you two must have practiced for days to get such perfect timing."

"He bought that?"

"We wouldn't have lasted fifteen years without allowing each other a masquerade now and then."

"Why didn't he tell me about your plans? I could have stayed away entirely."

He laughed. "He intended to leave a note in your room but got flustered after he saw you in the bathtub."

"Is he blaming me for that, too?"

"He'll be okay." John reached down to the chair next to him and gently picked up a sleeping white puff. "I promised him we'd throw a party this weekend for Liza's debut."

x x x

John With insisted that our temporary roommate arrangement continue, and because every minute on my bedroom floor the night before felt like it had expanded into an hour when it accumulated in my back, and because he was so darn sweet about everything, I agreed.

I ate, showered, and dressed, but I didn't have anything to do until my Pizza Pig inspection, so I called my cousin, Daisy, to tell her I would meet her for yoga at Namaste Y'all.

The eight o'clock class is usually full, but instead of blending in with all the other yogis, Daisy and I stand out among the young, thin, muscular UT students who believe that sweating is something football players and day laborers do, so they don't do it. Daisy and I have the muscles, but we also have twenty additional years, a few extra pounds, and no such beliefs about perspiration.

Daisy had saved me a spot, and together we breathed and sweated our way through an hour of warriors, triangles, and downward-facing dogs, with the added torture of something the instructor called donkey kicks. I'm pretty sure ancient yogis didn't balance on their hands and kick their legs into the air, but after I figured out how to place my hurt hand on the floor without stressing it, I got the hang of them. The final pose, Savasana, is a time for quiet meditation, but I usually do the only thing you're not supposed to: think.

I wondered what John Without would say to me the next time we saw each other, what I would say to Drew the next time I saw

132

him, and what Jamie would say when I told him that Drew was back. All of those thoughts made my shoulders tense up. Our instructor reminded us to relax, to say hello to our thoughts and then goodbye, which started me thinking about Troy and why he hadn't said good-bye in a suicide note. Even if he had killed himself, given the nature of the restaurant he wanted to open, he would surely have had some final words—one last bid for attention.

By the time our instructor said "Namaste" and bowed the light inside her to the light inside us, I knew I had a lot more work ahead of me.

After class, Daisy and I walked next door to the University of Java. We sat at an open table near a picture window that overlooked the Greenbelt, gulping tepid water and smiling at the double takes people gave us. Our mothers were sisters, and we look enough alike to be twins, except her hair is much longer than mine.

Daisy leaned down and looked under the table at my silver and purple spandex pants. "Where on earth did those come from?"

"My yoga clothes didn't survive the fire," I said. "John With pulled these out of a pile John Without is planning to give to charity. Apparently his Prince phase is over."

"Even Prince would be embarrassed to wear those. It would be more charitable to throw them away." She updated me on happenings with her husband, Erik, her thirteen-year-old daughter, Logan, and her eleven-year-old son, Jacob. "But that's boring family stuff," she said. "I'm sure your life is much more exciting than ortho appointments and volleyball camps."

"Are you wearing your big girl panties?" I asked.

She laughed. "Are you kidding? I have a teen and a tween. My big girl panties are the only things holding me together most days."

I started with Drew Cooper and the brief conversation we had at Markham's.

"Drew Cooper," she said wistfully. "There's a name I never thought I'd hear again. How does he look?"

"Really good," I said. "What am I going to do?" Like the Johns, Daisy and Erik have been together for double-digit years, since freshman year of college. She's well-versed in boy-girl stuff.

"What do you want to do?" she asked.

"Who's on first?" I said with some frustration. "Don't shrink me, Daze. Tell me what I should do."

"Ignore him and hope he goes away."

"That's not practical."

"Tell him you love him and you want to get married."

I answered her with a look that said, "That's ridiculous."

"Okay, then. Why don't we start with what you want to do." She put a spin on the words like she had already sent them around once before.

"I don't know," I said. "First Drew and then Jamie. It's not a question of *if* they'll cheat, but *when*."

"You don't know for sure Drew cheated."

"What else could it be? We were blissfully happy, all rice milk and peanut butter sandwiches, planning our life together. And then one morning he stopped answering his phone, cutting himself off from me, Mitch, Markham's—everything he loved. Or claimed to love."

"He told you his mom was sick," she said.

"And he didn't call for three years?" I shook my head. "He may have left because of his mom, but he stayed away because of another woman. And if he fell for someone that fast, he was already on his way out."

"I think you need to stop assuming and hear his whole story. If you're right, you can say 'I told you so.' But if I'm right…"

"You're not right."

Daisy already knew about Troy's death, so I filled her in on some of the details and my suspicions that his death had not been self-inflicted.

"I would say you're stretching things," she said, "but you're right that he loved having an audience. You remember that I had a couple of dates with him senior year?"

"That's right," I said. "Didn't he get drunk?"

She rolled her eyes. "Very. We went to Hill's Café after a game. I thought it was going to be a normal first date, but a lot of the other players were there. All the ones who had fake IDs. They spent the night reliving every play. We won in the last seconds of overtime against Del Valle."

"I remember that game," I said. "It took five minutes to pull their entire defensive line off Todd in the end zone, but he came up with the ball."

"Todd was at Hill's that night, too, but the way those guys were talking, you'd think Troy was the only one on the field. Every time they'd start talking about something else, Troy would start talking about his brilliant plays. He got so drunk, Todd had to take me home."

"And you went on a second date after that?"

"It was high school, and it was Troy the Train. You would have done the same thing."

I smiled. "Probably."

"I don't think he really liked me," Daisy said. "I think he took me out to get back at Ginger Krueger for asking Todd to be her lab partner."

"Troy married Ginger."

"No!"

"She was at the restaurant the first time I was there. They got into an argument in front of me and Todd."

She sipped her water. "Do you remember that cheer she made up and had the squad do during a pep rally?"

"I forgot about that!" I said. "Something about which twin is better."

"The train is number eight/The catch has better freight/If you want to win/You've got to pick the twin/Who gives it to you straight."

"Not a nice girl, that Ginger Krueger."

Daisy looked at her watch. "Oh! I have to go. Erik is expecting me home right about now." We gathered our yoga mats and walked outside into an invisible fog of humid heat. "Why don't you come over for dinner tonight?" she said.

"I'd like that."

"Bring Jamie."

"Maybe."

Daisy hugged me, then pulled back and looked me in the eye. "I want to say one thing to you, and I don't want you to respond, okay?" I nodded. "Jamie is a good man," she said. "He made a mistake. It's not fair to keep punishing him for what you think Drew did."

"What! I thought you were going to tell me I need to color my hair or drop my heels in down dog."

"Erik's waiting," she said. "I just want you to think about it."

I caught her wrist. "Erik can wait a little longer. Do you really think I'm confusing Jamie and Drew?"

"Not confusing them, but confusing your feelings."

"Betrayal feels the same regardless of the traitor. I'm very clear about how I feel."

Daisy held my eyes. "Jamie didn't leave you. He made a mistake, an error in judgment, and you have to decide if you can forgive him for that. But betrayal is not the same as abandonment."

"Goodness," I said, my nose starting to prickle with the beginning of emotion. "Where have you been hiding that?"

She hugged me hard. "I love you, Pop, but you spend too much time in your head. You need to follow your heart on this."

"That's not practical," I said.

Daisy laughed and opened her car door. "Come over around six, and bring a bottle of wine if you want to drink good stuff."

I got into my Jeep and pointed it toward Markham's so I could hear Drew's story and tell Daisy "I told you so."

SEVENTEEN

THE CLOCK ON MY penance for ruining the Johns's anniversary dinner had some time left on it, and I needed to gear up to face Drew, so I sat in my Jeep in the Markham's parking lot roasting like a Peking duck while I pondered Daisy's insight. She wasn't right that I had crossed Jamie with Drew, but I did feel abandoned by Drew in addition to feeling betrayed, which was only compounded by all the other things going on in my life at that time.

Drew had to help his mother, of course, but why did he withdraw from me? I loved and trusted him, and I thought he felt the same. At the time, I had played through the usual scenarios of sudden death, amnesia, and Russian double agent, but after months of silence on his end, I knew he had made a life with someone else. And after I moved on to Jamie, I hardened my heart against Drew. I wanted to hear the rest of his story, but only to cross that T.

A knock on the back of the Jeep brought me back to real time. I glanced up at my rearview mirror and saw a bandaged arm wave at me through cigarette smoke, then Trevor came around to my open door.

"Those were some deep thoughts," he said.

"How many times have you cheated on Ursula?" I asked.

He coughed smoke out of his mouth. "What kind of question is that?"

"I'm doing research."

He put both hands on top of the Jeep and leaned into me. "You lookin' for some action, Popstar?"

I pushed him back. "Not today," I said. "How many times?"

"Define cheat."

"Trevor."

"We don't have that kind of relationship. You know that. One week she's callin' me into the dry storage and I'm her MVP, the next week she's callin' me an immature churl and I'm a free agent." He looked toward the kitchen door. "A guy can get restless during the off-season."

"The dry storage?"

He waggled his eyebrows. "Or the walk-in."

I put my hand up. "Forget I started this."

"Yes ma'am." He said it the cute, flirty way.

He dropped his cigarette on the ground, and I stepped out of the Jeep and onto it. "Is Drew Cooper inside?"

Trevor crossed his arms and squinted at me. "Not you too." He sounded jealous, which could only mean one thing: Ursula was paying too much attention to the new GM.

In a restaurant, the term "private life" does not mean that your life is private; it means that you know about your business before everybody else does. Usually. It's not unusual for a waitress to find out that her bartender boyfriend dumped her when her coworkers tell her that he showed up the night before to give the new hostess a ride home. It's a lot like high school.

If Trevor suspected that Ursula was interested in Drew, the entire staff and some of the regular guests probably did, too. In a well-tended rumor mill like Markham's, Drew and Ursula could already be dating or engaged. And if Ursula were to gain a couple of pounds or wear a baggy chef's coat, then she's having Drew's baby.

"No, not me too," I said. "Just business to discuss."

"I hope it's not serious business," he said, looking down at my pants. "Did a gay man dress you today?"

"As a matter of fact."

I followed Trevor through the back door and ran into Ursula coming out of the dry storage room with a jar of mayhaw jelly in her hand. "Poppy!" she chirped, then threw her free arm around my neck and kissed me on the cheek.

Trevor turned around and winked at me. Ursula's back was to him so she didn't see him rub this thumb and first two fingers together and mouth "June sixth."

"Seventh," I said out loud to him.

Ursula pulled away. "What?"

"Seventh heaven is where I am," I said. "Is Drew in the office?"

"Oh, that reminds me," she said, backing me into the little room. "I want to know everything you can tell me about him."

Thank goodness I'd had a dollop of advanced warning from Trevor. "Why are you asking me?"

"He used to work here, right?"

"A few years ago." I did not want to have this conversation with Ursula and hoped that if I stalled long enough, a prep cook's sudden need for bread crumbs might rescue me. "Why don't you ask Mitch?"

"I haven't seen him. He's helping Mom redecorate the guest bedroom. Love your pants, by the way."

"Thanks. Does Nina allow overnight guests in her house?"

"I stay there sometimes," she said. "Now, dish on Drew."

I hadn't been employed by Markham's for the past couple of years, so rumors about my private life had been moldering on the top shelf of the walk-in behind opinions about whether Kate should be with Jack or Sawyer, but it was only a matter of time before someone pulled them down, garnished them, and presented them to Ursula. Better she hear the unembellished truth from me. "You know it's not a good idea to date someone you work with, right?"

"We're not dating," she said, then grinned. "Yet."

"What about Trevor?"

"We're not dating either."

Why did Trevor put up with her volatility when he could pluck practically anyone from the Markham's garden of waitress flowers? Ursula is ten years older than Trevor, which he probably sees as a coup. And she does have *Executive Chef* embroidered on her chef's coat, which means he's dating the boss. And she's also that perfect combination of confidence, beauty, and unpredictability, which a lot of men find enticing. And now she wanted to entice Drew Cooper.

"You don't need to know the details," I said, "but I had just become chef when Drew was GM. It was around the time my mother died, and we started dating." I stopped my narrative to decide how much to tell her. The story was in the details.

"So you two were involved…what? Three years ago?"

Maybe it was the cavalier way she lifted one shoulder or the way she twitched her head slightly to indicate that it had happened so long ago, it was no longer relevant. Or maybe it was her choice of the word "involved" that reduced my relationship with Drew to what she did with Trevor. Glimmers of the real Ursula York, Nina's selfish little offspring who believed that anything that wasn't about her couldn't be important.

Fine. Let her fall in love with Drew the deceiver, and let Drew fall in love with this immaculate version of Ursula. She might be all harps and rainbows now, but she is who she is, and she couldn't keep this plate spinning much longer. A cook would forget to drop a couple of well-done steaks on a Saturday night and throw off her timing, or one of her cookbook recipes wouldn't turn out right, or she wouldn't be able to get an appointment with her hairdresser, and then it's goodbye *The Sound of Music* and welcome to *Jurassic Park*. If I were in charge of karma, I couldn't have come up with a better arrangement than for Drew to have his feelings swindled by Ursula. I just hoped it happened the day after her birthday.

"It was thirty-five months ago," I said. "We were engaged." Let her think he was the marrying kind.

She stared at me. "But…you…and Jamie."

"We broke up a few months before I started dating Jamie."

"What happened?" she said softly.

"It just didn't work out." I had meant to sound indifferent, but somehow the pain and sadness of my entire history with Drew had come out in those five words.

"Oh, Poppy." She placed the jelly on a shelf, then embraced me in a tender two-armed hug. "I'm so sorry."

"It was a long time ago."

Our topic appeared in the doorway. "Trevor said you—" Drew took in the scene and smiled at me. "Oh, hi Sug…Poppy."

"We're finishing up," I said. "Can I talk to you for a minute?"

142

"I'd like that," he said, then looked at Ursula and held up some paperwork. "I'd also like to discuss these food costs later."

"Sure thing, Drew!" she said, as if she could think of nothing more wonderful in all of Camelot than to justify her food costs. "Some of it's for my cookbook."

Drew and I went into the office. He shut the door and dropped stiffly into the chair next to mine. "Mitch told me how you hurt your hand," he said. We both looked at it. I had taken the bandage off for yoga class and never replaced it. It looked raw and vulnerable. "You've always been brave."

"You know why I'm here," I said. My desire to hear flattering words from him had long since passed.

"Are you going to listen to me this time and not jump to conclusions?"

I nodded, thinking *I'll jump to all the conclusions I want to jump to, and you can't stop me.*

After the story Drew told me, Daisy would be the one saying "I told you so."

EIGHTEEN

"Do you remember when Iris died?" Drew asked. He stopped and dropped his eyes. "Sorry. Of course you do." He started again. "She contracted food poisoning at a Sunday brunch."

"*Clostridium botulinum*," I said. "Botulism." Why was he bringing up my mother? To add another layer of pain?

"And by the following Wednesday, she had…passed away." He looked hard at me. "I just now put that together. That explains why you became a health inspector."

"But it doesn't explain why you made a life with another woman."

He held up his hand. "Please just listen, okay? When my mom was diagnosed with kidney failure a few years ago, I went through the tests to see if I could be a donor. I was a match, but she didn't want me to do it unless it was an emergency, so they put her on dialysis. The dialysis had stopped working, and she needed my kidney immediately. I already told you I drove all night. The doctors had us in the OR two hours after I got there."

Not even three minutes had passed before someone rattled the door handle, trying to enter the office. It saved me from having to respond. I couldn't think of anything that didn't make me sound like a jerk.

"She was coherent but in critical condition after surgery, and the doctors didn't know if she would make it or how long she had." He shifted in his chair. "They had her on a mess of immunosuppressant drugs, so I couldn't be in the same room with her, but I could see her through a glass window and talk to her through an intercom. I thought about you a lot and remembered what you went through when Iris passed so suddenly. I spent every moment I could with her and told her all the things I've always wanted to."

"I'm so sorry, Drew. Is she okay now?"

He shook his head. "She hung in there for a few days, but her system was weak, and she contracted pneumonia. Contracted. Like she agreed to it." Drew made a fist and rubbed his left quad muscle. "Mine was weak too, and I caught some sort of super bug. It locked onto my leg and started eating away the fascia." He pulled up his left pant leg to show a prosthesis. "They cut me off at the knee," he said with a self-conscious laugh.

I must have looked horrified, not only at what I was seeing but because of how I had been acting. Conclusion jumping is often followed by tripping on your assumptions, then falling on your face. My stars, what he must have gone through—was *still* going through. I felt the beginning of tears.

"Please, Poppy." He put his hand on my knee. "Don't make a big deal about this. I went through lots of rehab and had lots of counseling. I've learned to live with it."

I met his eyes. "Why didn't you call? I would have been there for you."

"I wish you had been," he said. "I was depressed for a long time, as you can imagine, and by the time I was ready to tell you, you were dating Jamie Sherwood." Had I not been looking at him so closely, I would have missed the anger backfilling his eyes. "I still keep in touch with some ABRA people and heard you broke up a few months ago."

"We did," I said, "but we're on a slow mend." I didn't want to discuss Jamie with him. "What brought you back to Austin?"

"I was tired of the snow and I missed…my friends. I came straight here and asked Mitch if he could use me." He smiled. "Or what's left of me."

What do you say to something like that? I didn't know, so I brought us back to a safe topic. "I know Mitch is happy to have someone he can trust running the restaurant."

"And you?"

I stood up, and Drew came up with me. "I'm happy it's not me."

"I'm here to stay this time, Poppy."

"Ursula will be glad to hear that. I think she's tired of breaking in GMs."

He laughed. "I read an article on Sherwood's website where people said Ursula was touchy and liked to throw things, but I haven't seen any of that. I've only been here a few days, but she's nothing like what I had prepared for."

I knew that Ursula was interested in Drew, and from his comment, I could guess at his interest in her. But if I told him that people aren't always as they appear to be or that no one at Markham's had thought it impossible that Ursula had stabbed a rival chef in the heart, he might think I was jealous. And I couldn't say with certainty that I wasn't. After the story I heard, I no longer thought that Drew and Ursula deserved each other. But I also hadn't been put in charge of karma.

"I'm glad to hear it," I said.

He pointed to my legs. "I also wasn't prepared for those pants."

"Neither was I."

✗ ✗ ✗

By the time I left Drew's office, I had just enough time to make a sandwich with Ursula's freakishly evenly sliced carrots and beets before driving over to Lunch and Larder. When I arrived at noon, I saw several snack trucks pulling into the parking lot to either knock off after their breakfast shift or restock for the afternoon. It presented a wonderful opportunity for a few sniper inspections, but it was one I had to let pass because I didn't want to jump Olive's gun and be put on disability leave.

I would have caught one or two mobiles with a blank food temperature log or drinking from uncovered cups. Not critical violations, but not something they should get away with either. Today it's a spilled drink in the potato salad, tomorrow it's an outbreak of *Streptococcus*.

I didn't know what the truck looked like, but if I had to guess, I would imagine that with a stupid name like Pizza Pig, it was painted pink and had a caricature of a fat, grinning pig gobbling a whole pizza. The parking lot was mostly empty, and I didn't see anything like that, so I went over to the dispatch kiosk to confer with the office manager, a skinny woman with bottle-red hair and teal eye shadow.

"Good afternoon, Poppy M," Magdalena Zapata said through a microphone grill.

"You're looking quite comfortable behind that glass, Magda Z."

147

"It's my little ice-cold piece of heaven. You want in?"

"You'd never get me back out," I said. "I'm looking for Pizza Pig."

"They already in trouble with the food police?"

"Not yet. I need to do a mobile permit inspection."

"Another one?"

"Not another, just one. They made the appointment a couple of days ago."

"What? They told me you did the inspection and they're waiting on the piece of paper."

"Not us." I wiped sweat from my upper lip. "We're experimenting with doing them on location. Pizza Pig is one of the first."

Normally the vendor has to bring the truck to our offices to prove that they're actually mobile. Keeping Olive away from customers is one of the special privileges of being an SPI.

"Lying jerks," she said, shaking her head. "Spot two-eighteen." She stood up to look past me into the lot. "Doesn't look like they're here. I saw them earlier, though."

"Have they been serving food?"

She plopped back into her chair. "I don't know for sure. They're not one of mine, so I don't pay attention to anything but their rent check."

"What does the truck look like?"

"Like a member of Congress."

I laughed. "Can you be more specific?"

"Plain old white one. Not new. A few dings here and there."

"Like a hundred other ones out there." I slid my card to her through the metal well. "Can you call me when they show up?"

"You got it," she said. "But it wasn't me, okay? And it wasn't me who told you to check out the Epicuriousitiness truck. One row back and two spots over."

"Epi what?"

"Curiousitiness."

Another stupid name for a snack truck. "Are they here?"

"Early, early morning, like five. I'm not here, but the cameras are. Something's not right. They never use the commissary."

"I'll set my alarm," I said. "Stay cool, Magda Z."

"I'll never be as cool as your pants."

I returned to my Jeep and called Olive to find out what she knew about Pizza Pig missing their appointment. She answered the phone coughing. "Hold on," she rasped. After a community theater production's worth of choking and what sounded like her performing the Heimlich maneuver on herself, she said, "How's it hanging, Markham?"

"Like the moustache on a walrus," I said. "Pizza Pig is on the trot."

"It's lunchtime," she said, swallowing a big messy gulp of something. "They're probably out serving pizza."

"Olive, this is a permit inspection. They *can't* be out serving pizza."

"We do surprise inspections at lunchtime, Markham, not permits."

"You're the one who scheduled this for noon. Can we reschedule them for next week or have them come to the office? And ask the other inspectors to keep an eye out for the truck in case they started slinging dough ahead of time. According to Magda Z, it's a plain—"

"You can wait for them."

Waiting would be the perfect excuse to cancel my shopping trip with Nina, and I would have agreed if the temperature hadn't started flirting with 90 degrees right in front of me and if Olive hadn't said that the way she did. Sometimes it's the little things.

"I'd rather make them wait," I said. "Losing a week's worth of business from drunk frat boys after the bars close on Sixth Street might encourage them to respect my time."

"Same time tomorrow, then," she said.

"But I thought we didn't do permit inspections"—*click*—"at lunchtime."

Whether I was busy with Pizza Pig and Capital Punishment or I was having a boomerang conversation with Olive didn't matter. I still had a good excuse to call Nina and cancel our mall crawl.

"Oh, what a pity," Nina said. She put a lot of effort into sounding disappointed, so my father must have been within hearing range. "I want to find your color. That black you always wear is so cliché for a blond. I'm thinking ruby, emerald, sapphire."

Jewel colors. No surprise there. "I don't always wear black," I protested. "In fact, I'm wearing silver and amethyst right now."

My stepmother was right, though. I wear black all the time, but only because I work all the time and black hides the gunk I have to slide around in. We lied to each other about rescheduling soon, and then I called Jamie.

"Hey, Poppycakes. What's the good word?"

"I'm a cliché blond who wears too much black."

"It works for Madonna," he said, "but your clichés look better."

"Thanks, but Nina doesn't think so. We're supposed to go shopping for jewel colors."

"Put me down for ruby red."

"You're down," I said. "How are you coming on those crime scene photos?"

"You may not believe this, but the record of physical evidence from an active police investigation isn't that easy to get ahold of."

"Aren't you the guy who got a Michelin guide reviewer to write an anonymous article about how their stars are awarded?"

"I am, and I'm calling in twice as many favors for this."

"Now I owe *you* a favor."

"Good," he said. "What—"

"But don't ask me any questions about the Sharpe place."

"—is one plus one?"

"Daisy invited us over for dinner tonight."

"Both of us?"

"One plus one. Six o'clock."

"Just making sure I heard you right," he said with a couple of ounces of joy in his voice. "I'll pick you up at five."

x   x   x

Like Miles Archer, the contractor fixing up my house specializes in home remodeling, but unlike Miles, he had not taken on a project beyond his abilities. He'd had to rebuild an exterior wall and redo the interior walls that had been damaged—basically every wall in the house—as well as pull up the carpet. I had asked him to finish it out like a ski lodge, with lots of wood everywhere, which he said would take a little longer.

On my way home to have a look-see at their progress, I passed CapTex Restaurant Supply and remembered that Jesse Muñoz figured into this story. Miles had asked Todd for cash for the sink that first day because Jesse had cut off their credit.

I hadn't seen Jesse since I left Markham's, so I decided to stop in and say hello. Maybe see what I could find out about Capital Punishment's financial situation.

I doubled back and drove past a long line of cars in the parking lot before I found a space. Inside were several chefs, managers, and owners examining stemware and flatware or turning dials and taking measurements of convection ovens. Jesse keeps every item on display and plugged in because a $1,000 deep fryer can be as much of an impulse purchase for a chef as a $100 sauté pan.

I walked through the showroom looking for Jesse and waving to people I knew, which had me raising my hand every few feet. Some people stopped and asked about Mitch and Ursula, some smiled briefly and went back to their browsing, and some suddenly needed to be somewhere else. It all depended on their last health score.

One of these days, when food service is done entirely by androids that are programmed to follow the rules, everyone will be happy to see the health inspector.

I found Jesse by the major appliances speaking with Herb Wolff and Dana White. Jesse threw a peace sign at me. I caught it with a nod, then played with high-speed blenders while I waited. Maybe I could make a frozen drink for Trevor. The Cool Kid. No, he needed something with teeth.

Jesse finally shook hands with Herb and Dana, then walked over to me. "Is that what they're making health inspectors wear these days?"

So that's why everyone was smiling at me as if I were wearing ridiculous silver and purple pants. "I'm testing my tolerance for humiliation," I said, extending my right hand, then made a fist before he could shake it. "Sorry. It's the hurt one."

"I can dig it." Jesse tapped his fist to mine. "How is Ursula liking the new slicer?"

"Ursula got a new slicer?" When I ran the kitchen, I used to ask Mitch for a new one at least once a month, but he said we didn't use it enough to justify the purchase, and I insisted that we would use it more if it sliced more carrots than fingers.

"Mitch told me it was to help her with the cookbook, but I got the feeling it was also an apology." Jesse doesn't miss much, so chances were good his feeling was right on. And even though he couldn't know that the unfairness of it had reached me all these years later, he could tell it unsettled me, so he changed the subject. "What brings you in?"

"I've been inspecting the Sharpe place going up on Slaughter."

He straightened a price tag under a $400 blender. "It's a stressful business, this restaurant business."

"Do you think Troy Sharpe killed himself because the stress got to him?"

"Opening a restaurant anytime is hard, but especially in this economy."

"Money trouble?" I asked, trying to sound as if it had just occurred to me.

"It's possible," he said. The great thing about people who like to gossip is that they never ask why you want to talk about something that's none of your business. But Jesse doesn't like to gossip. "Why are you interested?" he asked.

I thought it might come to this and had prepared an answer. "One of the cooks at Markham's is thinking about jumping ship and I want to make sure he's not going to sink before they get started.

He's a good cook, but Ursula wouldn't take him back if things don't work out." I shrugged. "Just looking out for Markham's."

It was mostly the truth. Whenever any new restaurant opens, every manager, cook, food server, bartender, dishwasher, and busboy at least considers applying for a job there, and that would include Trevor. It's also true that Trevor is a good cook. And it's true that Ursula wouldn't take him back if he left.

"Danny MacAdams seems to know what he's doing," Jesse said.

"Then let me ask you this. Why would you take someone off credit and make them pay cash?"

He seemed surprised that I knew that, but said, "If they don't pay their invoices, but I'll let them slide depending on the situation. Or if I find out they've stopped paying their linen and food vendors and it looks like they may start doing the same with me. Or…"

Herb and Dana arguing over whether a fine-dining restaurant should have a microwave in the kitchen had taken my eyes away from Jesse, but I turned back when he didn't continue. "Or?"

"If they request to be cash-only."

"Did they?"

"We're talking what-ifs, Poppy."

Of course they requested it. Why else would Jesse make sure he had my attention before he told me? "Okay, in general, why would someone request to be cash-only?"

"I don't know," he said. I didn't think he was keeping it from me. "I will say that in thirty years of selling restaurant supplies, this is the first time I can recall anyone doing that."

NINETEEN

JESSE HAD GIVEN ME another something to puzzle over on my way home. When Miles had asked Todd for money for the sinks, Todd told him to charge it to their account, which meant that they had been on credit at some point. So why change? Had they made the same arrangements with other vendors? Did Miles receive his payments in cash?

Todd and Danny had seemed surprised when Miles told them they were cash-only, so it must have been Troy who made the arrangement with Jesse. Unless Todd and Danny were pretending they didn't know. But why do that?

And did this have anything to do with Troy's death? I couldn't see it, unless it was somehow related to Troy's personal financial situation. The only people I could ask were the very people who would want Troy dead, and not even I could finesse an answer for why a health inspector needed to know about a dead guy's financials. But Jamie could. I would ask him to help me on our way to Daisy's for dinner.

Whether for love or money, whoever killed Troy knew about his rope trick and had used it to make his death look like a suicide or an accident, so it had to be someone who had been inside the restaurant.

Ginger had the strongest motive in the love category, and the only car in the parking lot that day had GSHARP on the license plate. After I discovered Troy, I assumed that he had driven Ginger's car there, but what if he hadn't? According to Miles, Ginger had accused Troy of being a no-good scoundrel. Maybe she'd had enough and went there to ask him for a divorce, because who wants to be married to a scoundrel? Especially an immature one who smelled like stale cigarettes and beer. Troy hangs himself from grief, and then she takes off in his car? Unlikely. I had seen Troy and Ginger in action. He would have been more upset to lose a gurney race to Todd than to lose his wife.

Miles also said that Troy and Ginger still had some nice left for each other, but it appeared to be sporadic. Maybe they made up and decided to stick around after everyone left. They drink a couple of beers in the kitchen, then Ginger coaxes him up to the catwalk and asks him to show her his rope trick. She ties the rope to the cell when he's not looking, then after he hangs himself, she…calls a taxi? No. Leaving her car at the scene would bring the police to her front door if they ruled it a homicide.

Todd was the least likely culprit, which meant that he should be at the top of my list. I have imagined killing a lot of people, but never my own flesh and blood. Not seriously, anyway. (Ursula and Nina are not my flesh and blood.) It was improbable that Todd had killed Troy, but not impossible.

In high school, they had worked as a team on the football field, but as quarterback, Troy got all the glory. I assumed that he and Todd were equal partners in the restaurant, but Troy was obviously still quarterbacking, still grabbing attention away from Todd with his antics and drinking and contrary opinions. Had Troy been the favorite at home, too? In the marines? Had Todd lived in Troy's shadow into adulthood? Assuming sibling rivalry was a good enough reason to kill him, Todd could have lured Troy to the catwalk as easily as Ginger could have and tied the rope to the cell. And then Todd stands back and watches his brother leap to his death? If that were the case, I would rather believe it had been an accident.

Danny had a similar history and motives as Todd, but not the family ties, so I could more easily believe him as the murderer. He confronts Troy with a list of grievances, saying he's tired of them blowing him off. They're not in high school, and the name-calling needs to stop. He's the only one with restaurant experience, and if they don't want him to walk, they need to start showing him some respect. Troy laughs at him, calls him a dork, tells him to take his whining to a daycare. Danny ties the rope to the cell, then gets his revenge and the last laugh as Troy realizes what's happening. And if Danny did it for those reasons, was Todd's life in danger too?

And what about Miles? Surely he had been a victim of Troy's humiliating rope trick. He said he was in the dog house for the delayed construction, but the only building projects that come in on time and under budget are built by five-year-olds and made of Legos. Troy had berated Miles about the sinks in front of his crew, probably not for the first time, but Miles had told me he didn't have any problems with Troy. Did Miles not consider it abuse, or was he so used to people taking out their disappointments on him that it didn't register? Or did he not care because he was already planning his deadly revenge? It may not be a perfect motive, but I didn't need it to be Michelangelo's statue of David.

By the time I turned onto my street, I had cooked up enough circumstantial evidence to keep several teams of defense lawyers working until Super Bowl LX. If one of my four suspects hadn't killed Troy Sharpe, I would start being nice to Nina.

For the first time in weeks, I felt content. I had solved the years-long mystery of why Drew left, even if it had presented new issues. My hand felt stronger every day. And my relationship with Jamie was on the mend. All I needed was my house finished, and everything would finally be back to normal.

The feeling lasted the length of five houses, with my contentment turning to dread as I pulled into my driveway.

TWENTY

JOHN WITHOUT WAS HOME and in the back yard playing with the puppy. Ordinarily, seeing him would provoke mild disgust in me, not dread. But two issues presented themselves.

First, I hadn't seen him since the previous night when he had told me with his eyes that he was hungry for cooked goose and mine looked delicious. It wasn't so much an issue, I realized, as an opportunity to apologize to him without John With there to referee. John Without could bring out both guns and unload, which I deserved. I had the smidgiest glimmer of hope that he might go easy on me because his normally stern face looked something like not-ticked-off, thanks to Liza.

This perfect opportunity, however, was spoiled by issue number two: I was wearing his pants.

He would see them as soon as I stepped out of the Jeep and know that I had been at their house—alone with his boyfriend, whom I have an innocent crush on—and imagine all sorts of things about how I ended up in some pants that had been in a bag in their bedroom. Especially since he had restricted the amount of time John

With and I spent together by making them leave for the gallery so early every morning.

Everything he imagined would be ludicrous, but I've always thought that the "by reason of insanity" defense meant not that the reason for their actions was insanity, but that they had used their own insane reasoning when deciding to commit their crime.

I couldn't leave because Jamie would arrive in an hour to pick me up for dinner at Daisy's. I had no choice but to approach the back gate.

John stopped pretend-kissing Liza with a fluffy pink stuffed bear and stared at me. "Get in here," he gruffed. "Now."

John Without has always been catty, not commanding, and his urgent tone scared me. Maybe it wasn't such a good idea to do this with no witnesses. But I couldn't turn back. I opened the gate to put my goose's neck on the chopping block.

"*What* are you wearing?" he demanded.

"I know it looks bad, but give me a chance to explain."

"Those are positively *hideous*. Get inside before the neighbors see you."

x   x   x

"He never recognized them?" Jamie asked as we browsed a shelf of California reds at Central Market.

On our way to the store for wine, I had hit the lowlights of the past twenty-four hours with the Johns.

"I guess they didn't register without the matching top," I said.

Jamie groaned. "Thanks for that visual." He held up a bottle of Franciscan Merlot.

"Perfect," I said.

On the drive to Daisy's, he told me that *Deliciousness Magazine* had accepted his proposal to write a monthly column for them on how to be your own food critic.

"Jamie! A column! This is huge."

"International," he said with modest pride. I couldn't see the dimple on his left cheek, but he smiled the kind of smile that brings it out. "I'm thinking of calling it *Variorum*."

"Sounds like a foodborne illness. What does it mean?"

"Literally, it's Latin for a text that contains notes from multiple scholars or critics. If it takes off, they say they want me to be part of their teaching team, giving workshops and classes around the country."

"I am so proud of you, Jamie."

"Thanks." He patted my knee but didn't leave his hand there. "Dana White said she saw you at CapTex today."

"Did she mention my pants?"

Jamie laughed. "Nina's false eyelashes would come unglued if she saw you wearing something like that. Is that why she wants to take you shopping?"

"She wants to take me shopping to prove to Mitch that she's making an effort with me. I called and canceled the first trip today, but she didn't try to reschedule. Yet she'll call twenty times to reschedule an appointment with a dog whisperer to discover why Dolce and Gabbana growl at the ficus."

"Make sure you buy some yoga pants. I can't have my girlfriend's wardrobe be a topic of conversation among my friends and colleagues."

"I'll get some ruby red ones."

"Why were you at CapTex?"

"Capital Pun—" *Whoa!* I couldn't let all of my guards down around Jamie. "Capital of Texas is supplying equipment to the Sharpe place."

Nothing gets by Jamie, and I knew he would make a note, but not a big deal, of my slip. "Not following yet," he said.

I told him what Jesse said about their switch to cash payments.

"It's unusual," he agreed, "but how does that tie in with Troy Sharpe's death?"

"Maybe he had financial difficulties."

"Paying cash would indicate a surplus of money, which is not usually a problem."

"Since I'm trying to think of reasons why Troy was murdered, help me think of problems. Why would someone suddenly start paying cash?"

"The most obvious is that they're laundering money."

"I can't believe I didn't think of that!" I said, then changed my tone. "I don't see them as drug dealers, though."

"It doesn't have to be drugs," Jamie said. "They could be hiding legal profits to avoid paying taxes."

"They haven't opened yet, so there aren't any profits."

"Money laundering or not, Troy was carrying cash on him at some point. Depending on what he had to pay for at CapTex, the bill could run into five figures."

"A robbery gone wrong," I said. "Which, dang it, would turn all of the construction workers into suspects, as well as pretty much everyone he came into contact with in the past couple of weeks."

"Assuming they knew he had money on him. Did you see any?"

"No!" I said, brightening. "If Troy had that much cash on him, he would have flashed every dollar of it."

"The police report didn't mention any cash."

"Which Todd or Ginger would have reported missing, especially if they did it and are trying to pin the blame on someone else."

"Did Troy gamble?" Jamie asked.

"Besides with his life? Can you find out for me?"

"Are you going to tell me what the restaurant is?"

"Not even if you put me in solitary confinement."

x — x — x

The blond, blue-eyed Forrest kids were waiting for us at the front gate, Jacob waving at us like Arnold Horshack at Mr. Kotter. As soon as we drove through, Logan hopped into the back seat, leaving her younger brother to corral their Dalmatian/Lab, Othello, and shut the gate behind us.

"Hey TeePee, hey JJ," Logan said.

Jamie and I don't like how kids nowadays call adults Mr. or Miss First Name. "Just Jamie," he had requested the first time she addressed him as Mr. Jamie, so that's what she called him. Eventually it had been shortened to JJ. TeePee was the best a two-year-old learning to talk could make of Auntie Poppy. Technically I'm Logan's second cousin, but I'm glad Daisy didn't try to teach her to say Cousin Poppy or I might have had to answer a page for SinPee at a Hannah Montana concert a few months ago when Logan lost track of me at the concession stand.

"What's for supper, Squirt?" Jamie asked.

"You'll see," Logan said with an I've-got-a-secret lilt. "And don't worry, TeePee, nothing had a face or a mother."

We arrived at the house, and after hugs, snacks, and wine, Erik and Jacob whisked Jamie off in the golf cart to show him the new rain barrel watering system at their plant nursery next door. As soon as the back door closed, I pulled Daisy onto the front porch, leaving Logan at the stove.

"I talked to Drew after yoga," I said. "Go ahead and say it."

Daisy lit a citronella torch. "You weren't wearing Prince's pants, I hope."

"He's been in Colorado dealing with some serious health issues." I relayed Drew's story, and she made the appropriate sympathetic murmurs and comments.

The front door opened, and Logan said, "Ten minutes, Mom. Ring the chow bell."

"Sure, sweetie," Daisy said, then turned back to me. "So he's been in Denver this whole time, recovering? Does Jamie know he's back?"

"No, but I can't keep it from him much longer."

"It makes things a little knotty, doesn't it?"

"Honestly, Daze, it doesn't. I'm still sorting through old hurts, but I don't feel a connection to Drew anymore."

"You only just found out what happened. You might feel differently after your emotions catch up to your reason."

"And I quote, 'You spend too much time in your head.'"

"It's true, but reason isn't all bad. If Drew hadn't left, you two would be married, and he would be here with you tonight instead of Jamie."

"If Drew and I were married, we would be running Markham's by now, and we would both be at the restaurant tonight."

"My point is that you two had a very strong bond, and it might be prudent to wait awhile before you decide anything."

"I've already decided I want Jamie," I said. "Unless he does something dumb again. In the meantime I'll watch things play out with Drew and Ursula."

"What?"

"Apparently."

"Wow."

"I know."

Over a dessert of blueberry pie, Jamie said, "I don't know if it's my wonderful dinner companions or that I've been eating out a lot lately, but this is one of the best meals my taste buds have enjoyed in weeks."

Daisy, Erik, and Jacob smiled at Logan. "Thanks, JJ," Logan said.

"You made this, Squirt?" Jamie asked, not hiding his astonishment. I was a little astonished myself.

"Every dish," Erik said.

That explained why the entire Forrest clan had been on point during dinner, paying special attention to Jamie. I thought it was because they missed him while he and I were broken up.

"The pie, too?" Jamie said.

Logan smiled as if she were an Olympic athlete standing in the center podium wearing a gold medal around her neck. And in a way, she *had* won the gold. It was food critic Jamie Sherwood, not her friend JJ, whom she had dazzled.

"She's going to be a chef," Jacob said, "and I'm going to be a race car driver!"

"Formula One or NASCAR?" Jamie asked.

Jacob looked at his dad, then said, "Both!"

"I'll be your first sponsor," Jamie said, then turned to Logan. "Well, Chef Squirt, with your permission, I'd like to write a formal review of this dinner and use it in my first *Variorum* column for *Deliciousness Magazine*."

Logan looked distressed. "I thought you liked everything."

"I do," Jamie said.

"*Variorum* sounds bad," I said, "but it isn't. It's Latin."

"This is the first we've heard about a column," Erik said. "What are you going to write about?"

"It's a monthly column for foodies and budding critics," Jamie said. "I'll describe how to assess dishes individually and as part of a meal, and give them tips for describing flavors and textures." He took another bite of pie and winked at Logan. "So instead of saying this is perfect, they could learn to describe it as tasting like you're eating the ripest berries straight off the vine. Readers can use what they learn to become better home cooks or maybe start a blog in their own neighborhood or city."

I looked at Jamie. "It needs a better name."

"How about Taste Buds?" Logan suggested.

Jamie nodded. "I like it, Squirt. Incisive and piquant but familiar."

After more pie and coffee, Jamie and I left a beaming Forrest family on the porch and headed back into Austin proper.

"You tired?" Jamie asked, lightly rubbing the back of my neck.

"I've got enough steam for a cappuccino. What do you have in mind?"

"Irish coffee at Markham's?"

Unlike Drew, who uses distance and a practiced serenity to mask his true feelings, Jamie is easy-going and really does take things as they come. He prefers to coax rather than force, question rather than assume, wait and see rather than lead a charge. When I let him back into my life a few weeks ago, he wanted to resume our relationship as soon as possible, but he also understood and respected the damage that had been done. And while he never poked his nose into my business, he would not be happy about the return of Drew Cooper.

He noticed me hesitate. "I hope you're paying those hamsters for overtime," he said. "Is there something you want to tell me?"

"Like what?"

"Like Philip Seymour Hoffman and Matthew Fox," he said, then added, "in bit roles."

I leaned my head against the seat and looked up through the sunroof. *My Boyfriend's Back.* "How did you know?"

"Ursula told me."

I shot up. "Ursula!"

"She called a couple of days ago. Said she'd trade the first interview with her about her cookbook for any information I had on a guy named Drew Cooper."

"You've known this whole time? Why didn't you say anything?"

He removed his hand from my neck. "Why didn't you?"

"I was waiting for the right time."

We rode in silence until he stopped at the light at the Y in Oak Hill. He was more annoyed than mad, and he was probably annoyed with himself as a reporter for being blindsided with something like this. He wouldn't stay in the dark for long, though. He would dig around and find out all he needed to know about Drew. Probably already had.

"Trust goes both ways," he finally said.

"I know," I said. "I should have told you sooner. I'm sorry."

He replaced his hand on the back of my neck.

"What did you tell Ursula?" I asked.

"I told her to talk to you."

"And you want to go to Markham's right now because…"

"I heard from a new source that George and Laura are going to be there, and I want to verify it."

The former president, my foot. More like Jamie wanted to satisfy his curiosity about his predecessor. He wanted to see Drew in person, size up the competition.

Better it happen while I was present to do damage control. "Giddyup," I said.

TWENTY-ONE

AT 9:00 PM, GLITTERY couples and groups of friends still jammed Markham's foyer and bar area, waiting to be seated for dinner. Food servers whizzed through the dining room with venison stew and stuffed quail, homemade sourdough bread and bottles of wine, Black Forest cake and double espressos.

It didn't take long to find who I had been scanning for. I saw Drew walking out of the kitchen and toward the far corner table, where he set down a plate for...oh goodness, George and Laura! Dining with Mitch and Nina.

I wondered if Ursula knew who she was cooking for, but how could she not? The advance contingent of Secret Service agents would have put her on notice, then Mitch and Nina would have both gone into the kitchen to tell her—Mitch to give her a pep talk, Nina to crow.

I recalled what I had told Daisy earlier about running the restaurant with Drew. If things had played out differently, I would be cooking for them. Or would they be here at all? If Mitch had handed over the reins to us sooner, he wouldn't have been at the hostess stand the morning Nina traipsed into the restaurant to ask directions to the new spa down the street. If there were no Nina, there would be no Ursula, and Markham's would have stayed a humble café with waiters in T-shirts serving the Surf 'n' Turf instead of catering to people who would rather pay extra to order the Mixed Grille from a waiter wearing a tie.

But if things had gone differently, Jamie Sherwood wouldn't be waiting for me at the bar. Cool, gorgeous, sweet Jamie, who never gave up on us and who always surprises me with his intelligence and patience.

Drew lingered at the VIP's table for a moment, then walked through the restaurant greeting customers, refilling tea glasses, and bussing tables.

Women love to see a man in action, regardless of what the action is. A man is so much more authentic, so much more attractive, when he is completely focused on a task or commanding a situation instead of making a fool of himself trying to impress a woman. This is why waitresses fall for cooks, why secretaries develop crushes on their toady bosses, why women love men in uniform, and why Shannon Tweed married Gene Simmons.

A flash of white by the kitchen caught my eye. In fact, it caught everyone's eye, except of the person she wanted. Ursula stood at the mouth of the wait station waving like a rodeo clown, trying to draw Drew's attention away from the people who keep us in business. It's common for the chef and the GM to confer throughout the night, more so with political royalty on the premises, but I had never known Ursula to leave the kitchen after the first order came in. If she needed something, she sent a cook or a waiter after it.

I suspected that this odd behavior had nothing to do with her new desire to buy the world a Coke and everything to do with her desire for Drew. Rather than back off after I told her about my history with him, she appeared to be mounting an assault and had abandoned her kitchen in the middle of the dinner rush to flirt with him. And on a night like this!

Didn't she care about the restaurant? Markham's success depended on Drew's commitment to the front of the house and on Ursula's commitment to the back. If they started to commit to each other, all kinds of things would start skidding sideways. I couldn't let that happen. I hurtled myself around tables and landed in front of her.

"Poppy!" Ursula said. "Hi!"

"What are you doing out here?" I asked. "You didn't stab one of your cooks, did you?"

She looked momentarily confused, then laughed. "Not tonight. I need to tell Drew to eighty-six the *pâté de foie gras*."

"I'll tell him," I said. "You scoot on back to the kitchen. Y'all must be in the weeds."

"Not at all." She took a step to the left so she could see past me into the dining room. "Trevor's handling things."

"Ursula, it's too busy for you to be out here gawking."

"I'm not gawking," she said. "I just want to see him."

"You see Drew every ten minutes."

"*Tch.* Not Drew, George."

Oh. "Why don't you go up to their table and say hello?"

Her eyes grew as wide as Vinnie Barbarino's bell-bottoms. "No, I couldn't do that."

"Come on." I took her hand. "Let them give their compliments to the chef."

"No!" She wrenched her arm up and back with such force that she backhanded a waiter who couldn't hold onto his loaded tray. Six heavily sauced entrées toppled to the floor. Everyone in the kitchen and a few customers started clapping.

Ursula glowered at me. "*Now* we're in the weeds."

They weren't in the weeds yet, but recooking six entrées at the last minute would surely put them there. I should have been concerned about the effect this would have on Ursula's crew, but those thoughts couldn't push through my disappointment that Ursula lost it earlier than June 7, which meant that I lost the Diva Pot.

Within seconds of the crash, Drew coasted into the wait station to see the end of the show, but he missed Ursula's closing remarks.

"What happened?" he asked.

"A little accident," I said. "Everything is back to normal."

"Did I see Chef out here?"

He called her Chef? He never called me Chef. "They're eighty-six on the *pâté*."

"I'll let the wait staff know," he said. "Nina wants her daughter, the food genius, to come say hello to their guests."

"Good luck with that," I said, patting him on the chest. "I'll be at the bar."

"Are you waiting for a table?" Drew asked.

"We had dinner at Daisy's and stopped in for a drink."

"We?"

"Jamie's with me."

"Good," he said, then turned toward the kitchen. I thought I saw him put his hand over his heart and cross his first two fingers, something he used to do on busy nights to tell me he loved me. Was that for Ursula? Already?

I went to the bar, intent on asking Jamie to take us somewhere else. He had gotten what he wanted. He had laid his eyes on Drew and done whatever it is current boyfriends do when they see former boyfriends. He also saw George and Laura and verified the reliability of his source. We could have a nightcap at any bar in Austin. We didn't need to stay.

But I had to play it cool or Jamie would see my discomfort and do the exact opposite of what I wanted just to watch me squirm. He had a seat at the bar and had been watching my exchange with Drew. He stood up when I approached.

I put my arm around him and kissed him on the cheek. "How about we go to the Ginger Man?" I said.

"Why?"

"It's crowded and noisy and hot in here."

"The Ginger Man will be the same."

"Yes, but—"

"And we're already here." He patted the bar stool.

"True, but—"

"And I ordered drinks."

"We can cancel them."

He looked at me, amusement in his dark eyes. He knew the real reason I wanted to leave. "And I want to talk to Drew Cooper," he said.

"What? Why?"

The bartender, Andy, delivered two Irish coffees. Jamie thanked him, then handed the one without whipped cream to me. "I want to interview him."

I dropped the hand that had reached for the cup and crossed my arms.

He laughed and placed my drink on the bar. "Not tonight. I'm working on a piece about what a restaurant has to go through when a former president of the United States decides to dine there."

"Since when?"

He brought his drink to his lips with one hand and patted the stool again with the other. "Since I found out George and Laura were going to be here tonight."

I saw Drew coming toward the bar and regretted my attraction to interesting, unpredictable men. Drew and Jamie could become instant best friends as easily as get into a shouting match. I sat down, hoping that their professionalism, the busyness of the restaurant, and the presence of several Secret Service agents would help keep their meeting headline-free.

"Drew Cooper," Jamie said, extending his hand. "We meet at last."

"Jamie Sherwood," Drew said, shaking Jamie's hand. "Glad you could make it."

This was too weird. I turned my back to them and watched this tennis match in the mirror.

"Thanks for the tip on George and Laura," Jamie said.

Drew was his source? I sat up straighter, and Jamie smiled at my reaction. He was enjoying this.

"Markham's can use some good press," Drew said.

"They'll get it from me," Jamie said. "How do you like the new place?"

"To tell you the truth," Drew said, "I prefer things the way they used to be."

"Do you?" Jamie dropped a land baron hand on my shoulder but kept his eyes on Drew. "I thought it was time for a change."

"Just because something is different, Sherwood, doesn't mean it's better."

Uh-oh. Last names.

"From where I stand, Cooper, everyone really likes the upgrade."

"Not everyone," Drew said. "Some people think we made a mistake."

"Then you'd be wise to keep an eye on them," Jamie said. "People who are dissatisfied have a tendency to walk the check."

"Sometimes it's not intentional," Drew said. "Sometimes they come back to square things up." They both looked at the back of my head, then Drew said, "Let me know if you need anything."

Jamie hadn't taken his hand off my shoulder. "Thank you, but I have everything I need right here."

I felt flattered to have these two guys verbally jousting over me, but I also knew it could turn tedious, which would mean a lot more work for me. I should have reassured Jamie that he had nothing to worry about, but that wouldn't be entirely honest. Knowing that I was wrong about the particulars of why Drew had left had made me start to wonder if maybe Daisy was right that I needed to give more thought to all of this. But that was for another time.

When Drew was out of earshot, I said, "This is the first time I've known you to fence your property."

"This is the first time it's been trespassed."

TWENTY-TWO

THE NEXT MORNING, OLIVE called as I walked out the Johns's front door for another trip to Capital Punishment. "Oscar's Optometry," I answered, "where we see you right away."

"Kowsaki ate some bad sushi, so you're covering for him."

"What is it?" I asked, alarmed.

"Don't know yet. Could be *Vibrio* or *Scombroid.*"

The first one, *Vibrio parahaemolyticus,* is caused by bacterium that takes up residence in raw or undercooked fish, and the second, *Scombroid ichthyotoxicosis*, is caused by a histamine toxin that develops in improperly stored or processed fish, so Gavin had eaten sashimi, not sushi. Both toxins cause nausea, vomiting, and some of the worst gastrointestinal pain I wouldn't even wish on John Without, resulting in a person's most miserable twenty-four to seventy-two hours on earth.

"Full duty?" I asked, trying to sound put upon. Olive might say she was pulling my leg if I let on how excited I was. I wasn't excited that my colleague had food poisoning, but a cowgirl needs to ride often to keep the saddle sores away.

"A day or two," she said.

"Is Gavin okay?"

"No, Markham," she said as if speaking to a simpleton. "That's why you're taking over his district."

"I mean…" My phone beeped with an incoming call from Jamie. "Never mind."

"Good. Get over to the scene of the crime. He had tuna at the Emperor's New Rolls."

"Yes ma'am!" I said, betraying my glee. A full recovery might keep Gavin out for three or four days.

I switched over to Jamie. "Hey."

"Can you come to my office?" he asked.

"I can't right now. Olive has me filling in for Gavin."

"Bad tuna at the Emperor is what I hear."

"That was fast."

"I take care of my sources and they take care of me."

"What do you hear about that new place on Slaughter?"

"Nothing," he said. "My unnamed county official is a Girl Scout."

"After she rats them out and gets her Snitch badge, she can earn her Shiv-in-the-Ribs badge."

"Two badges from one project isn't a bad day's work."

"What's at your office?" I asked.

"How much do you love me?"

"I plead the fifth on that, but I could be compelled to testify for the right reasons."

"I'm looking at a computer file named APD hyphen Sharpe hyphen Confidential."

"That's a very right reason. See anything interesting?"

"Not really," he said. "A wallet, some keys, a couple of empty beer bottles. Maybe you'll see something I don't."

Two minutes ago I was like the cast of *Friends* with nothing to do. Now I had to choose between two things. I needed to return to Capital Punishment, but they probably weren't waiting on me, so I could be later than the 8:00 AM I had indicated in my note. Besides, the way things had been going there, Miles probably stained the ceiling instead of the floors and forgot all about the hot water. I wanted to review the photos before I inspected them again. If I didn't see anything amiss and, by some miracle, they passed the inspection, I could close the file on that one. And now that I had Gavin's district, I had plenty of things to occupy my days.

"Are you at your office this early?" I asked.

"Catching worms," he said. "Coffee will be ready."

x x x

"You were right," I said to Jamie as I clicked through the photos on his computer a second time. "Nothing stands out." The police contact who had sent the photos to Jamie had blacked out Troy's face, thank goodness.

"Sorry," Jamie said. "I was kind of hoping you would find something."

"Really?"

"I don't know any of these people, but I trust your instincts. I don't always like them, but I trust them."

"I wish it would have been worth your while to call in all those favors."

"It was," he said. "It brought you here this morning."

"Did you figure out what the restaurant is?"

The crime scene photos had shown small bits of the restaurant—part of the metal staircase leading up to the catwalk, the rail-

178

ing surrounding it, and a few metal bars that could be anything if you didn't know they belonged to a cell—but any details were photographed up close or with a blurry background. Still, Jamie has a good imagination and could piece it together if he tried.

"Besides a place where someone hangs by the neck until dead? No."

He may have phrased it that way to let me know he figured it out, but supposing he knew that the building had been fashioned after a prison, he wouldn't be able to guess the menu. "Keep thinking," I said.

My happiness at being back on full duty so delighted me, I wasn't too disappointed that the crime scene photos had been a bust. They were a long shot, anyway. If the police didn't already suspect murder, then the killer hadn't left any obvious clues.

I thanked Jamie for his help, then drove across town in pursuit of rotten fish. I decided to put the idea of murder out of my head. All evidence pointed to Troy Sharpe being responsible for his own death. Whether accident or suicide, the police would have to call it. From what I had determined, they had a fifty-fifty chance of being right, so they may as well flip a coin.

x x x

The Palatine is a monstrous shopping complex on the southwest side that uses words like *luxury*, *impeccable*, and *urban lifestyle* in its ads, which translate to "overpriced," "snobby," and "lifestyle I don't have the right clothes for."

The sushi place had managed the double offense of two high-dollar references in their name with Emperor and Rolls, as in Royce. I couldn't wait to bust them.

The Palatine has several phases, some of which are still under construction, which makes it all that much more exciting to maneuver. After locating and parking in the garage for Phase III, I wound my way through a labyrinth of restaurants, shops, salons, and spas so complex it would make the Minotaur stop and ask for directions.

I came upon the restaurant's awning printed with their logo—predictably, a man togaed up like Caesar sitting in a Rolls Royce and using chopsticks to hold a fat sushi roll in front of his open mouth. I went around the building, walked down the alley, and knocked on a beige metal door.

Olive didn't say when Gavin had eaten the bad tuna, but it would have been the day before, either lunchtime or early afternoon. Seeing what a health inspector sees all day every day has turned a lot of us into home cooks. We all have our weaknesses, though, and sashimi is Gavin's. Or it was. He was probably already planning to make that at home, assuming his intestines wouldn't seize up at the sight of raw fish.

A banged-up mobile food truck started down the alley on its way to the job site at the far end. I raised my hand to wave it down to find out if it was Pizza Pig, but just then a towheaded kid answered my knock, holding out a $20 bill. The truck rumbled past, and the kid whipped his hand back as soon as he saw I wasn't who he assumed I would be. The dishwasher from the looks of him, wet from chest to knees, conducting a transaction at the back door for what? Azaleas for his girlfriend? Barbeque ribs? Calculus homework answers? Let's pencil-in answer D: drugs.

I held up my badge and savored the look of panic on his face before I announced, "Austin/Travis County health inspector."

He turned his head and yelled, "Back door!"

A Japanese woman with delicate features that Nina had to pay good money for took his place at the door. "Yes, can I help you?" she asked, the words accented but carefully enunciated. She wore a bright blue chef's coat and clean black pants that matched the color of her hair.

"Are you the chef?" I asked, still holding up my badge.

"Chef, owner, manager," she said. "Ayame Kobayashi."

"Can I come inside, please?"

"Gavin was here yesterday."

I'm pretty good at distinguishing between stalling and genuine confusion. She sounded confused, but she might be a good actress. "What time was that, Ms. Kobayashi?" I asked as I clipped the badge to my waistband.

"When we opened at eleven."

I would double-check Gavin's inspection sheet. Knowing when he inspected them—and therefore, when he may have eaten the bad fish—was important to my investigation because pathogens incubate at different rates. And keeping her speaking to me in English would help me notice if she suddenly gave some command in Japanese that would put me in the middle of a samurai movie, looking at the business ends of a dozen sushi knives.

"Have any of your employees been ill recently?" I asked. "Sneezing, vomiting, bleeding from the eyes?"

"What is this about?" she asked, now sounding confused and distressed.

I accused her with my glare. "Mr. Kawasaki was rushed to the emergency room soon after eating in your establishment. Have you received any other complaints of food poisoning?"

I hoped there hadn't been. If so, and if at least one other food-borne illness—FBI, we call them—had been confirmed by a doctor, we would have an outbreak on our hands. Should I be so lucky that remnants of the actual food still existed, I would take samples and send them to the state lab for testing. Then I would have to ask this sushi restaurant not to serve raw tuna for the two to seven days we would have to wait for the test results.

If there were no remnants, I would investigate, step by step, how the sashimi is made, from receiving to storing to preparing to serving. Any misstep would lay the blame on the Emperor. Criminal charges could be filed against them, and Gavin could even take them to court.

If the fish was bad out of the box, the toxin could have journeyed all the way to the Emperor from the supplier, which would open up a whole other can of parasitic worms. We would have to contact the USDA, who would launch their own investigation of the supplier, which could result in a recall, a revocation of their permit, and heavy-duty federal fines.

"No one has been sick," she said, certain of her words. "The inspection sheet is on the bulletin board. We scored a ninety-nine."

"Good," I said, stepping inside. "I'm going to take a look around. When I'm done, I'd like to see your Food Manager and Food Handler Certificates, and this week's employee schedule."

In Travis County, every restaurant is required to have an employee with a Food Manager's Certificate onsite while food is being prepared and served, which is basically at all times. The certificate is awarded after a day-long health and safety class and successful completion of a written exam. The cost for the class is around

$100, so usually only the managers, chefs, and upper-level cooks are sent for training.

I'm of the opinion that every food service employee, from dishwasher to waiter to hostess, should be required to attend this in-depth training instead of the hour-long food handler training they get, but that idea would be as welcome to Olive as a sprout salad. Not because she wouldn't agree with me, but because making it happen would involve both thought and work.

Surprise health inspections, which are performed twice a year, act as a sort of practical pop quiz to make sure everyone has been paying attention in class. On first glance, the Emperor didn't look like the kind of place that flouted health regulations, and if they lacked only a single point for a perfect score, they probably didn't. But inspectors can't go on looks and seems. I washed my hands, then wrestled them into rubber gloves and entered the walk-in to visually and olfactorily check the tuna.

The Emperor is a tiny place, and the walk-in took up only a fraction of the kitchen, which meant that they probably got daily or twice-daily deliveries, further complicating my efforts to pinpoint the source. The overhead light bulb was out, so I pulled my backpack around to the front of me and pulled my flashlight from the side pocket. As soon as I flipped the switch, I knew that Troy Sharpe's death had not been an accident.

TWENTY-THREE

But I had a more pressing mystery to solve. If I didn't figure out the source of Gavin's food poisoning, many more people could get ill or even die. I went outside and stood near the back door to call Olive and tell her that the fan was on high and I was fixin' to throw buckets of poop at it.

She answered her phone with, "Call it off, Markham. Kowsaki's appendix busted."

"You could have told me."

"Sounds like I just did," she said, then hung up.

I walked into the middle of the dusty alley and began to count to ten, imagining myself floating up into the cool, quiet, Olive-less stratosphere, moving higher with each count. And because I'm a multitasker, I also began to count the number of seconds it was taking the mobile food truck headed in my direction to reach me. By the time I hit four and the first layer of clouds, the truck had covered significant yardage.

I held up my badge but the truck didn't slow down, and at the count of seven it was bearing down on me. The sun reflected off the windshield and I couldn't see the driver's face, so maybe he couldn't see me. I waved my badge and sidestepped into the building's shadow. "Stop! Health department!" The driver gave it some gas and angled the truck toward me. I yanked open the Emperor's back door and vaulted inside right before the truck's side mirror smashed into it.

"Dude, what happened?" the dishwasher kid asked.

I brushed pieces of mirrored glass from my clothes as I tried to think of an answer. The driver could have been texting or blinded by the sun or intoxicated or changing the radio station or eating an oyster po' boy, but those explanations seemed unlikely. "I think someone tried to kill me to avoid an inspection," I said.

× × ×

I knew I was right about Troy's murder, but before I went to Capital Punishment and started questioning suspects, I figured I should do the smart thing and make absolutely sure. I raced to Jamie's office downtown, pulling in next to his car in the parking lot around noon.

I threw open the office door and could not believe what I was seeing. Jamie stood by his desk, embracing another woman, both of them smiling like they had won the lottery. She was one of the freelance writers in his office, Kimberlee. The very young one. This is how Jamie shows me he loves me? This is how he proves he can be trusted?

I would have left, but I had to see the crime scene photos again. Why hadn't I thought to ask him to print them or email them to me? Because I didn't know I would be walking in on a lunchtime tryst in his office while he thought I was working on the other side of town.

I angrily cleared my throat. "Sorry to disturb."

They pulled apart and Jamie said, "Poppy? What are you doing here?"

"Spoiling the moment, apparently."

"What?" he said.

Kimberlee thrust out her left hand and did a bouncy wiggly happy dance. "I'm getting married!"

The thing about being wrong is that it takes your face a few seconds to catch up to your realization. But it took Jamie no time to figure out my assumption process. "You've got to be kidding."

"Congratulations," I said to Kimberlee.

"Thanks, Poppy." She hugged me, then turned to Jamie. "I have *so* much to do, but I'll be back this afternoon to proof your Taste Buds column, 'kay?"

"Sure thing, honeybunch."

She frowned at his term of endearment, then said, "Toodles."

"Toodles," we said.

Jamie hung his head and tapped his finger on the desk. "Sorry you had to find out like this."

"What am I supposed to believe, walking in on a scene like that?"

"You could believe me when I say it will never happen again."

"I'm trying to, Jamie."

"I haven't seen that person since that night and will never see that person again." He sat in his chair and pulled me onto his lap. "You have to trust me."

I nodded.

"Now that you've spoiled my moment with Kimberlee, you may as well tell me why you're here."

"I need to see the crime scene photos again."

"Why?"

"Troy Sharpe was murdered."

I stood up so he could reach his keyboard and pull up the file. As he clicked through them, my scalp began to tingle as photo after photo confirmed my theory.

"What are you seeing?" Jamie asked.

"It's what I'm *not* seeing," I said. "There's no flashlight."

"You're right, but…so?"

"The power was out at the restaurant, right? And it was as dark as the black stripes on a convict's uniform. With all the equipment and building materials everywhere, there's no way Troy could have gotten through the dining room, much less up the stairs and across the catwalk without a flashlight. Especially as drunk as he was. I saw him drink four beers, and there were four more empty bottles in the kitchen and"—I pointed to a photo—"two more on the catwalk."

"Hang on," Jamie said. He opened a document on his computer and together we scanned the list of items that had been photographed. "No mention of a flashlight."

"Troy went upstairs with his killer, who needed the flashlight to get downstairs and out of the building." I bounced up and down like Kimberlee. "I have *so* much to do."

Jamie took my hands in his. "You know what I'm going to say."

"You think it's a great idea for me to investigate this on my own, and you hope I catch the murderer before he or she can kill again." I kissed him before he could say the exact opposite. "Toodles."

✗ ✗ ✗

I didn't see Miles's pickup when I drove past the front, and it wasn't parked in back. So much for my assumption that he would always be available for questioning. I did, however, see a silver BMW with the license plate 88. At least Todd wasn't too broken up or busy creating a defensive playbook with Suzi Grimm to be at work.

Construction workers filled the kitchen, most of them watching two others on ladders snaking a long silver ventilation duct out of a gap in the ceiling tiles. I recognized my almost-rival gurney driver, Mingo, and said *hola*. I pointed to the scene and asked what was going on. "*Que pasa?*"

"*Esta quebrada*," he said. It's broken.

Well, obviously. I didn't think Miles would waste time fixing things that were working. I didn't know enough Spanish to ask if it was only the duct or if the entire ventilation unit was out. The system had worked during my first inspection, but it seemed like Miles's guys broke two more things for every one they fixed.

The office door was closed, but I heard Todd's and Danny's voices. I turned my back to the door and eyed the workers while I listened to their conversation. If the office door opened, I could say I was trying to decide if the ventilation issue belonged to my health inspection or to the mechanical inspection.

"This makes it look like Troy killed himself," Todd said.

"Right," Danny said.

"But it's better for all of us if the police think it was an accident."

"I don't care what they think as long as they make a final ruling," Danny said. "And I think you should be the one to tell Ginger."

"Negative," Todd said. "Troy didn't want her to know, and if she saw this we'd have to explain what it means."

Neither said anything, and I imagined Danny staring at Todd, trying to think of what to say to convince him to tell Ginger about whatever they were at odds over. It sounded to me like they might be discussing how to keep their part in Troy's murder a secret from both the police and Ginger.

That would make it a conspiracy. And it raised all sorts of questions about how Todd and Danny got this far into cahoots against Troy. And what didn't they want Ginger to see? Troy's last will and testament that left everything to Todd? His cell phone bill with midnight calls to a strange number? A credit card showing purchases of inappropriate entertainment?

I couldn't dwell on those questions because Danny said, "I don't think we should sit on this just to spare Ginger's feelings."

"I need some time to think about it," Todd said.

"Don't take too long," Danny said.

I heard the handle click and quickly turned around to face the door. I raised my hand and knocked a millisecond before Todd opened it.

"Is everything okay?" I asked.

"Yes," Todd said stiffly. "Why?"

"This is the first time I've seen the office door closed."

"The guys were noisy out there," Danny said. He was sitting at the desk holding my yellow sticky note in his hand.

"Sorry I'm late," I said. "I had to fill in for another inspector this morning."

"No problem," Todd said. "We just got here ourselves."

"Miles told us about the hot water," Danny said. "It's supposed to be working now."

It didn't escape me how easily they both went from discussing Troy's murder to the practical business of getting their permit. "I'll check the water," I said, "but the ventilation system needs to function properly above the grill."

"I thought the hot water was the last thing," Todd said.

"Everything has to be working at the same time," I said.

Todd looked back at Danny. "Get Archer."

"You keep thinking," Danny said on his way out the door.

"Do all permit inspections take this long?" Todd asked.

"Not usually. Most restaurant builders know the health code requirements."

Todd looked out into the kitchen and chewed his molars as he watched the workers.

"Ginger told me that Miles usually does home remodeling," I said.

His head jerked back to me. "When did you talk to Ginger?"

"Tuesday. Right after you and Danny left for Suzi Grimm's office. She came in looking for you."

"You didn't tell her where we went, did you?"

"I didn't know it was a secret."

Todd shook out his hands, then sat behind the desk. He didn't say anything else, and I had nothing else to say. I had come straight from Jamie's office with proof that Troy had been murdered, but I hadn't had time to think through my approach for questioning any-one about it. I couldn't tell him I overheard his conversation with Danny and ask him if he killed his own brother. Could I?

The success of a health inspection depends on two things: the element of surprise and the offensive nature of the attack. If I called ahead to a restaurant and made an appointment to observe their daily operations, I would never know if they left uncovered tubs of frozen ground beef in the alley to thaw or whether cooks licked cream gravy from their fingers during lunch service.

Surprise offensives work in a lot of other situations, too—football games, courts of law, marriage proposals, police interrogations. I decided to come at Todd head-on to catch him off-guard. "What are you and Danny trying to hide from Ginger?"

Todd laughed uncomfortably. "What makes you say that?" Classic evasive tactic: answering a question with a question.

"I overheard part of your conversation. Did you and Danny have something to do with Troy's death?"

His face flamed under his tan. "That's sick! How could you even think something like that?"

"Danny wants to go to the police, but you don't, and you don't want Ginger to see something. And two days ago you both visited a criminal defense attorney. What else could it be?"

"I don't see how any of this is your business."

"Nefarious conduct is always of interest to a county employee, Mr. Sharpe." Individually the words implied a threat, but strung together, they didn't say much of anything. I counted on Todd being too caught up in his own defense to parse it out.

"Troy left a suicide note," he said finally.

No!

There wasn't a note at the crime scene.

There was no flashlight.

His death was not his fault.

I am not wrong.

"That can't be," I said. Todd squinted at me, and I heard my choice of words. "I mean, I didn't know there was a note."

"We just found it," Todd said. "Some papers had been moved around on the desk and it surfaced."

"Which proves it was suicide," I said, disappointed, "and his life insurance won't pay, which is why you don't want to show it to the police."

Todd nodded but didn't say anything more.

Curiosity about what the note said and what it would tell Ginger consumed me. I stood there looking completely uninterested, hoping he would offer to let me read it. Instead he picked up his walkie-talkie. "Eighty-eight to Danny, over."

"Miles isn't here," Danny responded. "I'm tracking him down."

Todd slammed the walkie-talkie on the desk and looked out at the workers. "June eleventh is looking more impossible by the minute."

I, too, felt like assaulting an electronic device. I had been grateful for Miles's incompetence when I had a murder to investigate, but a suicide note now made the delays a waste of my brain power. "You still have eight days," I said. "It'll take me a little while to check the hot water today. Maybe they'll get the ventilation working by the time I'm done."

"Yeah."

I picked up Troy's hard hat and walked a familiar course across the kitchen and through the silver doors. One look at the dining room and I knew it was a good thing my murder theory had been disproved.

TWENTY-FOUR

THE SPACE HAD BEEN transformed. Gone was the litter of tools, machines, and building materials, replaced by construction workers on their knees and applying sealant to the stained brown floor. It was beginning to look like a restaurant rather than a concept. Throw out a few tables and chairs, and June 11 looked quite possible.

I stepped behind the bar and had the memory of serving Troy a beer Monday morning, fresh from his gurney race victory. He had monkeyed around with my badge and been so excited about choosing a name for the restaurant. He was going to order a guillotine. Morbid and creepy, but doggone it, he didn't act like a guy who planned to kill himself in a few hours. Without a flashlight.

I couldn't refute his suicide note, though. Unless...

Unless the killer planted the note!

Todd said that papers had been moved around on the desk. It had to have been done by me when I was snooping. I hadn't seen anything that looked like a suicide note, so someone must have put it there after I left. Which meant I didn't have to look any further than Todd, Danny, Ginger, and Miles. They had all seen his handwriting, and Troy was drunk before he died, which meant that forging it precisely wouldn't be critical.

Ginger was the most obvious suspect because she had the desk to herself when she shut me out of the office. And, clever girl, writing something that she wasn't supposed to know about.

Danny wanted to give the note to the police to settle things once and for all. Maybe the police had started to look at it as a murder, and Danny wanted to hand them proof it was suicide.

Todd didn't want to give it to the police because it would affect the insurance payout. Wouldn't that go to Ginger anyway? Perhaps the real reason is that he wrote the note as his own insurance policy in case the police started investigating him. He purposely wrote something Ginger shouldn't see as an excuse not to turn it over to the police unless absolutely necessary.

And what was Suzi Grimm's part in all of this? Todd met with her on Tuesday—two days before he "found" the note—so had he and Danny consulted her about something else?

Miles had access to the entire job site any time he wanted and was alone in the restaurant the day before while his guys stained the floors. He could easily have left the note, but why kill Troy?

That was the question for all of them. And why plant the note now? Either the police really were investigating a murder or…oh, no! They suspected that I was. And I had asked Todd if he killed his brother.

I started across the dining room toward the main entrance to call Jamie but stopped when I heard someone whistle. I looked around and saw Rudy by cell block B waving me toward the gift chamber door. He didn't want me to dirty up the floor while they were sealing it, which meant that I wouldn't be able to get to the bathrooms.

Good thing I hadn't arrived at eight o'clock like I had planned or they might have gotten their permit.

I made it halfway through the small room when I noticed the "gifts." Since they had settled on a name only three days before, there were one or two representatives of what they planned to stock, each resting in a cubbyhole or on a shelf. Plush German shepherd, Rottweiler, and pit bull dog toys; black-and-white striped T-shirts variously printed with INMATE, D.O.C., and PRISONER in fluorescent orange; ball-and-chain keychains; handcuffs and different styles of metal badges; several types and sizes of shot glasses; toy guns; and, curiously, golf balls.

I pushed through a door marked Final Exit and into the parking lot, then walked toward the only shady spot near the back fence and called Jamie.

"There's good news and bad news," I said when he answered.

"Is it a high school and they're serving cafeteria food?" he asked.

"Negative, but it's something the general population would enjoy."

"What's the bad news?" he asked.

"Troy left a suicide note, but you'll think that's the good news."

"No murder means you don't have anything to investigate, and that means I don't have to worry about you."

"I think the note is a fake."

Jamie sighed extravagantly.

"Hear me out," I said.

Two workers unlocked a separate fenced area on the other side of me and began loading cinder blocks into a wheelbarrow. They wouldn't care about my conversation, but I moved to the unshaded front gate anyway as I explained my reasoning to Jamie.

"The papers on the desk could have been moved again later by someone else," he said.

"They looked pretty much the way I left them on Tuesday."

"Pretty much?"

"Well, I was having to deal with Ginger catching me in the act, so my full powers of observation weren't on the desk. And I didn't know it would be important. I'm ninety-five percent sure the papers look the same."

"The note could still be real."

"I know, but the missing flashlight is real, too." My phone beeped with a call from Olive, which I ignored.

"What's your next step, Miss Marple?"

"I'm wondering why the killer decided to fake the note now. I'm thinking they're spooked because the police reconsidered their original conclusion and are looking at murder. Can you find out?"

"My contact wouldn't have sent me the photos if they thought it was a homicide."

"Okay, so what's putting pressure on the killer?"

"I assume you're still looking at Troy's inner circle," Jamie said. "Maybe they've started to suspect each other."

"Good thinking," I said. I glanced at the locked gate and remembered something from my first day there. "Do you remember a waiter from Markham's named Philip Anthony?"

"No, but you said he was one of the protesters on Monday."

Olive called again and I ignored her again. "Can you find him for me?"

"Do you think *he* killed Troy?"

"I hadn't thought about that. If he and his buddies did time in jail because of Troy, they might want revenge, but that's kind of thin. Regardless, maybe he knows something."

"I'll find him."

"Philip with one L," I said. "I also need to know if Troy requested COD with their other suppliers. I saw paperwork from Lone Star Supply and Waterloo Linen on the desk."

"Would you like fries with that?"

"Yes, I know you have your own work to do, but they're going to pass the inspection at some point, and Olive is going to put me back on full duty. I don't know how much time I have to get this figured out."

"Is it a monastery and they're going to make people take a vow of silence when they walk through the door?"

"Like where monks live?" I said. "Not even close."

As soon as I hung up with Jamie, Olive called a third time. "House of Joust," I answered. "Lance speaking."

"Fast-track me on Pizza Pig," she said.

Shoot a biscuit! I forgot all about that inspection. "I thought since I'm filling in for Gavin, you would assign that to someone else."

"I would have said so, Markham."

It's true, she would have. Micromanagers don't let their employees make their own decisions. "I can do it right now."

"Let's hope they waited around for you," she said, then hung up.

My trek to the kitchen to tell someone that the inspection was delayed again would have been shorter and shadier through the restaurant, but I couldn't walk on the sealed floor, and the gift chamber door had locked itself behind me, so I circled the building. The two workers I had seen loading the wheelbarrow stood near the snack truck, drinking sodas and helping to slide the awnings down and prepare the truck for travel. Surely Miles would have given them a more important assignment—like meeting their impossible deadline for completing construction—but Miles still wasn't there.

197

I heard frantic yelling and turned around to see the snack truck back into a concrete pylon, which had been painted bright yellow to bring attention to it so something like that wouldn't happen. The two guys who had tried to prevent the accident went behind the truck to check out the damage, further delaying their return to work.

—— x —— x —— x ——

I had to take the Jeep off-road twice, but I made it to Lunch and Larder in seventeen minutes. That was one of those times where my thoughts didn't make sense. I didn't expect Pizza Pig to be there, but I also didn't expect them to be gone. Yes, I was three hours late for our noon appointment, but they should have waited. Nothing should be more important to them than getting their permit—not buying raw ingredients or scouting for good lunch spots or getting their truck painted pink. They cannot legally sell food without a permit and they should have waited.

I went back to my Jeep, reflecting on the irony that even though I had seen Capital Punishment almost every day for the past four days, they were in the exact same permit-less position as Pizza Pig, which I had never seen.

Westbound traffic was as vile as eastbound traffic that afternoon, and I decided to delay my trip to the Palatine. I left a message for Jamie asking if he had made any progress on either of my requests, then left a message for Olive about Pizza Pig, then made a phone call I had been dreading but could put off no longer.

TWENTY-FIVE

"Poppy who?" Nina said.

"Markham. Mitch's daughter. Your stepdaughter."

"Oh, I didn't recognize your voice."

"How many people do you know named Poppy who would call your cell phone?" She had apparently also deleted my number from her phonebook again.

"Just you."

The only reason I didn't point out the inanity of her response was because it was time to ask for that favor. Except I couldn't call it a favor or have it in any way resemble a favor. "I'm calling to reschedule our shopping trip," I said.

She hesitated. "When would you like to go?"

"I know it's last-minute, but my afternoon freed up."

"Why do we have to switch sides?" she asked. I didn't answer because I knew she wasn't talking to me. "I'm at my tennis clinic right now."

"That's right," I said. "I believe you mentioned it at dinner."

"But the sun is going to be in my eyes," she whined to someone.

"There's a chichi clothing boutique at the club, isn't there?"

"Will I have to switch the racquet to my left hand?"

"I can be there in half an hour."

"Okay," Nina said.

"Looking forward to it." I hung up before I found out what she okayed.

Inside of twenty minutes, I pulled up to the valet at the Silver Niche on Barton Springs, a private country club for members age fifty-five and older, with a conservative dress code and a minimum guest age. That age had been recently lowered to twenty-five when several members complained that the age of thirty-five barred their girlfriends from joining them for dinner and spa treatments. The dress code for women had necessarily been relaxed as well, which is why the valet attendant sneered at but did not question my jeans. Everyone calls it by its acronym, the SNOBS club.

Nina must have okayed our shopping trip because she had arranged for a guest pass to be waiting at the check-in desk. A runway model named Lola escorted me outside, past the Ilie Nastase and Vitas Gerulaitis tennis courts, and left me at the Evonne Goolagong court, where Nina, CiCi Chesterton, and two other women stood by the net listening to Ginger Sharpe explain the scoring system.

Nina glanced at me, then excused herself and came over to the bleachers. "I'm so glad to see you," she said.

"You are?"

"My brain was starting to fizzle with all that talk of fifteen-loves and love-all." She sat down and patted her dry neck with a hand towel. "This isn't the *Newlywed Game*. Why can't they keep the scoring simple, like in bridge?"

"I don't know," I said, more interested in Ginger's state of mind than Nina's state of confusion. Troy had died four days ago and Ginger was giving tennis lessons to a group of overindulged, out-of-shape seniors wearing full makeup in 90-degree heat.

"Let's get you out of those dreary black clothes," Nina said. "You're what, a size ten, twelve?"

"I'm a six. What about your tennis clinic?"

"It's almost over."

Shopping for clothes at the club had been a pretense to get close to Ginger, and I had never intended to actually go through with it. "You know," I said, "I hadn't planned to go shopping when I left the house today and I'm not wearing any underwear."

Nina gaped at me as if I had said exactly that.

Ginger looked at her watch, then dismissed the remaining three ladies. She went to the opposite bleachers, unzipped a tennis bag, then pulled out her cell phone.

I waved to CiCi, who didn't recognize me but returned my wave in case I was someone important. "I'm wearing a bra," I continued, "but not undies, so I can still try on dresses and tops."

Nina turned her Botoxed brow toward the approaching trio of women. "I just remembered I'm having a massage in thirty minutes," she said. "Why don't we reschedule for when you're, ah…" She didn't want to say the reason out loud in front of her cronies.

"Wearing undies?" I asked, louder than I needed to.

She stood. "We'll go to the Palatine. Can you find your way out?"

"I can find my way anywhere."

As soon as Nina flew off with her friends, I walked across Evonne Goolagong. "Ginger?" I said.

"The clinic just ended," she said.

201

"I'm not here for a lesson."

She raised a hand to shield her eyes from the sun. "You're the inspector from the restaurant."

She sounded combative, so I changed the subject to talk about her. "I didn't realize you were a tennis pro here. When did you start playing?"

"About a year after I married Troy." Now she sounded angry. "I have an MBA, but no one wants to hire a military wife who moves every few years. So I worked retail and took up tennis."

"And now you're teaching my stepmother, Nina Markham."

Ginger looked as if she had caught a whiff of rotten tuna, then recovered and said, "She's doing very well."

"It's okay. I'm pretty sure the only reason she's taking lessons is so she can buy tennis outfits. She'll quit in a couple of weeks."

Ginger laughed. "She wouldn't be the first."

Now that I had chipped away some of the frost, I said, "Since we're both here, do you mind if I ask you some questions?"

"So Todd can get the permit?"

We weren't in the restaurant, and as far as I was concerned, I was a private citizen, but I would never misrepresent the badge or risk my job. It didn't hurt that she made that assumption, however, and I didn't correct her. "It should happen soon," I said. "How well do you know the manager, Danny MacAdams?"

"Not well. We all went to high school together, but we weren't friends back then. After Troy hired him, we had dinner with him and his wife a few times, but after construction started, we stopped seeing them socially." She looked toward the club house. "They're not really our kind of people."

Not SNOBS kind of people, she meant. "Did Troy have a problem with Danny?"

"Not so much Danny as Danny's brother-in-law."

"Who is that?"

"Miles Archer," she said. "He's married to Danny's sister."

Whoa! "Was Troy upset with him about the construction delays?"

"That was part of it. Miles complained to Danny all the time about Troy not wearing his hard hat and making so many changes and playing around with his guys."

"Do you know why Troy never wore his hard hat?" It was an innocent question, or so I thought, but Ginger's stare made me backpedal. "I figured maybe all those years of wearing a football helmet turned him off to putting big plastic things on his head."

"Troy had a brain tumor," she said. "He claimed the hat irritated it."

Double whoa! "I didn't know. How awful for all of you."

"Very few people knew about it."

"I'm really sorry about Troy," I said.

She pressed her lips together and looked down, assuming a posture of sorrow that looked practiced. "Thank you."

"I only spent a few hours around him, but I can't believe he would take his own life."

"He didn't."

"Oh?"

Her face hardened. "He was playing around as usual, drunk as usual, and things got out of control. As usual."

Yes, except he didn't take a flashlight upstairs with him and someone faked a suicide note. "You know I was the one who found him."

"It looked like an accident to you, right?"

Because you staged it to look like one? "I couldn't really say. I thought it was you at first."

"Me-ee?"

"Your car was the only one in the parking lot when I got there."

She laughed. "Oh, because even on my worst day, I do not have that much hair on my legs."

Yikes. "Were you with him then?"

"No," she said quickly. "One of his tires was low, so he took my car." She bounced the strings of her tennis racquet against her open palm. "You're awfully curious about my husband's personal life."

"I'm curious about why he would return to the restaurant when the electricity was out and no one was supposed to be onsite," I said. "I'm wondering if it had something to do with the permit inspection." I hadn't wondered that at all, but I could have. "Do you know why he went back there?"

She bent over to zip the racquet onto the side of her bag. "He told me he had a meeting."

"With who?"

Ginger stood and crossed her arms. "With you."

"Me-ee?" She had to be making that up. "Are you sure?"

"That's what he said. That you were coming back to finish up and he needed to be there."

"I told Todd I would be back around two o'clock. You were standing right there. It could hardly be considered a meeting with Troy."

"All I know is that my husband left to meet you at the restaurant." She sounded triumphant and suspicious at the same time, as if she could hang this whole thing on Troy's romantic interest in me.

I should have thanked her and wished her good day, but I didn't know when or if I would speak with her again, and I had to know. "Is it true that you wanted to divorce Troy?"

She dropped her hands by her sides. "Who told you that?" Answering a question with a question.

"Just a rumor I heard."

She picked up her tennis bag and slung it over her shoulder. "You'll have to excuse me," she said curtly. "I'm teaching a private lesson at Martina Navratilova."

— x   x   x —

While I waited for the valet to bring my Jeep around, I thought about Ginger's three bombshells, starting in the order they had been dropped. Miles Archer was Danny's brother-in-law! I didn't know what it meant to the big picture, but this nepotistic detail—which would force Danny to choose sides between his wife's brother and an immature business partner who didn't respect him—couldn't be unimportant.

From what I had seen and heard, Danny mostly sided against Troy. I couldn't blame him. Twenty years on, Troy still called him Danny Dull, still treated him like a high school dork instead of a successful businessman. Troy's similar treatment of Miles would only compound Danny's hatred. And if Danny's wife knew about all of this, she could have Lady Macbethed him into killing their tormenter.

I had been thinking that Danny and Todd were plotting together, but now I had to consider a new alliance. If Danny killed Troy, he could have enlisted Miles in a cover-up. Did he have Miles plant the suicide note the day he stained the floors and everyone else was away so Danny could later "find" the note and insist Todd take it to the police? For the same reasons, Miles could have killed Troy and then Danny planted the note to protect him. I needed to find out where everyone was the afternoon Troy died.

A brain tumor would explain Troy's eccentric behavior and his medical discharge from the marines. I wish I had thought to ask Ginger if the tumor was inoperable and how long he had to live and did he act crazy because of the tumor or because he had a death wish? With all the smoking and drinking he did, he may have known he didn't have many more days on this earth. Is that why he refused to change the grand opening date?

Ginger had not denied wanting to divorce Troy, which was as good as an admission. If it was because of the brain tumor, that would make her more heartless than she appeared, and she already looked like the dictator of a South American country. Unless she was leaving him for a more altruistic reason, like she loved him so much, she couldn't watch him kill himself. Nah. But if he was dying, why would she kill him? Why would Todd, for that matter?

Jamie called as my Jeep came around the corner. I held up a finger to the valet, then went inside to take the call. "Did you find Philip?" I asked.

"Yes," he said. "And you're not going to believe where."

TWENTY-SIX

"Markham's Grille and Cocktails," Jamie said.

"It's Cocktails and Grille," I said. "How did you find him?"

"I called Mitch to see if he still had Philip's personnel file with a phone number or address."

"Good thinking."

"Mitch told me you sent Philip over there for a job."

"Is that what he told you?"

"And you didn't mention this because…"

"I forgot," I said, and then I had to change the subject because one of the reasons Jamie likes me is because I'm always on top of things. "Would you like to have an early dinner?"

"Where oh where shall we meet?"

"I need to freshen myself," I said, walking out to meet the SNOBS valet. "First one there gets a table in Philip's section."

I wouldn't have anything nice to change into after I showered at the Johns's house, and I refused to go through another day wearing a gay man's clothes. Maybe I really should go shopping with Nina. Or…I could shop while Nina was in the vicinity. I asked the valet guy to hold the Jeep for a few minutes, then ran into the boutique.

I picked up a sleeveless black linen dress that was on sale and black sandals that weren't, and charged them to Nina's account.

x   x   x

Philip was not waiting tables. He was working as a host, which would have been perfect on any other night, because at 6:15 PM when I arrived, he would have been mostly standing around chatting up waitresses and could have answered hundreds of questions. But Four Corners was having a gallery opening for a photographer who took black-and-white portraits of circus performers in the seventies, which meant that every restaurant in the area had an early dinner rush.

Philip sailed around the dining room bussing tables, taking appetizer orders, and opening bottles of wine for waiters who couldn't spare the five to seven minutes it took to do it themselves. He told me that one of the cooks had burned his hand and Drew was in the kitchen cooking, so I helped out with hostess duties. I asked him questions as we walked through the restaurant together after seating guests or when we met up at the hostess stand. The good thing about doing it that way was that Philip didn't have time to think about my questions, so he answered quickly. The bad thing was that I couldn't always look him in the eye to know if he answered truthfully.

"When did you start protesting the Sharpe place?" I asked.

"About a month ago," Philip said, then picked up a stack of menus. "How many in your party?" A woman indicated five adults and a small child.

"How did you find out about the restaurant?" I asked.

"When I applied for a job there. Do you need a high chair, ma'am?"

"Wait…you wanted to work there, but you protested the construction?"

"Troy asked me to," he said. "Can you follow me with a booster seat?"

"Troy asked you to what?" I said after we settled the six-top.

"Protest construction," Philip said. "We have about a ten-minute wait, sir. May I have your last name, please?"

"Sherwood," Jamie said. "Two for dinner."

"*Jamie* Sherwood?" Philip said, his words tinged with awe. "I'm honored to meet you in person."

"No need to alert the kitchen," Jamie said. "I'm not reviewing anyone." He looked at me. "Wait for you at the bar?"

"Drinks are on me," I said to him, then to Philip, "Troy asked you to protest construction of his own restaurant?"

"The protest was just a cover."

"That explains why it was so lame," I said. "A cover for what?"

Philip laughed. "What do you expect from a bunch of waiters and business majors? Troy said he would pay me and some buddies to hang around and watch the place." He checked the wait list, then announced, "Treehorn, party of four."

As I watched Philip seat two couples at what would forever be known to me as George and Laura's table, someone approached the hostess stand from the bar. I didn't have to turn around to know it was Jamie because two women who had been chirping about where to go dancing after dinner suddenly stopped and smiled at something behind me. It's not easy dating a beautiful man.

Jamie handed me a glass of red wine. "This okay with dinner?"

A lot of people, Jamie especially, like to choose a wine after they decide what to eat so that the wine complements the food—

Chardonnay with shrimp, Cabernet Sauvignon with filet mignon, Muscat Canelli with raspberry sorbet—but I drink red wine with everything, so Jamie orders his meal to complement the wine.

I sipped the crimson liquid. "Malbec?" I asked, trying to impress him.

Jamie hung his head in mock disappointment. "Pinot noir."

"I like it," I said. "Troy hired Philip and his friends to watch the restaurant about a month ago."

"That's interesting. Why?"

"I'm fixin' to find out."

Jamie scrammed as Philip returned. "I think we're finally winding down," Philip said. "Thanks for your help."

"Sure thing," I said. "Why did Troy want you to watch the restaurant?"

Philip wiped a menu with a damp towel. "He didn't tell me. He said to hang around as much as possible and keep our eyes open."

"For what?"

He hesitated, then said, "Why all the questions about Troy?"

I was pretty sure Philip wasn't the killer, and revealing my suspicions might make him interpret something he had seen in a different way. "I don't think he killed himself," I said.

"You know, I don't think he did either, but I can't say why."

"Mine is just a hunch, too," I said. "So, why did he hire you?"

"He didn't tell me. We'd meet every couple of days and I'd report on what we saw. The first few times, he handed me an envelope full of cash, but then he started giving me excuses why payment would be delayed."

"What did you report to him?"

"Construction workers coming and going, building material deliveries, the snack truck arriving and taking off, when the other bosses were there."

"Nothing unusual about that."

"That's what I thought," Philip said. "But Troy wanted to know everything."

"Did he ever ask about anything in particular?"

"Sometimes he would want to clarify what time something happened. But mostly he would stand there and write stuff down."

"Troy took notes?"

"Yeah," Philip said. "He kept a little notebook in his back pocket."

"Did anyone else know about your arrangement?"

"I don't know. It didn't seem like it."

A waitress asked Philip to water her section and said she had a two-top ready to be sat. I took those two single women to her table in the second dining room, far away from Jamie.

When Philip and I met up at the hostess stand again, I asked, "Are you sure it was Troy, not Todd, who hired you?"

"That was one of the first things Troy talked about," Philip said. "He wanted me to make sure it was him before I reported anything."

"How did you do that?"

"We had a code. I would say something like, 'I hope your restaurant fails.' If it was Troy, he would always say, 'Say that in Latin.' I'd know it was Todd if he said something that made sense, like, 'You're wasting your time, slacker.' After a while, I could tell them apart, but Troy insisted we always use the code." He looked at me. "Do you think Todd had something to do with this?"

"It's possible," I said, not wanting to get him off-track with my theories. "Did your friends know that you weren't really protesting?"

"Troy didn't want me to tell them at first, but there was so much going on all over the place I couldn't watch everything, so we paired up and covered a side of the building."

This was too good to be true! "What happened when Troy went down behind the restaurant?"

"When?"

"That morning I saw you. He said someone knocked him out."

"I can't help you there. We were all in front gearing up to rush the gate. We did that once in a while to make the protest look legit."

"What happened after the police came?"

"Nothing. Troy never pressed charges."

"Did you leave after that?"

Philip shook his head. "Not until after the power went out and the construction manager cleared the site."

"Did everyone leave?"

"Most of the workers had gone, but all the fancy cars were still there when we took off."

"Troy's too?"

He nodded.

"Where did y'all go when you left?"

"Most of us went downtown to shoot pool at Buffalo Billiards."

That alibi would be easy enough to check, if necessary. "Are you sure Troy never told you why he wanted this information?"

"I asked him once and he said he was documenting construction, but I didn't really believe him. I mean, why keep it a secret from everyone?"

That sounded familiar and I remembered John Without doing the same thing with photos. What had Troy been up to?

"Thanks, Philip. If you remember anything that might help, let me know."

He nodded, then looked at a foursome walking through the door. "Looks like we're getting our second rush. Are you and Mr. Sherwood ready for your table?"

✕ ✕ ✕

"Your clichés look fetching in that dress, Poppycakes," Jamie said as he poured pinot into my wine glass. "Did you go shopping with Nina?"

"Sort of," I said. Then before I had to explain that I had essentially shoplifted my outfit, I told him about Troy hiring Philip to watch the comings and goings at the construction site.

"If Philip is telling the truth, it sounds like Troy was spying on someone."

"Or everyone," I said. "Miles told me that Troy had accused Todd and Danny of ganging up on him, and they both said Troy was paranoid."

"Wasn't he worried about someone stealing his restaurant idea?"

"Then why not hire a security company instead of Philip and his friends?" I put my napkin in my lap. "No, he wanted to do it on the sly, so he was spying on someone in particular."

"Troy could have discovered a secret and was blackmailing someone," Jamie suggested.

"Possibly, but blackmail is a lot of work, and Troy wasn't that focused and organized."

"If the secret was damaging enough, Troy wouldn't have to organize anything. All they would need is the suspicion that he discovered it."

"So I have to uncover some secrets," I said.

Jamie reached across the table and took my right hand, then turned it palm up so that we both could see the red slash that had finally started to heal. "I know I say this a lot," he said, "but please be careful. If they killed Troy to keep their secret, they'll kill you too."

I looked into his brown eyes and stayed there for a moment. I didn't want to do anything that would separate me from the love I found there. But I couldn't let someone get away with murder, especially someone with a murder-worthy secret. "I promise I won't let anyone kill me."

Jamie released my hand. "It's a good thing you always tell the truth."

Drew arrived at our table wearing a smudged white apron over his dress clothes and carrying a big black ceramic bowl. Philip must have told him we were here. "Asian Curried Cauliflower," Drew said as he placed the bowl and two appetizer plates on our table. "With my compliments."

Jamie pushed his plate away. "You shouldn't have."

Drew looked at me. "It's my pleasure," he said, then went back to the kitchen.

I spooned two helpings of the cauliflower onto our plates and pushed Jamie's toward him. "It smells good," I said, then took a bite. "Yummy in my tummy."

Jamie rolled his eyes at my silly attempt to lighten his mood, but he ate a bite anyway. "Heavy-handed and overdone," he said, dropping his fork on his plate.

I thought it was just right but didn't say so.

Philip delivered glasses of ice water to our table, promising that our regular waiter would be with us soon.

"Philip told me Troy took notes on his reports in a little note-book he kept in his back pocket," I said. "I don't remember seeing it in the photos or list of personal effects, do you?"

Jamie shook his head. "I'll double-check, though."

"I'm pretty sure the killer took it. It's probably why they killed Troy."

"Maybe Troy left the notebook at home or in his car. Why don't you check with his wife first?"

I sipped my wine and squinched my mouth to the side.

"Why can't you do that?" he asked.

I told him about my meeting with Ginger at the SNOBS club and her abrupt retreat.

"I know this is only the second wife of a dead man you've questioned," he said—the first being BonBon, wife of Évariste Bontecou, who threw Jamie and me out of her hotel room when she discovered we weren't lifestyle reporters profiling her for the Sunday paper—"so can I give you some advice?"

I leaned toward him, anxious for any expert guidance from this master interviewer.

"Stop ticking them off."

I gave him a wry smile. "I'll try that next time. Meanwhile, I have a motive for Ginger to kill her husband. Death instead of divorce."

"A few minutes ago, the notebook was the motive."

"Maybe Ginger didn't want Troy to know a divorce was on the horizon, but with all his spying, he found out, and then Ginger found the notebook and discovered that he knew, and when Troy found out she knew he knew, he started funneling all his money into Swiss bank accounts so Ginger couldn't get any of it, which is why he went cash-only with his vendors."

Jamie sat quietly, trying to untangle my logic, and I took time to do the same. "Or Troy wanted to get rid of Ginger," he said.

"Okay, then Ginger reads something in the notebook and thinks Troy wants to divorce her, and since there's no alimony in Texas, she decides on assassination instead."

"Why not let the brain tumor do it for her?"

"She couldn't take the chance that he would live long enough to divorce her," I said. "Or maybe he was faking the whole thing. Another practical joke."

"And got a medical discharge from the marines?"

I threw myself against the back of my chair. "Dang! Nothing makes sense."

"That's because you're making things up," Jamie said.

"I'm theorizing and postulating."

"They're good theories and postulations, but only one of them is supported by the facts."

"So I should start with the facts."

"That's what I usually do."

I fortified myself with a gulp of wine, then said, "Assuming that the crime scene photos are accurate and everyone I've talked to so far is telling the truth, I know that there was no flashlight on the catwalk; there exists a suicide note allegedly written by Troy that Todd doesn't want Ginger to see; Troy was documenting secrets in a notebook that the killer stole—"

"You don't know that for a fact."

"Troy kept a notebook full of secrets I haven't seen; Danny and Todd had an emergency meeting with a criminal defense attorney the day after Troy died; Troy had a brain tumor; and Miles is Danny's brother-in-law."

"Do any of those facts support your theory that Ginger and Troy were divorcing?"

"Not directly," I said sulkily.

"Do those facts support any other theories?"

"I'm not wrong about this, Jamie. Someone killed Troy Sharpe. If not Ginger because of a divorce, then Danny or Miles or Todd for some other reason."

"You actually have a lot to go on," he said.

"Pft."

"You could find out what he wrote in his suicide note or find the notebook or find out why those two went to see Suzi Grimm."

I smiled at him. "I guess my thinking had gotten really uptight. Thank you."

"My pleasure," he said. "Is it a microbrewery?"

"More like a microcosm."

Our waiter, a new guy I had never seen before—who obviously didn't recognize me or Jamie because he stored his pen behind his ear until I pointed out that it was unhygienic—took our dinner order. Cucumber salad for me, salmon cakes for Jamie.

After he left, I asked, "Is it kosher to pair salmon with pinot noir?"

"Of course," he said. "I don't make those kinds of gastronomic errors."

"Were you able to find out if Troy arranged to pay cash—another *fact*—with any other vendors?"

"They're COD with Lone Star and Waterloo."

"Did they say why?"

"Only that Troy made the request a few weeks ago."

"Maybe Troy didn't trust whoever was signing on the account. It would have to be Todd, Danny, or Ginger."

"Is that a theory or a postulation?" Jamie asked.

"A little of both."

Our meals arrived, and after the first bite of his entrée, Jamie said, "I may have lied to Philip earlier. These salmon cakes are review worthy."

"That's my recipe, you know."

"Yes, I know, but I review chefs who do amazing things with food, not girlfriends who do amazing things to their dresses."

We passed the rest of dinner talking about the various projects he was working on, the progress on my house, and the latest antics between Dana White and Randy Dove, who were both running for president of the Friends of the Farm at Good Earth Preserves.

Jamie invited me to the Cove to listen to his jazz band, Zzaj. I don't care for jazz, but I love watching Jamie play the drums. I would have gone for a little while, but I had one more stop to make. We said good night around nine o'clock, and I drove down the street to the Johns's gallery. I needed to view some photographs, but not ones of circus freaks.

TWENTY-SEVEN

THROUGH THE PICTURE WINDOWS of the gallery I saw the Johns standing with two other couples, everyone happily drinking champagne. The door was locked, so I knocked on the glass. John Without looked up first. He stopped smiling and crossed his arms as John With came over to open the door.

"Hi there, Poppy Markham," John With said, standing aside to let me in. He waved his champagne flute at the room. "We sold every piece."

"The midget lion tamers, too?" I asked.

"That went first," he said, then hugged me.

The look on John Without's face would not have been out of place hanging with all the other photos. Under normal circumstances I would have played it up, but I had gone there to ask him for a favor and didn't want him to harbor any more feelings of animosity toward me than he already did, so I pulled away.

"Come meet our friends," John With said.

He introduced me to Sean and Jason, then Rob and Emmanuel. "I told you about the fire," John With said to them. "Poppy's staying in our guest room while her house undergoes renovations."

"Which are being done by a deaf, dumb, and blind contractor," John Without said, "who doesn't own a clock or a calendar."

Everyone sensed his mood change, and the other guys said they needed to shove off. John With let them out the front door, saying, "Our back yard, Saturday at noon. Don't forget Ricky and Winston."

"What's happening Saturday?" I asked John Without, hoping to get him talking about something that sounded like fun.

"Liza's debut picnic," he said, "but you can't attend unless you bring a dog."

"Oh, stop it, J," John With said as he returned with a champagne bottle. "You don't have to bring anything."

The thought of borrowing one of the stuffed dogs from Capital Punishment's gift chamber flitted through my mind, but that might be considered antagonistic, so I let it go. "I can find something else to do on Saturday," I said.

"You'll come to the party," John With said. "And bring Jamie. A friend has been asking about him."

I didn't know of any friends Jamie had in common with the Johns, but I could tell that John Without wasn't happy that his dog-required ploy had already failed to keep me away, so I nodded noncommittally and looked around at the photographs of bearded ladies and tattooed strongmen. "These remind me of Diane Arbuckle's photos," I said.

If I didn't know better, I would have said that John Without looked impressed, but I did know better and he wasn't. He said, "Would that be Fatty Arbuckle, the infamous twenties comedian, or Diane Arbus, who photographed society's fringe?"

John With tried to deflect his snark with, "What brings you here so late, Poppy Markham?" But it didn't work.

"Yes," John Without said. "A couple more hours and we would have gone an entire day without seeing you."

I envisioned the next few moments, me asking John Without if I could look through the photos he took for Troy at Capital Punishment, him snorting and saying, "Fat chance," then John With saying, "Oh, just let her see the photos." And that's how it went down, except John Without said, "Fatty Arbuckle chance," and John With sugared the request by saying John's photos were really good and they should frame some of them and hang them in the gallery.

"They're in the office," John Without said.

I followed him to the back and he pointed to the computer on the desk.

I didn't move.

"They're in a file called Sharpe, with an E," he said.

I still didn't move.

"They're digital," he said loudly.

"I don't know how to use a Mac."

"Figures." He sat at the desk and pulled up the files for me. Troy's smiling face filled the screen, his dilated pupils shining with a secret. "This is a mouse," John said. "You press the left button—"

"I know how to use a mouse."

He stood and we switched places. "What are you looking for?" he asked.

"Something to prove Troy was murdered."

"Is that so?"

I looked up at John and wondered why I hadn't thought to discuss this with him before. He had spent time with those people and had been everywhere in the restaurant. He could have seen and heard all kinds of suspicious things. Maybe some arguments or threats against Troy. Maybe even taken pictures of them.

And then he said, "You solve one little murder and suddenly you're Jessica Fletcher."

Yeah, that's why.

"How did Troy hire you?" I asked.

"He and his wife came into the gallery a couple of months ago. When he found out I was a photographer, he asked me to take pictures of the restaurant."

"That seems beneath your talent," I said. I didn't like giving him a compliment, but it was the truth. John Without is a respected fine arts photographer, and that was a job for someone hungry and just starting out.

"It is," he confirmed, lifting his chin a couple of inches, "but it was obvious he was waiting for me to accept the job before he bought a bronze bust Ginger said she wanted because it looked like him."

"Did it?"

"She was being sarcastic."

"How did he pay for the bronze?"

John Without looked at me like it was none of my business, but then he said, "His AmEx was declined, so he wrote a check."

"How did he pay for your photos?"

"He didn't. I told him I would invoice him at the end of the job."

I could only imagine that I was having a civil conversation with John Without because the topic was him. "Do you remember photographing anything unusual?"

"That whole shoot was ridiculous," he said. "Troy had me take pictures of him posing in various places around the restaurant, pretending to bartend or paint or hammer a nail."

"For what purpose?"

"Arrogant self-indulgence."

"That makes sense," I said. "Did you know he was a star quarterback in high school?"

John yawned. "And a captain in the marines with the highest security clearance, and a brilliant stock trader, and a multimillionaire, and yadda, yadda, blah."

"A multimillionaire?"

"That's what he said, which is funny because his check for the sculpture was returned NSF."

"Troy's check bounced?"

"He paid cash the next time he saw me at the restaurant."

"Did you ever photograph his rope trick?"

John sneered. "Not the first time."

"He got you too, huh?"

"Not as bad as he got you." John used the mouse to scroll through the pictures until he came to one of me running toward Troy, eyes as big as tambourines, my mouth frozen in an O. I felt the humiliation of that moment all over again.

The photo had been taken from above, and I could see Todd smiling behind me. And then something jelled: the flashes of light coming from the catwalk and John's appearance out of nowhere when the protesters showed up. "You were upstairs Monday morning?" I asked.

"Jessica Fletcher strikes again."

"Show me the rest of the pictures from that day."

He clicked a left arrow on the screen and the pictures scrolled back in time—Todd and me standing in the dining room, looking up at Troy on the catwalk. Troy looking back at the camera as he put a leg over the railing. Troy putting a noose around his own neck.

"Go the other way," I said.

He clicked the right arrow and moved past my imitation of Mr. Bill to the coin toss before the gurney race. Troy shoving Todd's gurney into the wall. Troy puking on the floor. The construction workers returning to work.

"Stop there," I said.

"A rare tender moment between Troy and Ginger," he said.

"That's not Troy."

TWENTY-EIGHT

IN THE PICTURE, GINGER and Todd stood by the bar, kissing. Not an in-law kiss but an on-the-lips, hands-behind-the-head, bodies-pressed-together, quick-before-we're-caught embrace.

"Of course it's Troy," John snapped.

I pointed to the bottom right corner of the picture. "That's Miles coming into the dining room from the gift chamber. Troy was outside dealing with the protesters and sent him to get you."

"So that's why he didn't want me to take his picture sometimes," John said. "It wasn't him."

I had so many more questions for him about what he had seen there, but it was late and we were both tired and my questions had nothing to do with him, which meant that the conversation would be as pleasant as trying to scrape plaque off the teeth of a partially sedated cat.

Maybe I could piece together something from the photos. "Can I get copies of these?" I asked.

"No."

"Please?"

"No."

"They might help me find out what really happened to Troy."

"No."

"I might get killed trying to solve this."

He picked up a CD case from the desk with "Sharpe Photos" printed on the label, then handed it to me and left the office.

———— x — x — x ————

No way could I sleep after discovering that Ginger and Todd had been having an affair, so I drove downtown to the Cove to share this new intel—this new *fact*—with Jamie. Zzaj was finishing up their first set, but I was too excited to wait for them to play two more numbers. I wrote a note on a napkin and asked the cocktail waitress to deliver it to Jamie along with a bottle of Shiner Bock beer.

"Good luck getting that one's attention," she said.

I saw her read the note on the way to the bar. I had assumed she would, so I had written "GSHARP + BRO" inside a heart.

The waitress pointed me out to Jamie, and he drummed the code to let his band mates know he wanted to take an early break. The sax player and piano player each sounded their code for 10-4. Jamie read my note, then used it to wipe the sweat from his face and neck as he made his way to my table. He leaned down for a kiss as the waitress returned with my glass of water.

"Lucky you," she said to me.

"Why are you lucky?" Jamie asked before he gulped down half my water.

"Because the most gorgeous guy in Austin is at my table."

He smiled and kissed my neck, his lips cold from the water, then dropped into a chair.

"Who do you know who's also friends with the Johns?" I asked.

"Just you."

"Are you sure? They said someone is asking about you."

"That's a wobbly circle I don't travel in." He drained the rest of my water. "So, the wife and the brother. How did you ferret that out in the past couple of hours?"

"I went to Four Corners and looked through the pictures John Without took of the restaurant. Troy was outside with the protesters when John took a picture of Todd and Ginger inside. Troy thought Todd was locking the back door."

"But he was locking lips with his brother's wife."

"Can you believe it?"

He laughed. "Sure. From what you've told me, Todd is a nicer version of Troy."

"I can believe Ginger, but to do that to your own twin? Right under his nose? In the restaurant you're opening together?" I shook my head. "Wicked."

"No more wicked than killing him."

I crunched an ice cube. "A theory now supported by a fact."

"I think you need more facts," he said. "Having an affair doesn't mean they killed him."

"Val Kilmer and Robert Downey Jr.," I said.

"*Kiss Kiss Bang Bang.*"

"Or in this case, hang hang. That's the best motive I have for any of them to do it. Too bad it's so mundane."

The rest of Zzaj started assembling on the stage, and Jamie stood. "You can't have everything."

"Can I have another kiss kiss?"

"Sorry, Poppycakes, but you've reached your hourly quota." He leaned down and said softly into my ear, "Ask me again after the next set."

227

I felt tingly and a little warm from his temptation, but as much as I wanted to hang out and watch Jamie in action, I needed to spend the next few hours sleeping in a bed down the hall from a wobbly twosome. "I can't stay," I said. "I have to be at L and L at five tomorrow morning. One of the independents might be up to something hinky."

"Oh?" he said, his sultry voice gone, replaced by his all-business reporter voice. "Something I should keep an eye on?"

"I'll let you know."

"Wait until after noon, please."

x   x   x

After working what most people consider normal business hours the past few weeks while on light duty, my body clock had somewhat adapted and I was afraid I would sleep through the alarm I had set for 4:00 AM. Turned out, I did sleep through it. Thankfully John Without is a light sleeper, and my alarm woke him up. He made sure I kept on schedule by pounding on the wall between our rooms and shouting, "Turn that blasted thing off!"

I had allowed enough time to feed and coffee myself, but if I wanted to start my day without a confrontation with an enraged elf, I would have to either find nourishment on the way or do without. I groomed and dressed, then tiptoed through the house and out the door to catch Epicrustinaceous doing whatever it is Magda Z wanted me to see. Tips like hers, from a reliable source who isn't trying to start trouble or get even, always pay off, and I felt wide awake from the excitement and the briskness of 80-degree morning temperatures, but I still needed coffee. Surprisingly, not many coffee places are open that early.

My choices were either a convenience store or an all-night restaurant, so I resigned myself to doing without. But then I remembered that it was Friday and Markham's baker, Hannah, would have been there since 3:00 AM preparing rolls, cakes, and muffins for Sunday brunch. She also prepares the most righteous breakfast blend.

I had two surprises when I pulled up behind the restaurant. The first was that there were two cars: Hannah's vintage gold Mercedes sedan, which she claims was a gift from an Arab oil sheik, and a gray truck. The second surprise was that the truck had Colorado license plates. What was Drew doing there so early? I sat in my Jeep trying to decide if I should go inside, because really, not even a stray dog would believe that I went there at 4:30 in the morning for coffee and Drew just happened to be there.

My idling Jeep motor must have made Hannah curious, because the back door opened to reveal her warm smile ahead of the noble fragrance of baking sourdough and cinnamon. Drew and the stray dog could believe whatever they wanted. I was going in.

Before I made it through the door, she bussed me on both cheeks and assessed my physical appearance. "I like you in black," she said in her lingering German accent. "Come, come, have some breakfast. It has been too long."

"You look wonderful, Hannah," I said.

She hugged me again, then waved me through the door. "In, in, before my babies are ruined." Meaning that the slightest change in kitchen humidity would turn her rolls into gooey blobs.

I waited while she put a warm lingonberry muffin on a plate, then poured coffee into a mug. I knew better than to touch anything under her gray-blue gaze. While Hannah was there, the kitchen belonged to her. Even Ursula deferred to her when their schedules overlapped.

Hannah set my breakfast on the counter. "Now," she said. "Eat."

She began to punch down a batch of dough on the counter as she dined on my moans and yums, filling with pride while pshawing my compliments. "A little flour, a little sugar," she said. "No magic."

"Is Drew here?" I asked, waving off another muffin.

She put it in a white paper bag along with a couple of warm sourdough rolls. "Drew who?"

"Cooper. Mitch brought him back as the manager. His truck is outside."

She sprinkled flour on the dough. "That was here when I came, but I have been alone all morning."

I excused myself to the bathroom but checked the office instead. Door locked, light out, no Drew. Had he gone home with someone? With Ursula? My heart revved with something that could have been either too much coffee or a little bit of jealousy. It had to be the coffee. Jamie and I were mostly mended, and as long as Drew and Ursula kept Mitch happy and Markham's prospering, why should I care what they did in private?

On my way back through the wait station, I caught sight of yesterday's date on the specials board: June 3. That put Ursula's birthday two days away. My heart decelerated. If Drew had gone home with someone, and that someone wasn't Ursula, and Ursula found out about it, someone else might win the Diva Pot.

— x   x   x —

By the time I arrived at Lunch and Larder at 5:15 AM, several go-getters had already prepped and loaded and were filing past the guard shack, eager to get a good location or defend their territory. I showed my badge to the guard and parked near the main building.

Shepherded by my flashlight, I made my way down aisle 100 toward my quarry. One row back and two spots over from 218 was empty in both directions, so Epicrustaceanality had caught a break, but spot 218 wasn't so lucky. Olive didn't say that our experiment doing inspections on location had to be done during certain hours, and while I would have preferred the assistance of daylight, Pizza Pig was getting inspected whether they liked it or not.

The truck looked as Magda Z had described: plain white with no markings, and the typical flap doors that opened into awnings during service. I saw no lights or activity, but thought I heard movement inside. I hoped the operators weren't sleeping in their truck. Serious no-no.

I stepped onto the running board of the driver's side and looked in, then tapped the window with my flashlight. "Health inspector," I called.

In less time than it takes for lightning to strike, a snout and fangs appeared in the window, barking out a very clear instruction. I did as ordered and backed off, falling off the truck and landing on my rump. How can anyone think it's okay to keep a dog trapped inside a food truck overnight? Not only for the health violations, but for the cruelty to the animal.

My rational mind assured me that the dog couldn't open the door, but my instincts insisted I get far away. I scooted toward the back of the truck and stuck the butt end of my flashlight between my teeth to free both hands to pull myself up. My light fell across something on the back of the truck, which I hoped might be some sort of identifier I could use if I saw the truck out on the street.

Indeed it was: scrapings of bright yellow pylon paint decorating a large dent in the bumper.

So, not only had Pizza Pig been hiding in plain sight at Capital Punishment, they were serving junk food without a permit. Olive and Jamie would both need to know, but not at 5:30 in the morning.

I had *so* much to do—confront Todd and Ginger about their affair; get a look at Troy's suicide note; find Troy's notebook and the secrets hidden inside; and look through John Without's photos. But my home computer was fried, and I couldn't use my office computer for personal business, so I would have to use Jamie's. Except letting Jamie see those photos might be considered a breach of confidentiality. I would have to work that out later.

I also had to check the ventilation system and who knows what else at Capital Punishment. Even if Miles was already working at this hour, it was unlikely that Danny or Todd would be there, so Miles wouldn't let me onsite.

If the Pizza Pig guy saw me hanging around his truck, he would never show his face. Better to catch him later at Capital Punishment. Plus, I didn't know how long he would be and didn't have time to wait.

I drove west to surprise a few sleepy breakfast cooks in Gavin's district and was able to inspect three restaurants before the smell of fried bacon made me sick. I knocked off around 9:30 AM and headed south.

As I drove down Slaughter, I could barely contain my excitement at finally coming face to face with my work nemesis. I hadn't even been inside the Pizza Pig truck and I already had so much on them—operating without a permit, keeping live animals in a food prep area, evading a health inspection. Okay, I'm making that last one up, but it should be against health regulations to miss inspection appointments. As far as I was concerned, they had already failed, and today would be their last meal service.

When I pulled around to the back of Capital Punishment, I couldn't decide if it was Pizza Pig's lucky day or mine.

TWENTY-NINE

THE FOOD TRUCK WASN'T there, but GSHARP and 88 were, probably celebrating their illicit love now that Troy was out of the way. "Not so fast," I said to myself as I walked through the back door.

The office door was open, and Todd sat behind the desk holding a piece of paper. Ginger stood behind him and dropped her hand from his shoulder when I appeared in the doorway.

"There's Poppy!" Todd said. "I hope today is the day." He sounded in high spirits.

"Me too," I said. "Where are Miles and Danny?" I hadn't seen their cars outside, but I wanted to make sure they couldn't get an earful of the conversation we three were about to have.

"The snack truck didn't show up," Todd said, "so Miles is out getting food for his guys, and Danny's on his way."

"So it's just you two love doves this morning," I said. Their faces changed to what? Anger? Shock? Guilt? All of the above. "I saw a photo of you two kissing."

"That's impossible," Ginger said.

"Why?" I asked. "Because you were so careful to hide your affair?"

Todd looked up at Ginger. "We're not having an affair."

Had I thought to print the photo and bring it with me, the part where I whipped it out would have been much more dramatic and effective. Instead I had to paint them a picture with words. "Late Monday morning. Troy outside dealing with the protesters. You two by the bar. You in your tennis whites. You with your hands all over her. Don't tell me you were searching for lost tennis balls."

Ginger said, "No one was in the building…"

"Except the photographer Troy hired," I said. "Up on the catwalk." I would never have another chance like this one, so I went for it. "If I were the police, I would think maybe you two killed Troy."

Todd shot out of his chair. "That is completely out of line!"

Ginger didn't surprise me when she insisted, "Troy killed himself," but she did surprise me when she got weepy and asked Todd, "Do you think because of us?"

"No, no," Todd said tenderly, pulling her to him. "The photographer hadn't given us those pictures yet. Troy couldn't have known."

"Did he say why he killed himself in his suicide note?" I asked.

Ginger pulled away from Todd. "What is she talking about?"

"I have no idea," he said, a warning in the look he gave me.

I ignored it. "Yes, you do, Todd. Danny wants to take it to the police, but you don't want Ginger to see what it says."

Her eyes held a mixture of danger and disbelief. "Give it to me."

"Ginger," he pleaded.

"Todd," she cautioned.

He opened the desk drawer and pulled out a yellow sticky note—the one with my handwriting. The note I had left on Troy's hard hat on Tuesday. What was he trying to pull? At that moment, though, my face was so neutral, I could have won the World Series of Poker with a pair of deuces.

Ginger wiped tears from her eyes then took the note from Todd. "I can't make this out," she said, handing it back to him.

I knew what I had written: *Checked sinks. No hot water. CU Th at 8.*

Todd said, "Checks sink. In hot water. Cut out eight."

I had written the note with my hurt hand, so those words and letters could have looked like what Todd read. But why would he think those were Troy's last words?

Ginger sniffled and took the note out of his hand. She repeated what Todd had read, then said, "I don't understand."

We both looked at Todd and waited for him to explain how that could be interpreted as a suicide note and what it meant. I also wanted to know what it told Ginger that she wasn't supposed to know.

Todd launched a handful of eye daggers at me, then said, "Troy got into trouble writing bad checks."

"Again!" Ginger cried. "That bum!"

"We hired a lawyer," Todd said. "She was working it out, but in the meantime, she told him to stop writing checks and start paying cash."

Shoot a doughnut! Everything had an explanation. That knocked out the mystery of the COD requests with his vendors and why Todd and Danny needed to meet with Suzi Grimm. A felony conviction for Troy would mean no liquor license, and an Austin restaurant that doesn't serve liquor is an abandoned building. And if my note was Troy's suicide note, that blew away my theory that it had been planted by the killer. Todd and Ginger had the best motive, but if they believed my note to be Troy's, could they still be suspects?

On the other hand, no authentic note meant that it was even more likely that Troy had been murdered.

"Why do you think it was Troy who wrote that note?" I asked.

"'Cut out eight,'" Todd said. "Since high school, Troy has always been number eight. He was cutting out, signing off."

"Does that look like his handwriting?" I asked. "It could be fake."

What Todd said was, "According to the autopsy report, he was pretty drunk when he died." What he didn't say was, "Why would someone write a fake note?"

"Troy really did commit suicide," Ginger said, "but not because of us." Apparently that was a load off her mind because her eyes had stopped drizzling.

I had a Hamlet-inspired question to answer: to tell or not to tell? Troy's killer was probably quite happy that the note existed. If the police started questioning their own ruling of self-inflicted death, he or she could trot out the note as proof that Troy did it to himself. If asked why the note hadn't surfaced until now, they could say they didn't want to bring attention to Troy's financial troubles. If I kept mum, Troy's killer might get comfortable enough to make a mistake. But if I revealed myself as the note's author, Troy's killer might get nervous enough to make a mistake. And these two might be the killers.

I decided to bluff and see if I could get them to go all in. "Now that Ginger knows about the note, there's no reason not to go to the police with it."

"No!" Ginger cried.

What was this? I raised a questioning eyebrow.

"The insurance company thinks it's an accident," she said.

"But Troy is a multimillionaire," I said. "You get his estate."

"A multimillionaire? Is that what he told you?" She glanced at Todd. "Troy had millions of lies, not millions of dollars."

"This place has all of us in serious debt right now," Todd said.

"Another reason for you to kill Troy and make it look like an accident," I said.

Todd took a step toward me, forcing me to step back into the kitchen. "First you accuse me and Danny," he said, "and now me and Ginger. Why are you so hot to prove that someone killed my brother?"

I had bet big and didn't expect them to raise, however small, and it stopped me. I couldn't tell them that I had seen the crime scene photos because I would have to explain how I got ahold of them. And I didn't want to tell them about the missing flashlight because it would reveal a key piece of evidence and give them a reason to kill me. I also didn't think it would be a good idea to let them know how invested I was in my pursuit of the truth.

"I'm not," I said. "This note proves that he killed himself, but if you want to keep it from the police and the insurance company, I'm not going to say anything."

They both relaxed, then Todd said, "Where are we on the permit inspection?"

"Close," I said. "The guys were sealing the floors yesterday and I couldn't get to the bathrooms and check the water, so I still need to do that, and I need to check the vents above the grill."

"Everything should be working."

I had heard that so many times, it should be their tagline. "Give me a hard hat and I'll get started."

Ginger and Todd wouldn't talk about anything important with me in the kitchen inspecting the vents, so I started with the upstairs bathrooms to give myself time to work out a new strategy and give my prime suspects time to conspire.

I went into the dining room to check progress. To keep the sealed floors looking nice, slightly elevated board planks had been placed throughout the room, with a network of boards leading to the bar, the double doors, and the downstairs bathrooms. Most of the construction workers ignored the walkways, imprinting the floor with their dusty footprints as they assembled the gallows scaffolding for the lights.

I turned back to the stairs in the wait station and ran into yet another obstacle, this one physical. The door to the stairs was blocked by a wheelbarrow full of cinder blocks too heavy to roll out of the way without help. I'm so used to doing things myself that I didn't think to ask one of the guys to lend me their brawn. I leaned across the wheelbarrow, opened the door, then heaved myself over it and into the stairwell. I felt on the wall for the light switch, but nothing happened when I flipped it on. I reached for my flashlight, except I didn't have my backpack with me. In my haste to confront Todd and Ginger about their affair, I had left it in my Jeep.

I also didn't have the rest of my inspector supplies, but I didn't need a thermometer to check the hot water. My fingers know what the heat from 100 degrees feels like. And I could feel my way up the stairs in the dark, which I decided to do.

As soon as the door clicked shut, I felt like the air had been vacuumed out along with the light. I heard scuffling and felt something bonk against my hard hat. It didn't hurt, but I lost my balance and fell forward onto the stairs, landing at precisely the right angle to knock the wind out of me.

x x x

Next thing I knew, I was sitting on the floor at the entrance to the stairwell, propping open the door, my hard hat and a paint can next to me. Miles sat on the second step, with Rudy and Mingo behind him, higher up on the landing.

"You hurt, ma'am?" Miles asked. He opened a bottle of water and handed it to me.

"I need to inspect the bathrooms. The hot water."

"It's working," Miles said.

"I believe you, but I still need to check it."

"The thing is, ma'am—"

I closed my eyes. "Now what?"

"We're staining the upstairs," he said. "We blocked the door so nobody'd come up. We toss the cans down the stairs as we empty them."

I sipped some water and decided that I didn't want to be a health inspector anymore. I should do what Nina did several times and marry well so I wouldn't have to work. I could concern myself with who should sit next to whom at tea parties instead of why someone thought it was a good idea to keep their teacup poodle warm in a soup bowl near the oven during the dinner service. I would dress like Joan Crawford instead of like Johnny Cash. I would never have to wear a hard hat or carry a backpack full of rubber gloves and alkaline strips. I would spend my days in air-conditioned department stores. And I would sweat only if I chose to sun myself by the SNOBS club pool instead of all day every day in hot kitchens.

That kind of life would surely bore me to alcoholism, but it would limit the number of corpses I stumbled upon.

"The grass is always greener, isn't it, Miles?"

"Ma'am?"

"On the other side of the fence."

Miles looked back at his guys, and they shook their heads.

"When will the floor be dry?" I asked.

"Tomorrow afternoon."

I picked up my hard hat, and Miles stood and held out his calloused hand to help me up. "Why didn't the snack truck show up today?" I asked.

"I couldn't say, ma'am."

I didn't ask Miles if he knew that Pizza Pig didn't have a permit to serve food. He had other things to worry about, like what would happen if he didn't get this place finished in six days. It could be done if everything really was working as he said and they got their permit, and if Danny had hired a good crew, and if everyone stayed on task, and if someone didn't get arrested for Troy's murder. It wouldn't be pretty, but pretty wasn't the idea behind this place.

"Is the ventilation system working in the kitchen?" I asked.

"Yes ma'am," he said. "Ever'thing is working now."

"But I can't see ever'thing working until tomorrow," I confirmed.

"Afternoon," he said.

— x   x   x —

Miles and his guys went back upstairs, and I went to the kitchen door. I didn't have my cell phone to check the time because it, too, was in my backpack, but I figured I had been away from Todd and Ginger for about fifteen minutes, and I might could overhear something good.

I put my ear up to the space between the door and the jamb and heard voices but couldn't make out any words. I put a finger in my other ear to block out the sounds of hammering. I still couldn't make anything out, so I used my knee to crack the door open an inch.

When I peeked inside, I spied with my little eye Danny Mac-Adams. I wondered if I had suffered brain damage during the few seconds I had been gasping for oxygen in the stairwell. He appeared to be searching Ginger for lost tennis balls.

THIRTY

I PULLED MY FINGER out of my ear and pushed through the door. "Oh, come on! You're cheating on Todd, too?"

Todd charged out of the office. "He's trying to comfort her. She's been crying since you left. Just how many conclusions do you jump to in a single day?"

Danny said, "What does she mean, 'cheating on Todd'?" He looked at Ginger and then Todd. "You mean you two…"

Oops.

"At ease, Danny," Todd said, then to me, "Are you done here?"

I didn't like the attitude with which he said that, either to Danny or me. I may have discovered his affair with his brother's wife and accidentally let Danny know about it, but I was still a health inspector on official business. He didn't have to respect me, but he had to respect the badge. I crossed my arms and gave them a couple of seconds to pay attention. "Do y'all hate the entire Travis County health department or just me in particular?"

Todd softened. "Neither. We're all—"

"Because I'm trying to do what should be a very simple inspection. I've been here about a hundred and twelve times since Monday, which was a holiday, if you recall, and if you also recall, it was the day I found Troy because none of you bothered to pick up a phone and tell me the power was out and I didn't need to come back. And now I'll be returning tomorrow, a Saturday. Maybe again on Sunday, or perhaps Monday. Or maybe you want me to keep coming back every day until June freakin' eleventh!"

"We appreciate your patience," Danny said. "Whatever it is, we'll get it fixed."

"Tell Miles I'm inspecting this place tomorrow whether you're here or not."

"Yes, okay," Danny said. "Tomorrow."

✕ ✕ ✕

By the time I swung into the driver's seat of my Jeep, familiarity had bred a rabbit warren's worth of contempt inside me. I despised Todd and Ginger for cheating on Troy. I despised Troy and Todd for the way they treated Danny. I despised Danny for being so spineless. And I despised Miles for taking on a construction job he wasn't qualified for. The delays kept my murder investigation alive, but all my digging hadn't gotten me anything except a bucket full of vexation.

As nice and neat as it would be for Todd and Ginger to have killed Troy because he discovered their affair, they believed that Troy wrote a suicide note, which didn't make sense if they did it, which meant that they probably didn't. So that left Danny and Miles, and the best motive I had ever come up with for either of them was poor treatment by Troy. Only crazy people kill someone because of name calling, and neither of them appeared to be crazy.

I had the rest of the day to kill, so I started running through my options. I could call Olive with an update on my permit inspections, but I didn't want to because I never want to call Olive. I could work Gavin's district, but driving in Friday lunchtime traffic makes my teeth hurt. What's so special about Fridays that people allow themselves to eat lunch in a restaurant? Why not Tuesday? I could go shopping with Nina, but the fact that I didn't want to was a good enough reason not to.

It wasn't quite noon, so I couldn't call Jamie. Besides, with my elevated level of contempt for everyone at Capital Punishment, I might blab everything I know about that restaurant. I could work on Trevor's drink, but I would get tipsy tasting all of my experimental creations, which would make me worthless for the rest of the day.

But since I didn't give a flip about the rest of the day, I fired up the Jeep and drove to Markham's.

x x x

Back when the Yellow Pages listed us as Markham's Bar & Grill, back when my mother was alive, back when Drew managed and I cooked, we opened for lunch and dinner. Now Markham's opens only for dinner and Sunday brunch. So instead of starting her day at seven or eight in the morning, Ursula could roll in as late as noon if she had stayed out late with the new GM.

When I walked into the kitchen at noon:10, no one was there. Except someone had to be there because I didn't need my key to get inside.

Just when I began to wonder if I had been left behind during the Rapture, I found Mitch staring at the ceiling of his little office off the second dining room, singing, "'Fly me to the moon…'"

"I know that look," I said.

"Hi, honey."

"Who do you have to fire?"

"Coop," he said.

"Seriously, Daddy, who?"

"When he left, he made you miserable and worthless, and now he's making Ursula happy and worthless." He picked up his signed Babe Ruth baseball. "I liked it better when she was seeing Trevor."

"You know about that?"

"There are no secrets in a restaurant."

"You can fire Drew, but you can't stop them from dating."

"Yes, but Ursula won't be very happy, which is what I'm after." He smiled. "The food she sent out of that kitchen the two weeks Évariste was here could restore sight to the blind."

"You can't fire Drew because Ursula is in a good mood."

"Yes, I know." He place his elbows on the desk. "What brings you here?"

"I had some time and thought I'd work on Trevor's drink. Where is everybody?"

"Coop is either getting a new battery for his truck or at CapTex looking at ovens, and Ursula took her guys to lunch at Mostaccioli's. She's trying to convince them to come in on their off days to help work on her cookbook." He looked at his watch. "They should be back by now."

Dead battery. That's why Drew's truck was here this morning. Wait… "Drew is buying Ursula a new oven?"

"I'm buying the oven."

"First a slicer and now an oven? Just for a stupid cookbook? How many times when I was cooking did I ask you, *beg* you—"

"Please, honey, the oven is for Hannah. The old one is ruining her babies."

Oh. "Well, as long as you've got your wallet out, I could use a new car and a new wardrobe and a London vacation."

"Nina still wants to take you shopping."

I looked at the wall behind Mitch, his "love me" wall, hung with a lifetime of photographs—Mitch with Governor Ann Richards before the rift, Governor George Bush and then President George Bush, Governor Rick Perry, Tommy Lee Jones, Oliver Stone, Willie Nelson, Anthony Bourdain, my mother—his beard and ponytail getting longer and grayer over the years until the last picture with Évariste Bontecou. Mitch's head is shaved, his full beard snipped into a goatee.

"Why does Nina try to change everything all the time?" I asked. "First you, then the restaurant, now me. Why can't she let people be themselves?"

"That's not fair, honey. She doesn't try to change everything."

"Come on, Daddy. She bought Chinese *Hairless* Cresteds, then rubbed them with Rogaine to make their hair grow."

"It was winter," Mitch said, smiling. "She didn't want them to be cold."

I laughed.

"She wants to thank you for helping Ursula." He stood up and came around the desk to give me a hug. "Give her another chance."

"I'm not buying anything pink."

He hugged me. "Oh, Penelope Jane."

"And can you please send Drew to the Toyota dealership to buy me an FJ Cruiser?"

"Sorry, honey. All my extra money is in the Diva Pot."

—— x x x ——

I picked up a champagne bucket in the wait station, took it to the kitchen and filled it with ice, then carried it to the bar. I dropped a few cubes into a highball glass and thought about Trevor. Young, cocky, flirty, tattooed Trevor Shaw. His drink should be something simple but different. Nothing blended or shaken. A little sweet but with an edge.

I started mixing, tasting, tossing, then mixing again. I poured sweet liquor into savory mixers. Southern Comfort and tonic. Gross. Grand Marnier and soda. Adult and boring. I tried savory liquor with sweet mixers. Scotch and Sprite. Gag. Vodka and Coke. Maybe.

Thirty minutes later I heard deep voices and chattering coming from the kitchen. Ursula and her guys were back, the restaurant coming alive with pans banging down on burners and knives hitting cutting boards.

I saw Ursula walking—no, bouncing—through the dining room, but she didn't see me until she had almost reached the bar. "Poppy?"

"Taste this," I said, handing her my most promising concoction. She sipped and made a face. "Try it again," I said. "It grows on you."

She gave me a look but sipped again. "Tastes like something Trevor would drink."

"Does it?"

"So that's why you're here." She came behind the bar and uncorked an open wine bottle. "What are you going to name it?"

"I'm still working on that. Any ideas?"

"Let's see," she said, tilting her head to the side. "Jealous Junior. Silly Shaw. Big Blue-Eyed Baby."

"I take it he's not happy about your interest in Drew."

She smiled. "Not one bit. How about Two-Timing Trevor?"

248

"Calling the kettle black, aren't you? With who?"

She sniffed our house red wine. "That awful waitress."

"Belize? That ended a couple of weeks ago."

"Ended or not, it happened."

"While y'all were on a break."

"So?"

Something about this whole situation didn't smell right, and I thought I knew what. "Things must be going really well with you and Drew for him to buy you an oven."

She uncorked another bottle. "I guess."

Her answer should have been enthusiastic agreement or at least a knowing grin. "Oh, Ursula."

"What?"

"You're not interested in Drew. You're mad that Trevor threatened Évariste over Belize, and you're using Drew to make Trevor jealous."

She smiled again. "You don't know what you're talking about."

"You've been in such a good mood because it's working."

"I'm in a good mood because I'm writing a cookbook and I'm going to be famous."

"If you think Trevor is going to put a meat cleaver to Drew's throat, that's not going to happen. Do you really think he's dumb enough to get in the middle of the chef and the GM?"

She stopped sniffing wine and I knew that she hadn't considered things at that level.

"Trevor is going to wait for you like he always does," I said. "Just make sure this little game of emotional blackmail doesn't hurt Mitch or Markham's."

Ursula's face darkened, but she recovered quickly. "You worry too much," she said, then picked up half a bottle of Merlot and walked, not bounced, back to the kitchen.

I wanted the old Ursula back as much as Mitch did, but for different reasons and not until June 7. My Diva Pot winnings wouldn't buy me a new car or pay for a trip to London, but it would give me something even better: bragging rights for life.

"What are you smilin' about?"

"Trevor, hey. I didn't see you."

"I seem to be invisible to women in this place," he said, looking at himself in the mirror behind the bar. "I'm thinkin' about cuttin' my hair and wearin' a tie."

"I vote no on both," I said. "Need a drink?"

"Yeah, actually." He hopped onto a bar stool. "Mr. Wonderful just got back from CapTex, and Ursula…" He completed his thought with a sigh. No wonder Ursula was having so much fun. Trevor was adorable when he was jealous.

I started mixing a weak version of his own drink. "I understand from Mitch that the Diva Pot is still on."

Trevor nodded, looking as forlorn as Snoopy laying on top of his doghouse. "Shannon started makin' plans for the money when we heard her yellin' at you in the wait station the other night, but when she came back to the kitchen, she was fine, so it didn't count."

"She freaked out when I tried to get her to say hello to George and Laura," I said. "It was weird."

"Ursula never goes out to meet guests. She gets stage fright."

"You're not serious."

"I thought everyone knew."

"No, but that explains quite a few things." I handed him the drink I made.

"I can already smell the Dr. Pepper." He drank half of it and grimaced. "Tequila?"

"What do you think?"

He drank the rest, and his face stayed smooth. "I like it."

"Good," I said, pointing to a black board behind me that listed the house drinks. "It's yours."

He smiled a big, happy, genuine Trevor smile. "Mitch named a drink after me?"

"He wants to thank you for keeping Markham's alive during that mess with Évariste. We both do."

"It was nothin'," he said. "What's it called?"

I went over to the board and picked up the white marker pen. I wrote the name, then turned to face him. If he felt hurt or offended, I would erase it and call it Trevor's Treat. After a dramatic pause, I moved aside and pointed to it.

He laughed. "Ursula gets credit for the name."

"I'll let Mitch know we have a new drink called the Immature Churl. Tequila and Dr. Pepper on the rocks."

"Thanks, Popstar." Trevor stood and raised his arms in a stretch. "This is just what I needed."

"Do me a favor?" I said. He lowered his arms and looked at me. "Don't cut your hair or start wearing a tie. You're still MVP, and you'll be playing first string again soon."

"How do you know that?"

Trevor was ready to run his own kitchen, but he stayed at Markham's because of his personal relationship with Ursula. If Ursula kept this going for much longer, Trevor might quit, which would not be good for Markham's. I said, "Promise me you won't use what I'm about to tell you to manipulate the Diva Pot."

"I can't promise until I know what it is."

"Ursula is using Drew to make you jealous."

His face got hard, then relaxed into another big, happy, genuine Trevor smile.

"Trevor, promise," I said as he bounced back to the kitchen.

x x x

I made and drank a double espresso with a weak head of foam that Jamie wouldn't award half a star to, then called him. "I want credit for letting you sleep two extra hours," I said when he answered.

"We didn't go that late," he said. "I could have met you at L and L this morning."

"You would have wasted your time." I told him about missing Epignaceous, the attack dog in the Pizza Pig truck and their unauthorized food distribution, confronting Todd and Ginger about their affair, and the suicide note that wasn't Troy's.

"Let me get this straight," he said, amused. "You were right about the suicide note being planted, but you're the one who planted it?"

"That's about the size of it."

"So this—"

"Compromises several of my theories. Yes, I know."

"No, I was going to say this narrows down your suspects."

"Pardon?" I said. "Did Jamie Skepticwood eat some Credence Crunch for breakfast?"

"I'm not the governor," he said, "and I haven't had breakfast yet."

"If it's not Todd and Ginger, then it's Miles or Danny, and I can't think of a good reason for either of them, so I think we can stick a fork in it because it's done."

"That doesn't mean a good reason doesn't exist. If you had to pick one of them, who would you arrest right now?"

"Aren't theorizing and postulating against the rules?"

"Not when you have facts on which to base them," he said. "Now we know that Troy wrote hot checks, he hired a lawyer who advised him to go cash-only with his vendors, and he may or may not have known that his twin brother and wife were having an affair."

"Troy hadn't seen the picture of Todd and Ginger."

"Troy may have hired John Without in the first place because he suspected something was going on between them."

"That could have been why he hired Philip!" I said, excited again. "He wanted to track Todd's and Ginger's movements."

"Where is Troy's notebook? Did you ever see it?"

"No, but the first day I was there, Troy claimed someone knocked him out behind the restaurant."

"What?"

"He went out back for a snack, and one of the workers found him. Danny and Ginger both thought he passed out because he'd been drinking. When Ginger asked what his attacker took, he felt his back pockets. I had assumed he was checking for his wallet, but it could have been the notebook."

"Was it missing?"

"I don't think so. He didn't seem distressed."

"If Troy thought someone was after his notebook, he might have thought he was in danger. Where were your suspects when Troy was knocked out?"

I took a moment to place everyone. "I was at the bar with Todd, Troy, and Danny when I named the restaurant, then—"

"You named the restaurant?"

"You're not the only wordsmith in this relationship."

"What is it?"

Was the name I came up with subject to the confidentiality agreement? I didn't want to risk it. "I can't tell you the whole name, but it has capital in it."

"Oh, that's really clever," he said. "Austin is the capital of Texas. Everything has capital in the name."

"That's true," I said. "Getting back to their whereabouts, I stayed inspecting the bar alone for about fifteen minutes, then caught up with Todd and Danny in the office. After Troy went down, I went back inside to get some water for him and ran into Ginger coming into the kitchen from the dining room. And Miles had gone to Cap-Tex for a sink but was there when Philip and the protesters showed up."

"Where were they?"

"I don't know. I didn't know they existed until later."

"And John Without?"

"Ditto."

"Any one of them could have knocked out Troy," Jamie said.

"Yes, but if they didn't take the notebook, why?"

"Figure that out and you'll have your motive."

"Brilliant, Jamie."

"I wish I could give you more."

"Who do you think did it?" I asked.

"Brad Pitt and Brian Cox."

Troy. "So you were just humoring me?"

"That's what the facts point to."

"The facts can kiss my hind end! Troy Sharpe did *not* kill himself."

"So figure it out, Poppycakes."

"Okay, I'll keep working," I said. "I forgot to tell you at the Cove that the Johns invited us to a picnic at their house tomorrow."

"Did they plant a new rose bush?" he asked. The Johns use every little excuse to throw a party.

"Liza's debut."

"Oh, brother. What time?"

"Gary Cooper and Grace Kelly."

"*High Noon,*" Jamie said. "I'll be there."

I hung up and saw Drew walking through the dining room, smiling. He looked handsome in a brown shirt and starched khaki pants. "Trevor told me you were here," he said when he got to the bar.

I took my espresso cup around to the sink. "I'm almost done."

"He also told me what you said about Ursula."

See? It takes no time for word to get around in a restaurant. "Sorry," I said, "but it's true."

"I knew what she was up to."

Of course he did. Drew is scary good at reading people. "So you're not interested in her?" I asked.

He held my eyes. "I prefer smart, quiet blonds."

I looked away. "Drew—"

"I wasn't entirely honest with you earlier about why I came back to Austin."

"Don't."

"I came back for you," he said.

"Coop!" Trevor called from the wait station.

Drew crossed his first two fingers and put them over his heart. "I'll wait as long as it takes," he said, then stood and walked off.

Poppycakes didn't want to hear that, but Sugar Pop? She thrilled a little at Drew's words. But why? I'm a one-guy girl, and Jamie is my guy.

Yes, Jamie is my guy.

x   x   x

I spent the rest of the day at the Palatine inspecting restaurants, working into the early evening inspecting bars to make up for the couple of hours I had spent at Markham's. It's the strangest thing that upscale establishments think that by virtue of catering to a wealthier clientele, they are somehow immune to surprise inspections. How dare the health department check up on them!

The Johns were out when I arrived at their house around 9:00 PM, which meant I could take a shower before I went to bed without feeling guilty about making noise. Too bad you can't bathe your brain and wash away the thoughts you no longer want in your head.

I would expunge my thoughts that Daisy was right about me feeling differently about Drew now that my emotions had caught up to my reason. I would scrub away my suspicions about Troy's death so I could relieve myself of the self-imposed responsibility to right that wrong. And I would stop thinking that I was probably going to accept Nina's imminent offer to decorate my remodeled house.

x   x   x

The next morning, the Johns rose early to make final preparations for the party. They wouldn't let me help, so I offered to fetch breakfast. After we ate, I went back to my room and stayed out of their way, finishing up my inspection paperwork from the night before. I planned to stay at the picnic for a couple of hours, then head over to Capital Punishment.

I heard snatches of the Johns's conversations as they walked in and out of the house. "We should have made more bones." "Do we have enough pink balloons?" "I think Liza is getting excited." "Yes, baby girl, this party is for you! For you! For you!" Each "you" punctuated with a kiss.

I also heard their end of phone conversations. "No, you can't bring your cat." "We're not Baptists. Of course we're drinking!" "John loves your fried gizzards." "You're allergic to dogs?"

For some reason, the Johns's friends are never late to their parties, not even fashionably, and the first guests started arriving at 11:45. Jamie called me at noon to tell me he was finishing up a story and to ask what everyone was wearing.

"Apparently it's a Cuban-themed picnic," I said, "so they're mostly wearing shorts and *guayaberas*."

"I don't have one of those shirts."

"Wear your blue linen and the dressiest shorts you have, and you'll be fine."

"What about shoes?"

"Yes, wear shoes," I said. Since when did he care about looking good for a bunch of gay men? "And you'll have to park down the street."

By noon:15, about fifty mammals had pranced through the back gate, some carrying their dogs, some leading their owners on leashes. I saw the Johns's friends I had met the other night at the gallery. Sean and Jason introduced me to their white standard poodle, Winston, then I met Rob and Emmanuel's boxer, Ricky. As the beer and Cosmopolitans flowed and the tiny back yard filled with Shih Tzus, Chihuahuas, Dalmatians, and dogs of unknown pedigree, it became difficult to distinguish the canine yapping from the human yapping.

Jamie finally arrived to appraising stares and a few growls. "Woof," I said as he walked up to me.

"So I look okay?"

"Like a model."

"Not the look I was going for today, but thanks."

"Did you finish your story?" I asked.

"Yes, but I need you to help me with the title before I post it." A wicked little smile revealed his left dimple. "It's about last meals at Capital Punishment."

I nodded, then heard what he said. "What?"

He laughed. "It's what I do for a living, babe."

"How long have you known?"

"For a while. You dropped enough hints about the menu. Then you almost said the name on the way to Daisy's, and Philip Anthony told me it was based on a prison. It was easy to figure out from there."

"You're amazing," I said, and kissed him. "How about 'Capital Comfort Food'?"

"Keep thinking, little Miss Wordsmith."

As we ate and drank and chatted with acquaintances from gallery openings and other parties, Jamie either held my hand or wrapped his arm around my waist. It would have been nice to believe it to be an expression of his devotion to me and how inseparable we are, but we aren't the types to hang all over each other in public. He wanted there to be no doubts about his straightness.

When the Johns started walking around with silver trays, handing out homemade dog bones imprinted with Liza's name, Jamie said, "I need to talk to you about something. Can we go over to your house?"

As we reached the back gate, two girls who had dressed to get the attention of straight men came through it. One of them said, "Jamie?"

I recognized his hairdresser, Tara, her short red hair moussed into spikes, the tips dyed electric pink. She looked like something from a Dr. Seuss cartoon.

"I was hoping you'd be here," she said, fingering his curls. "It's been forever! I thought you had switched salons, but you've been letting your hair grow. It looks good long."

"Thanks," Jamie said. His hand tightened around mine.

"Don't you think so, Poppy?" Tara hugged me. "I miss seeing both of you."

And then I smelled it. The sweet, flowery stench that had curdled my happiness seven months ago.

I looked at Jamie, his face as white as sour cream. He gripped my hand tighter. "Poppy."

"Tara?" Disbelief heated my face, and I threw his hand out of mine. "*Tara?*"

THIRTY-ONE

TARA WAS ALL MY mind would process. That's why he hadn't had his hair cut. That's why he wouldn't tell me who she was. Tara the party girl. The tall, skinny party girl who is half his age.

Conversations near us softened to murmurs as I backed away from Jamie, rage retarding my motor skills. I stumbled into dogs, trampled sandaled toes, spilled expensive beer.

John With saw the commotion and rushed over to me as I reached the back door to the house. "What? What?" he asked, distressed at my distress.

"Tara," I choked out. "It was Tara."

John opened the back door and walked me inside. He let me fume for a few seconds, then said, "I'm so sorry, Poppy Markham. I didn't know."

John Without came through the back door. "What happened? Did a dog bite you?"

John With said, "Tara is who Jamie cheated with."

"Her?" John Without said. "She's such a skank."

"What do you want to do?" John With asked me. "I can ask her to leave."

I shook my head. "I'm leaving. I have to do an inspection. Go on back to the party."

John With sat down at the table, sweetly having no intention of abandoning me, which forced John Without into a decision between strutting around the back yard among his guests or leaving his boyfriend alone with me in a vulnerable state. His ego won and he made a huffy turn, then flew out the door.

"I'll be okay," I said to John With. "It's a shock, and I need some time to process everything. I thought we were mended, but this is a new breach." A huge one. "Get back to your guests."

John stood and hugged me, then opened the back door, letting in sounds of happiness. He turned back to me. "I know you don't want to hear this right now," he said, "but Jamie Sherwood is a good guy, in spite of his bad judgment one night. Believe me, I know. Straight or gay, most of those guys out there aren't any better than their dogs."

"You're right, John. I don't want to hear that, but thank you."

I changed clothes, then hurried outside to my Jeep to make a triumphant getaway. Except I had parked under my carport, and the Johns had told their friends they could park in my driveway, which they did. I had the time to wait for the cars to be moved, but it wasn't a good idea to hang around. I had controlled myself fairly well, considering, but now that my hurt and disbelief had festered into disgust, the likelihood of a scene being caused if I saw the booze-crossed lovers was quite high. And John Without would never forgive me if the post-party gossip focused on the drink I would have thrown in Tara's face instead of how adorable he and Liza looked in their matching rhinestone collars.

John Without, on the other hand, had the foresight to park on the street. I called John With's cell phone. "I need to borrow John's car," I said when he answered. "Mine's blocked in."

"The extra keys are hanging by the front door," he said. "Bring it back today and he'll never know."

Jamie knew that coming after me would only make things worse, but he called my cell phone several times, hanging up without leaving a message. What could he say? "Of all the girls at all the clubs who buy me drinks and slip me their phone number, of all the girls in Austin who could have turned my head away from you, I picked Tara."

Tall, skinny party girl Tara, who is half his age.

When I first discovered that Jamie had cheated, and then figured out that it was someone we both knew, I examined every possibility: the regular waitresses we had at our favorite restaurants, the checkers at the grocery store near his house, the bartenders at clubs where he played, the freelancers he shared an office with, Ursula. I had never even considered Tara.

She flirted with him during his hair appointments, but she flirted with everyone. And she dated everyone. Seriously. *Everyone*. Jamie would return from the salon making fun of Tara's latest drama with her boyfriend of the week. She usually dated club bouncers, personal trainers, and bartenders, so Jamie Sherwood, the famous food writer, was dozens of steps up.

I didn't want to think about that, about them. Together. They were probably still together, doing Zeus knows what, and I didn't care. If that's who Jamie wanted, then I wouldn't stand in his way. I hoped they would be very happy together, actually. Him with her nice haircuts and her with his movie-naming game. Kate Hudson and Matthew McConaughey. *How to Lose a Guy in 10 Days*. The movie based on Tara's life.

One of my greatest assets is my ability to switch mental gears quickly, but not today. I had to fight to keep Jamie and Tara out of my thoughts, but they kept fighting their way back in. At first I had resented having to finish Capital Punishment's inspection on a Saturday, but now I could think of nothing I would rather do. Funny how fate paves the way for what you need.

— x   x   x —

Capital Punishment looked like it had most every other time I had been there—on the verge of completion. Several workers trudged in and out of the double doors ferrying construction supplies to the cage in the back corner. Maybe they were finally wrapping up. What could Jamie possibly see in her? The fact that she is the literal opposite of me: a health-conscious, law-abiding, faithful girlfriend who is his age? Could it be her smoker's cough? Her boney elbows?

As usual, I parked near the back door, taking care that John's car stayed on the blacktop and I didn't get grass stains on the tires or dirt in the wheel wells. I didn't see Danny's or Todd's cars and hoped they had told Miles to let me onsite. But Miles's pickup wasn't there either, so it didn't matter. I had been around so often the past week, the construction workers probably assumed I worked there, so they paid no attention to me as I walked through the back door.

I didn't trust that nothing else had been broken while something else had been fixed, so I started my inspection from scratch. To my dismay, everything worked as it was supposed to in the kitchen. Water flowed into the three-compartment sink, and the mop sink had a back-flow valve. The hot water and the vents worked. All of the refrigerators were cooling to 41 degrees or below, the freezers to freezing. Same thing in the wait station and bar. Jamie had said that Crown Royal was on special that night, but he doesn't usually drink hard liquor. Why did he that night? Why Tara? Because of her hedgehog hair? Her man hands?

Before any of the guys, or the gal, showed up, I went upstairs to see if I could figure out anything about Troy's murder while I had the time—something I should have done when I first got there, had I been thinking clearly. Had Jamie said he couldn't make the party, had Tara not worn that revolting perfume, had I not spoiled the Johns's anniversary party in the first place so Liza's apology debut picnic wouldn't have been necessary.

Even the light in the stairwell worked when I flipped the switch. Would we be in this situation if Jamie had told me who she was at the time? I would have broken up with him regardless, but would I have mended things with him as I had? Probably. And now I was back in the fifth circle of hell, anger, and we were starting all over. Or ending all over.

I stood at the top of the stairs and looked toward the railing. Usually, fear and panic were either thrust upon me, as had happened the first time on the catwalk, or I knew in advance to avoid such a thrust. But for the first time I would have to brave my fear of heights, and I didn't know how to go about it. Should I creep up to the edge and let myself get used to the idea inch by inch? Or should I rush to the railing so my body didn't have a chance to figure out what my mind was doing?

I had never understood the point of conquering fears until I looked at the twenty feet of catwalk I had to cross. I remembered reading that G. Gordon Liddy, one of the Watergate burglars, had a fear of fire, so he held his hand over a flame until his skin burned black. To conquer his fear of rats, he roasted and ate one. At the time, I thought those were extreme and disgusting ways to conquer fear. I had also wondered if the rat had inadvertently been cured of his own fear of being eaten by a crazy bald man.

If I could be where Troy had been, maybe something would speak to me—like Tara's perfume had done. Shrieked, actually. How could Jamie's finely tuned sense of smell tolerate that stench for any length of time? Had he been desensitized by all that Canadian bourbon?

I put the question of my courage on hold and inspected the bathrooms first because I didn't have to conquer anything in there. The toilets flushed, and the hot and cold water worked. It looked like Capital Punishment would pass their inspection, and this would be my last visit.

If I wanted a chance to come back, I knew I would have to make it happen. I didn't have much to work with in the bathrooms, but I could be extremely picky about something in the kitchen, like there was no soap in the dispensers. I wouldn't arrange a violation because that would be unethical. Not immoral and conniving, like what Jamie had done.

As I dried my hands on my pants, I heard a ding, a pneumatic slide, and male voices. Since when did the elevator work? I stayed put, hoping to overhear something, like maybe Danny and Todd congratulating each other on getting away with their diabolical scheme.

"You're keeping them up *here*?" a man said.

I didn't recognize his voice, so I slowly pulled the door handle and applied my eye to the crack to see who he was. He had his back to me, so I couldn't say if I knew him. I knew the other man, though.

"No one ever comes up here," Miles said.

The man turned to look at Miles. Tall and dark, but not even within squinting distance of handsome. "Except for Troy and that food inspector," he said.

I had seen him recently, but where? A protester? No. Too old for one of Philip's buddies. Nina's country club? Not old enough.

"I had to put the brakes on ever'thing somehow so we could move all of this out of here." Miles lifted his chin toward the cell they stood in front of, the one that held a bunch of cinder blocks and brown boxes. "I can't just drive off and avoid her like you did." Miles unlocked the cell door. "We'da been done already if you'da showed up yesterday."

"I told you. I had to take over for Hugh while he got his side mirror fixed."

I didn't know him from Markham's, neither employee nor guest that I could remember. Maybe from another restaurant or bar? He could have been a vendor, but with his dirty jeans and scruffy cheeks, he looked too grubby to represent clean linen or the expensive seafood and steaks Capital Punishment would be serving.

"How many more?" the man asked.

"Twenty," Miles said. "Can you take all of 'em?"

"Not in a one load," he said. "Get started. The truck's unlocked."

I had been so busy trying to figure out who the man was that I hadn't processed their conversation. Why was Miles talking to him about cinder blocks?

"I gotta take a leak," the man said. "These bathrooms working?"

"They are now," Miles said.

I didn't close the door when the man walked toward the men's room because the sudden movement would have drawn his attention. I watched Miles walk to the railing and lean over the edge, easy as you please, no hesitation, no quaking from fright. He whistled and waved to someone on the first floor, then went into the elevator and came out pushing a wheelbarrow. A minute later, Mingo and Rudy emerged from the stairwell. Miles unlocked the cell door and pointed to a stack of broken cinder blocks on the floor. So that's what they were doing—salvaging unusable building materials.

Miles's foremen moved the broken ones aside and loaded whole cinder blocks into the wheelbarrow. Miles stood behind them, supervising, so I didn't have an as-the-crow-flies view, but it looked like the cinder blocks had been stuffed with something and wrapped with plastic. And the something was white and powdery.

THIRTY-TWO

MILES GOT HIMSELF MIXED up in a drug operation? How was that possible? He didn't even have the smarts to keep the restaurant construction on track. Of course, that may just be me jumping to a wrong conclusion about Miles based on his good ol' boy demeanor.

Regardless, it was brilliant—muling drugs through building supplies. The cinder blocks could be delivered on a pallet, specially marked somehow. Miles unloads the blocks and places the drug-stuffed ones under lock and key. Or the blocks come in empty, and Miles stuffs them with drugs. And gets rid of them how? Oh! Pizza Pig! That's where I had seen that man. Serving food and drinks to Miles and the other construction workers. Food and drinks—and drugs!

All I needed to do was stay put and wait them out, but then the men's room door opened and the reason the man had spent so much time in there wafted out with him. And I sneezed. A loud one because I hadn't expected the cigarette smoke, but nobody noticed over the din of construction on the floor below. Plus their attention was on Mingo and Rudy guiding the full wheelbarrow into the elevator.

I was prepared for my second sneeze, which shook my shoulders, but I let go of the door at the same moment Miles looked up at Mr. Pizza Pig, and I could tell by the way Miles's mouth opened that he had seen me.

Trapped in the bathroom, my best option was to lock myself in a stall and stall for time. But there were only two toilets, and even a good ol' boy drug mule could narrow down those choices in less than five minutes. I had one other option. I pulled a thermometer from my backpack, then turned on the hot water at one of the sinks just as the door opened.

"Hey, Miles," I said breezily.

"Come on out of there, ma'am."

"Didn't Todd tell you I would be back today?" I pretended not to notice the gun in his hand so he could put it away and we could both pretend everything was fine. Except he didn't and we couldn't. "I'm almost finished."

"You're finished now," he said.

I slung my backpack over my shoulder.

"Leave it."

I dropped it in the sink under the running water and stealthily pulled the stopper so the sink would eventually overflow. I didn't know if it would come in handy, but it couldn't hurt. If nothing else, my wet backpack would raise suspicions with someone if I turned up in a ditch.

Miles held the door open and waved me onto the catwalk with the gun. The elevator door was closed, which meant that Rudy and Mingo had gone down with the drugs. I hoped the Pizza Pig man hadn't gone with them. Maybe Miles wouldn't kill me in front of a witness.

"Mr. Pizza Pig!" I shouted. "You can come out now."

"Mr. what?"

"Nothing," I said. "What's with the gun?"

He stared at me.

"Are you going to shoot me, Miles? With all those people down-stairs?"

"No ma'am," he said, waving the gun toward the railing. "You're going to jump."

"I'm afraid of heights."

"Then we'll call it a case of the jim-jams and you fell."

"I really don't want to do that, Miles."

"Well," he said, pushing up the brim of his hard hat with the barrel of the gun, "I'll tell you like I told Troy. Either jump and make this easy and you're the only one who dies, or don't jump and make this hard and the rest of your family dies, too." He sniffed. "Your daddy owns Markham's Grille and Cocktails, don't he?"

"It's Cocktails and Grille," I said. I suddenly knew what I wanted my last meal to be. Forget health, I wanted fat and sugar and ani-mals—a thick porterhouse steak, a medium-rare filet mignon, salmon cakes, macaroni and cheese, and a big piece of Italian wed-ding cake. As it turned out, it looked like my last meal would be the glass of orange juice and carrot sticks I had eaten at Liza's picnic.

"If it's all the same to you," Miles said, "we'll have to do this with-out beer."

"Why kill Troy?"

"He was up here one time when he shouldn'ta been and saw us doing what you just saw. Then he had the idea to bleed cash out of me."

"And you lured him up here on Monday with the promise of a payment but killed him instead."

"I got partners, ma'am. I just needed a few more days and we'da had ever'thing out of here, but then Troy showed me all them notes he'd been taking about our activities and such. Said I had to give him more money or he'd go to the cops."

I felt a grotesque combination of terror and victory at finally discovering the truth about Troy's death. "Did you knock him out behind the restaurant on Monday?" I asked.

"That was Mingo, trying to get the notebook."

"I guess you got it after you killed him."

"He handed it over before he jumped." Miles pointed the gun at me. It looked like a .22, so the report from the gunshot would blend in with the rest of the construction noise. It also wouldn't kill me unless Miles stepped closer, which he did. "We're burning daylight, ma'am."

I didn't need beer. My terror at having to move toward the railing mixed together with my alarm at a painful death, and they both combined into a potent adrenaline cocktail. I had one plan and one chance.

Miles came up behind me and I felt the gun poke my back. "If you're thinking about hollering for help—"

"I'm not. But I need some room. Back off."

"Yes ma'am."

As soon as he moved away, I closed my eyes and gripped the railing. I jumped off the ground and thrust my legs back in a powerful kick that would have qualified me for the Yoga Donkey Kick Invitational. I hit something solid, so it couldn't have been his belly.

Miles *ghrfed* and I heard the gun clatter to the floor. I opened my eyes and whirled around to pick up the gun but saw Miles on his back on the floor, still pointing it at me. The clatter had come from his hard hat.

"Fire!" I yelled. "Fire! Call nine one one!" I dropped and rolled and rolled and rolled, banging into cells and knocking against walls. I felt dizzy and stopped rolling, locating Miles by his grunting. He had scooched toward the railing but didn't take his eyes off me as he pulled himself up to standing. Sweat leaked from his red face, and he took a moment to catch his breath.

And aim the gun.

I scrambled into the open holding cell full of drugs where he couldn't see me.

"Come on out, ma'am," Miles said, making an effort to sound harmless. "I won't hurt you."

"I didn't just fall off the turnip truck, Miles." I dropped to a crouch and peeked out of the cell. Miles fired, but he expected me higher up. I was right about one thing—the sound blended in with the construction noise.

If someone wasn't calling 911, if I didn't think of something pronto... I looked around the cell and found an open box of medieval death implements. I grabbed one of those sticks with spiky iron balls attached to a chain. It looked like Tara's hair. What was that called? It was also a spice. Cinnamon? Nutmeg? Mace!

My adrenaline and bravery were gone, replaced by something better: fury. *Stupid murdering Miles!* I flung the mace in his direction. He answered with a shot that struck the far wall. *Stupid cheating Jamie!* I threw another, harder. Another shot from Miles. *Stupid skinny Tara! Stupid lying Pizza Pig!* Another and another. *Stupid greedy drug dealers!* I wound up with another and let it fly. *Stupid jealous Ursula!* I stopped. Out of maces.

How many shots had Miles fired? How many did he have left? How many shots did a .22 hold? Why did he stop firing? Was he reloading?

I couldn't trick him again by looking out from the bottom of the cell, so I stepped onto a couple of cinder blocks and slowly poked my head out close to the top. Miles lay on his back near the railing, bleeding from a gash at his hairline. A hit!

"Miles?" I called. "I'm giving up."

I inched out of the cell in case he was playing opossum. The gun lay within reaching distance of his right hand, but he didn't reach for it. I ran over and kicked the gun away, then picked it up and pointed it at him with a trembly hand. I tapped his foot with mine. "Hear those sirens, Miles? The cops are on their way." They were probably fire trucks, but that was good enough for now.

Miles opened his eyes and wiped blood from his forehead with the back of his hand. "How in the name of Davy Crockett did this happen?"

"You messed with the wrong cowgirl."

x x x

The following Tuesday I ignored my contractor's wishes and moved into my house. He had refused to connect the central air conditioner, so I bought a window unit for my bedroom with my Diva Pot winnings. Trevor had enlisted Drew in a scheme to get Ursula back to normal. They pretended to butt heads over her during prep for Sunday brunch. She was so happy, she threw an egg at the first waiter who special-ordered a Denver omelet, saying that Markham's wasn't an IHOP.

After I arranged to have a refrigerator delivered, I went to Daisy's to borrow her blow-up bed and eat lunch.

"Did you see Jamie's story?" she asked as I helped her prepare avocado sandwiches.

"The one about Capital Punishment and last meals? Yes."

"The new one he posted this morning about Troy's murder."

"No."

"Logan printed it out. She wants you and Jamie to sign it." Daisy used her knife to point to a piece of paper on the counter. "Go ahead. I'll finish these."

I sat at the kitchen table and read that Miles had confessed to everything. He and Mr. Pizza Pig, real name Donny Lee Rogers, were part of a small drug operation involving several construction sites and mobile food trucks, including Epicuriousitiness. When Troy discovered what they were doing, he blackmailed Miles to get the cash he needed to make purchases because he didn't want Ginger to discover his hot check trouble. When Troy threatened to go to the police if Miles didn't triple the amount of his payments, Miles killed him.

Miles had tried to delay the opening of the restaurant by sabotaging the food permit inspection to give himself more time to move drugs. "Perhaps," Jamie wrote, "Mr. Archer would have been more successful had he tried to impede the building inspection instead."

Within hours of Miles's arrest, the restaurant's theme was no longer a secret. Danny or Todd must have agreed to an interview with Jamie because he wrote that they decided to push back the grand opening to November 24, Ted Bundy's birthday. I read the final line of Jamie's story out loud. "Ted Bundy did not request a special meal the night before he died in the electric chair. He was served the traditional meal of steak, eggs, and potatoes, but did not eat it."

"Creepy," Daisy said. She placed our sandwiches on the table, then poured us each a glass of iced tea. "Did you help Jamie with the article?"

"He came over on Sunday to interview me, but we didn't get very far. He refuses to discuss Tara."

"Did you break up again?"

"I said I needed more time, and he said I could take the rest of the summer because he's going to be traveling around the country giving workshops with *Deliciousness Magazine*. So, yeah, we're taking a break."

"Does Drew know?" she asked. I had already told her about his "as long as it takes" proclamation.

"I'm going to tell him tonight at dinner," I said. "Am I awful for doing this to them?"

"Of course not," she said. "You're not deciding between two couches. This is important, and you need to know if you want Jamie or Drew."

Daisy said grace, then we started on our lunch.

"What would you have for a last meal?" I asked.

"I've been thinking about that. So far, I've come up with Erik's barbeque pork ribs, Ursula's crawfish bisque, and Logan's blueberry pie. You?"

"Rice, beans, tater tots, and a chocolate soy milkshake."

The End

WWW.MIDNIGHTINKBOOKS.COM

From the gritty streets of New York City to sacred tombs in the Middle East, it's always midnight somewhere. Join us online at any hour for fresh new voices in mystery fiction.

At midnightinkbooks.com you'll also find our author blog, new and upcoming books, events, book club questions, excerpts, mystery resources, and more.

MIDNIGHT
INK
TM

MIDNIGHT INK ORDERING INFORMATION

Order Online:

- Visit our website, www.midnightinkbooks.com, select your books, and order them on our secure server.

Order by Phone:

- Call toll-free within the US and Canada at
  1-888-NITE-INK (1-888-648-3465)
- We accept VISA, MasterCard, and American Express

Order by Mail:

Send the full price of your order (MN residents add 6.875% sales tax) in US funds, plus postage & handling, to:

> Midnight Ink
> 2143 Wooddale Drive
> Woodbury, MN 55125-2989

Postage & Handling:

Standard (US, Mexico & Canada). If your order is:
> $24.99 and under, add $4.00
> $25.00 and over, FREE STANDARD SHIPPING

AK, HI, PR: $16.00 for one book plus $2.00 for each additional book.

International Orders (airmail only):
> $16.00 for one book plus $3.00 for each additional book.

Orders are processed within 2 business days.
Please allow for normal shipping time.
Postage and handling rates subject to change.